# Stormwalker Series
# Connections In Time
# Bain's Story Book 1

## By S.G. Boudreaux

ISBN: 978-1-960091-03-1  (Paperback)

ISBN: 978-1-960091-04-8  (Digital)



Zanchier Publications

Printed in the USA

Sgboodro2@yahoo.com

www.SGBoudreaux.com

# Glossary

LSS - Loradin Secret Society - An organization that secretly operated from a base in Loradin, Zanchier. They swore to protect the innocent and help to control and deal with any unlawful activity. Not many knew of their existence until the Three Army War broke out.

LARS - Loradin Animal Rescue and Sanctuary - A facility on the island city of Loradin that found injured creatures and nursed them back to health to return them to the wild. But things there began to change when some of the children were found to have special gifts of communicating with the creatures telepathically. LAPS was born during the Three Army War.

LAPS - Loradin Animal Patrol Services - The resident students of LARS rode creatures and patrolled the territory borders of Praxtingen and Loradin for Scaither movement.

Scaithers - A ruthless, cutthroat group of men and women led by the biggest crime boss in Zanchier.

Rhial (Ree all) - A city or colony in the world of Harilhia.

Harilhia (Ha reel hee a) - The second h is nearly silent - A planet that has four moons. Each moon sits slightly askew off to the side of the first and vary in size. Dihendra is situated on the opposite side of the planet from Zanchier. In Zanchier only the largest moon was visible from their position on the planet and its rotational direction. On rare occasions Zanchier scientists could see one of the smaller moons behind the largest but assumed it to be a small planet that orbited close by during certain cycles.

Eathreon – (E ATH ree on) A wild, beautiful land in the northern region of Harilhia. It is full of wild Baiskreet. This is where the untrainable Baiskreet are taken to live.

Dihendran Guard - There are fifteen squadrons of guard employed at Castle Dihendra by the Dihendran Council. The guard have approximately one-hundred recruits, two to three Captains, and one Commander per squadron, making the guard's count to be over fifteen-hundred people. Rounding out the high chain of command is the Lieutenant Commander and the General who is the highest-ranking military official. The Tenth, Eleventh, and Twelfth Squadrons are known as the High Patrol, and are normally the only ones who deal with the Baiskreet. Each squadron is assigned their own particular duties in and around the castle and throughout Dihendra Rhial and surrounding territories.

Trendelow (trEn de low) - A large creature resembling an elephant. Its thick skin is dark, olive-green. It has three horns on its head which are white at the tips and fade into a light green near the skin, and two long curved tusks below the eyes on each side of a long trunk which are the same color. Its ears are wide and long, nearly dragging the ground, dark green fading into a lighter shade at the edges.

Wrotmond (Rot mond) - A beast with a long, outstretched, neck that sways as it moves like the motion of the strikers from Zanchier. It has an elongated head which protrudes on both the front and back of its neck. The other end of the neck nestles between two protruding shoulder blades which sit above long arms. It has a thick torso which connects to two strong back legs, and a short stub of a tail finishes off the beast's odd appearance.

Baiskreet (Bay skreet) - winged beast, like a dragon, some of which are bred and raised by the Dihendran Guard. Native to Zanchier in the Dihendran territories. There are many variations, but all are four-legged, winged beasts who are trained and ridden by the Guard, specifically the tenth, eleventh, and twelfth Squadrons known as the High Patrol. The Baiskreet is a generic term for all breeds. Beneath that are 10 different breeds that are hatched and cared for in the Baiskreet hatching ground. The most common ten breeds are listed below.

Verassuan (Ver A Sue on) - Colors - reds, yellows, and oranges. Size - mid-range with a thick, bulky, build. Abilities - powerful tail and legs for thrashing. All four legs have long sharp talons. It can shake the earth surrounding it when it stomps the ground and thrashes its tail.

Copasedrom (Co pa SE drum) - Colors - purples, golds, and grays. Size - smaller to mid-range. Has a sleek, powerful, build made for speed. Abilities - a fast flier and quite agile in the air, especially if it catches airstreams. Its screech can disorient its prey or enemy, allowing it ample time to attack.

Brundwedim  (Brund WE dum) - Colors - browns, greens, creams. Size - Very large range. A burrower by nature. Likes to dig and can even dig through softer types of rock. They are not very fast and need a running start to take flight due to their size and weight. They have very thick skin and use their body to slam into things to bowl them over. Their roar is deep and loud, and often behave as bullies.

Lurepture  (Lure EEP chur) - Colors - Reds, pinks, whites. Size - Small to mid-size.  Abilities - quick flier, belches fire, and has a playful nature. They are quite the prankster and they enjoy annoying others.  However, it is fiercely loyal, and quick to react, making them deadly.

Nassureptic  (Nas your EP tick) - Blues, greens, and yellows. Size - mid to large. A very laid-back creature that can fly fast after they build up speed. Abilities - can turn invisible, along with its rider. Belches ice spikes when threatened.

Durnestrum (Durn E strum) - Purples, blacks, grays, and whites. Size - smaller than average. They are hard to see at night due to their dark smooth skin. They are one of the few Baiskreet breeds that do not have scales. They can emit a nasty pungent odor to drive away anything that threatens them. Because of this ability, few people wish to bond and ride with them, so not many are bred in captivity. They can also breathe fire, are lightning fast, and are very good at disguising themselves. They have a defensive nature, often avoiding conflict whenever possible.

Triastrium (Try AS tree um) - Yellows, browns, and grays. Size - small to mid-range. Abilities - belches a pungent and intoxicating gas though it is not deadly. This gas can cause it's victims to experience a euphoric state of mind for up to thirty minutes, giving it plenty of time to escape or attack, whichever avenue it decides to take. Its riders must carry air filtration masks that can quickly be snapped into place. These masks cover the nose and mouth and have a strong filter made specifically to protect them from this gas.

Vurcransu  (Ver cron SUE) - Colors - Blues, purples, and blacks. Size - mid to large range. Abilities - A quick flier that can camouflage to its surroundings which also aids its riders. They like to swim and can do so quite well by holding their breath for long periods of time. They can take in large amounts of water into their stomachs and expel it in a defensive manner. They are often used for putting out fires.

Viigisur (VIE gi sure) - Colors-tans, grays, and whites. Size - small to mid-range. Abilities - Their long arms and legs allow them to scale and hang from the sides of cliffs, buildings, or whatever they like. They are fast flying, fire-breathing, and can fill any space with a thick smoke as a defensive measure.

Kriesletrope (Kree ES la trope) – Color - Golds, silvers, coppers, and bronzes. Size - large. Abilities - can breathe fire, and it swims well, although will avoid water if possible. They are considered to be the most beautiful of all the Baiskreet; regal in appearance and stature. They have soft looking spikes that lay flat along their backs but will raise up and stiffen when they feel threatened. They can throw these spikes but use this defense as a last resort since it takes weeks for them to regrow. They are characteristically snobbish but are also loyal to a fault. They are often the dominate species among the Baiskreet, and the largest male is seen as the Alpha by the other Baiskreet.

Brendelwren (BRIN del ren) - A very large, kelpy-looking creature whose head resembles a seahorse, it has an eels body, but with four large, sinewy, fins, and a long tail that can produce poisonous spikes from beneath its kelpy looking fins. It is bioluminescent and can turn translucent when needed. It once lived in the deepest, most recessive part of Everly Lake in Zanchier, near the forgotten coast, often passing between the brackish lake waters and the ocean beyond. It eventually left Zanchier and set out across the vast ocean of Harilhia.

Dot – An unknown breed and singular creature discovered on the smaller chain of the Phorellian Islands in Southern Harilhia by Jillian Porter, a young LARS telepath. Dot is a large beast, average man height but thick in the chest and shoulder areas. He has a large head, wide mouth with a powerful set of jowls. He has medium length fur which is white with grayish-black spots. Although he looks quite intimidating, he is mild tempered but fiercely protective of his bond-mate.

Hobbling – A large, four-legged beast slightly larger than a bull. They have long hair which sticks out wildly in most directions and varies in color. Their floppy ears vary in length as well. Their large wet nose, long rough tongue, big eyes, and whiskers make up a round face. A long shaggy tail and a very amiable temper and personality round out this unusual beast. They love attention and their whole body will wiggle incessantly when happy. They eat mostly foliage and grass. They do not live long in the wild because they have a very timid nature. Hobblings are often kept and used by farmers to pull plows and help with work on farms.

Bigfooted Loper – similar to rabbits but larger than the average wild bunny. They have very large feet with long toenails, shorter ears than your typical rabbit, and two sets of three eyes on either side of it's face. Large protruding front teeth and a full set of large back teeth complete this creature. Their colors vary. They are fast and hard to catch as they can jump quite far or high if needed.

Hardhead Hopper – similar to frogs – This breed of Hopper resemble toads. The have larger back legs, are more round in the torso, and have a large, bulbous, hard plate on the tops of their heads. Males use this plate to knock heads with other males to establish dominance in the wild. Female head plates are smaller and flatter.

# Planet of Harilhia and its four moons

# Chapter 1



**Earth, Cairo, Egypt, 1940's**

Nineteen-year-old Bain Brinley stood in the middle of the street, staring at his surroundings. He tugged at the offending winter jacket and hat as the hot sun beat down on him. Just a few seconds earlier he had been standing in the blue, snow-covered mountains of Zanchier. Now, he wasn't sure where he was.

*What had just happened?* he thought.

He turned one more time to see if the glowing light he had passed through just moments before was truly gone. Yep! He was stuck here, at least for now, wherever here was. Had he really just stepped through a time portal to another world? In academy he and some friends had always speculated over there being other dimensions in time. Other places and worlds than just Zanchier had to exist, and now it seemed that he had found one. Bain never expected to actually travel through time, which is exactly what he supposed had happened to him when he stepped into that glowing light in the middle of Storm Valley.

He once overheard his father, Wilkins, talking about a similar experience many years earlier where he had time-traveled and disappeared for six years. He had found a way home, so Bain should be able to as well.

Sweat began to bead and run down his face. The thick beard he had grown while hiding in the Xantifal Mountains for two months began to itch some with the heat and sweat. He stuffed his toboggan hat in a pocket and shrugged out of the thick winter coat he wore, shoving it in his backpack. He was fortunate that he had all his clothing and travel supplies with him in his pack. He scanned the area for a place to duck into and change into some clothing that was more appropriate to the dry, desert, heat of this world.

He noticed a small cafe' across the street and walked across to use the bathroom. He hoped the owner or manager would allow him to do so, especially since he wasn't a paying customer and had no idea about the culture here. He doubted they took rhedon in this world, the currency that was used back on Zanchier.

As he walked into the establishment, he paid close attention to what people were saying and using to purchase food. He had some dried meats, nuts, fruits, and berries in his pack to hold him over for about a week, but he knew he would soon get tired of that and want real food. He needed to find work and fast. He would also need a place to stay. There were no forests, or mountains anywhere near here, so he would need to scout the area for cover.

Bain inconspicuously ducked into the men's restroom and quickly changed into something more suited for the stifling heat. He looked at his appearance in the mirror and decided it was time to shave. He locked the bathroom door, took out his razor and soap, and quickly shaved his thick beard and mustache. He was just finishing up when someone began to pound at the door.

Bain unlocked the door and swung it open. "Sorry," he stated to the perturbed looking man standing before him.

The man just glared at him and entered a stall.

Bain exited back into the cafe', the smell of the food making his stomach rumble. It was nearing dinner time and he was growing hungry. He left the cafe' and took to walking the streets of the desert city. Off in the distance he could make out some very large, triangular shaped structures. Taller than any of the buildings he could see around him.

A loud alarming sound shook him from his thoughts and he turned to see a rather primitive-looking Module behind him. The sound blared again, coming from under the front of the module, making him jump. He stepped aside to allow the offending module to pass but it didn't move. The driver waved him over to the window and Bain reluctantly walked over.

"I say, old chap, are you daft?" The man behind the wheel spoke with a rather odd accent.

"Roderick," a woman from the back seat scolded, "don't be so rude. The man is obviously lost or confused."

Bain leaned down to peer at whoever was talking to the man driving. To his surprise, it was a young woman. A very attractive young woman wearing a long skirt, a button-up, tucked-in, shirt with a high collar and a beautiful brooch that sat just at the hollow of her throat. Her curly, red, hair was piled high upon her head and a small hat sat just a tad sideways, like her hair was pushing it to the other side.

She leaned forward to look up at him and questioned with a smirk, "Are you lost?"

Bain grinned a little sideways. "I do believe I am, ma'am."

"Ma'am, goodness, I'm not that old!"

"I'm sorry, I didn't mean to offend you."

"Oh, posh," she said with a wave of her hand. "Can we give you a ride somewhere, Mr...?"

"Bain, Brinley. I would say yes, but I'm not sure where I'm going. I'm a stranger to this land and not sure where to go next."

"Well, may I call you Bain?"

"Sure."

"Well, Bain, perhaps we can help you with that," she said, gesturing to herself and then the driver, who glared at her and rolled his eyes.

"Not another stray, Lilith. You know your father will have a fit!"

"Oh posh, Roderick. It's been months since I brought home a stray anything." She turned to Bain and opened the door. "Climb on in, Bain Brinley and let's see what we can make of you." She smiled brightly as he climbed into the back seat beside her.

Roderick put the module in gear and they began down the road once more.

Bain took in his surroundings. "This is a strange looking module."

"Module? What on earth is a module?"

"Sorry, wrong word?" Bain cleared his throat suddenly growing a bit nervous. "It's what we call transports like this where I am from."

"I've traveled to a lot of places, and I've never heard that term used to describe a motorcar before."

"I doubt you've ever been to where I'm from."

"And where exactly is that?"

"Zanchier."

"Well, you would be right. I've never heard of the place. Is it in Europe? Perhaps South America? It does sound a bit African."

"I don't believe so." Bain decided to quickly change the subject. He doubted this woman had ever heard of time-travel before and might likely have him locked up. He didn't even know about it back on Zanchier until it happened, so he wasn't entirely sure how he had managed to do so himself.

"Where exactly are we going?"

"Does it matter? Being a stranger to this land, would you even know anyhow?" She smiled teasingly at him, trying to size up what sort of man he was.

Bain cleared his throat again, unsure what to say to that.

"For heaven's sake Lilith, stop tormenting the poor lad," the driver scolded her.

Bain noticed that she just grinned and giggled at the scolding which obviously did not faze her in the least.

She smiled again then said, "We are headed over to the site of my father's latest dig. He's a type of archaeologist."

Bain looked at her confused, unsure what an archaeologist was.

She raised her eyebrows questioningly, realizing that he didn't understand. "My goodness, Bain, where have you been living? Under a rock? You really don't know what an archaeologist does?"

"I'm afraid not," he said sheepishly.

"Well, they dig up old civilizations to learn more about the past in an effort to try and better our future. Although, some do it just to find buried treasure."

"And your father is which kind?"

Lilith smiled broadly at his quick wit. "The first kind, most definitely. He's extremely wealthy already and doesn't need the money. He wants to save things for posterity reasons. My father is known as an Egyptologist, a specialist on all things Egyptian."

"Sounds like a good man, and very interesting as well."

"He is both. Brilliant and kind; the very best of men. And you shall soon meet my special fellow, Simon Lane. He's the main archaeologist working for my father at the dig site. He's very Irish, temper and all. But still, the sweetest of men. I'm hoping to get a proposal out of him any day now."

Bain looked over at her and grinned. "I hope you get it. I'd say he's one lucky man."

"Thank you, Bain. I'd say that I am just as lucky. Now, what about you? Any special ladies where you're from?"

Bain's countenance fell abruptly and a searing pain shot through his heart at the memory of Raila.

"My goodness! I've said something to injure you. I'm so very sorry."

"No, it's all right. It's just that there was someone. Her name was Raila Orman. She died in combat just a few months back."

"Combat? What sort of world do you hail from that puts women in wars?"

"One where everyone fights or we all suffer. I come from an archaic society. Where evil men rule with a firm and cruel hand. Women, and often younger teens, fight beside the men. They use weapons, sail ships, fly airships, build machinery, and talk to creatures. Do your women here not do these things?"

"Heaven's no! We barely leave the house most days. None are quite so brave as to take on the tasks you've described. We're more of a garnish for the arms of our men. We keep house, raise children, sew, draw, paint, play the piano, that sort of thing. However, I am a bit more liberated than many in my gender. My father spoils me quite frivolously and allows me to tag along on many of his digs. You see, my mother passed away when I was young, and instead of hiring a nanny and never seeing me, he chose to drag me along. I have to say I've rather enjoyed my upbringing and the things that I've been able to see and experience. Just imagine, if I was home with a nanny, we'd have never met and you'd still be standing back there in the street. That is, if someone hadn't run you down by now with their motorcar." She smiled and giggled slightly.

Bain couldn't help but smile and chuckle a bit with her. Lilith seemed to be quite a character, a blend of honesty, integrity, and playfulness. Of course, Bain's experience with new acquaintances was limited. It had been years since anyone in Zanchier got to visit or meet anyone new unless they were born in Zanchier. No one ever came from anywhere else. Zanchier was like a large world unto itself. Land locked on all four sides by devastating lands that no one ever crossed, until he found a way out. But he would never be able to tell others about the secret pass he discovered unless he could find a way back. What about his parents and siblings? Were they safe? What was going to happen to them if they never got to escape the Scaither's overbearing rule?

They sat in relative silence for the next few minutes as Bain looked out the window of the motorcar and took in the landscape before him. The closer they got to the triangular shaped structures, the larger they became. Once they arrived at their destination, he was overwhelmed by the sheer size of them. They were nearly as large as some of the smaller mountains back on Zanchier.

Bain stepped from the motorcar and whistled lowly, grabbing Lilith's attention.

"I suppose that means you've never seen the pyramids either," she stated rather than questioned.

Bain smiled at her. "You'd be right about that. I haven't traveled from my home-land before. So everything is a first for me."

"I see. Well, I'll have to be your tour guide while you're here. Tell me, Bain, do you have a place to stay?"

"Not exactly. And my form of currency, I doubt, is accepted here so I'll have to find some work as well if I want to eat."

"I'm sure we can remedy both of those situations for you. My Simon happens to be looking for laborers in the digging of the site. That is if you're not afraid of hard work. Many of the natives here are superstitious and won't dig in some of the areas here."

"Hard work isn't a problem."

"Wonderful. Now, let's get you over to meet the man in charge shall we?" Lilith slipped her left arm into the crook of his right as they walked across the desert sands in the direction of one of the large pyramids, her driver Roderick close behind holding a rather large umbrella over them to block the hot evening sun. They walked between the giant structures toward the back where a large crew of men were digging out what looked to be a set of steps that went underground, possibly buried from years of sandstorms. They soon came upon a man who looked to be near Bain's age. Perhaps in his early twenties, such as Lilith.

"Darling," Lilith called out to him.

The man spun around just as he and Lilith stopped in front of him.

"Hello Sweetheart. What brings you out here today?" He leaned over and kissed the cheek she offered.

"Well, two reasons. You, of course, and I wanted to introduce you to a most interesting young man I recently met." She smiled up at Bain. "Simon Lane, this is Bain Brinley."

Simon reached out and took Bain's hand, shaking it fiercely. "Hello Bain, nice to meet you."

Lilith smiled at Simon's exuberance. "Bain is looking for a job darling, and a place to rest his head after a hard day's work."

Simon smiled. "You're in luck. I can help you with both. We need diggers and laborers, and since you're new and know no one else here, you can bunk with me in my tent. It's plenty large enough for the both of us, and frankly, has a few added bonuses being that I'm the head archaeologist here."

"Sounds great, thanks," Bain replied with a smile. "So, when do I get to work?"

"Well, the day is nearly gone now, so how about Lilith and I show you around a little, and you can start tomorrow morning."

"Sounds good."

Lilith turned to Roderick. "Roderick, you can return to the car, I think the sun is dimming enough now as to not burn us alive."

"Thank you, miss. I'm sure Mr. Lane will escort you back to the car?" he questioned in Simon's direction.

Simon replied, "Of course, Roderick. I would never leave her side if given the chance to linger." Lilith smiled brightly up at him as he gazed down into her violet-colored eyes.

Roderick rolled his eyes slightly at the mushy reply as he turned to head back to the 1920's Maybach motorcar belonging to his employers, Mr. Maxwell Cantrell and his high-spirited daughter, Miss Lilith.

Bain smiled at the look Roderick gave the young couple who obviously adored one another. He and Raila were just starting to experience that sort of freedom with one another right before she died. But he wondered what it would be like to be in love and not have to worry about the constancy of war. He looked at Lilith and Simon chatting and giggling quietly at what each other said. Bain's heart longed for that sort of love. His heart longed for Raila.

# Chapter 2

The next morning Simon took Bain to where he would be working, helping to dig the recently found staircase that led underground just outside one of the pyramids. Simon spoke to Bain the night before about the excitement of finding the hidden entrance. Bain asked if it had actually been hidden on purpose, or if it were simply covered by years of wind-blown deserts. Simon informed him that it could have been either. After the death of the pyramid's keepers and the collapse of the Egyptian society after the Jewish slaves were freed and left Egypt, the Egyptian society never fully recovered with the loss of so much slave labor.

Bain found it interesting that there had been slaves and oppression in this world as well, but it didn't seem to reach the time-period he now found himself in. The oppressors died out and it appeared that men were paid fairly for the work they did. If only Zanchier could be so fortunate. His thoughts returned to his parents and siblings. Were they all right?

He shook his head to clear his thoughts and got back to work shoveling the sand from the staircase. He and about nine other men worked continuously, stopping only long enough to drink some water. By lunch time, they had another four steps uncovered making a total of eight, wide, stone steps down into the earth beneath. Bain had to admit, he was just as curious as Simon about where they could possibly lead. Not only were they soundly constructed, but also intricately and colorfully designed. The stones that survived the grinding of the desert sands were still mostly intact. Some of the hieroglyphics, as Simon called them, were worn nearly completely off, but others were clear and readable. Bain looked over the strange drawings and carvings, wondering how people had communicated with the strange images.

When lunch was over, they were just beginning to get back to work when Simon looked to be stressed about a message he had just received.

"Simon, is everything all right?" Bain asked the man.

"No, I'm afraid it isn't, Bain. I've just received word from Lilith that her father, Maxwell, had a massive heart attack early this morning and has passed away."

"Wow, I'm sorry Simon. Can you send my regards to Lilith as well?"

"Certainly, Bain. But I suggest we get cleaned up and go visit Lilith together. I think she would like you to be there."

"Sure. If you think so." Bain said, surprised.

"I do. Let me give the dig foreman orders to continue until we return. You can head on over to the tent and get cleaned up. I'll meet you there shortly."

Bain did as asked, taking a washcloth, and some of the water provided in a basin and washed the sweat and sand from his skin. He wet his hair and washed with some soap found nearby. By the time Simon returned, he had nearly finished dressing, pulling on a clean shirt.

"Give me just a few minutes to clean up as well, Bain. My car is just on the other side of the tents here near the road. If you'd like, you can wait for me there."

"Sure."

Bain walked out of the tent and toward where Simon said his car would be. Since there was only one transport parked there, he assumed it was Simon's. It was different than the other owned by Lilith. And there was no driver waiting to take Simon wherever he needed to go. As Bain stood looking at the transport, Simon appeared. He watched Bain quizzically inspect the vehicle.

"It's called a Willy's Jeep. The latest model in land touring vehicles. I had it delivered just a few months back. We had to have something that could handle the desert terrain and it boasted sixty horsepower, four-wheel-drive, and a whopping forty-five miles an hour." Simon smiled brightly as they climbed into the car and started it up.

"It's interesting."

"Not like the cars where you're from?"

"Not really, no."

"Well, let's be off." Simon accelerated and they began their journey. "It's a bit of a ride to the Cantrell estate. Nearly an hour. Maxwell and Lilith keep a flat in Giza here during the week to be close to the dig site, but Maxwell must have been tending to business at home when he passed away. This is going to tear Lilith apart. He was the only family she had left."

Bain sighed. "Yeah, being alone has its benefits for short term, but to have no access to any sort of family is daunting."

"It sounds like you speak from experience."

"Yes, only recently so, but I have little hope of ever seeing my family again."

Simon noted the dejection in Bain's voice.

"Chin up, Laddie. You never know what fate has in store for you." Simon grinned at Bain, his expression soon turning sour. "Of course, on a day like today, that fate looks rather grim doesn't it?"

Bain nodded in agreement and the two men spent the next forty-five minutes in relative silence, lost in their own thoughts of present and future prospects. Only commenting on questions Bain had about the landscape or structures they passed.

They soon arrived at the Cantrell estate in Heliopolis just east of Cairo. Bain noticed that the architectural designs of the house mimicked those of the rest of the city he had seen so far. Large, curved archways turned and stepped down inward, toward a singular, round, wide, columned leg that connected it to the ground. Live tropical plants were scattered around most of the entryways, and wood-latticed window screens allowed the breeze to pass through the building's interior rooms. The scent of spices lingered on the air, filtering from the many different rooms, each containing an incense burner in a hanging pot, which swung in the slight breeze. Bain caught glimpses of each as they passed through the long portico-style walkway toward a central room.

Stepping into the room, the scent of polished leather along with Jasmine filled his nostrils. The room was decorated in earthy tones of deep rich browns, reds, and softer muted greens, with touches of deeper blues and gold in the relics and artifacts that were scattered about. Potted plants and trees adorned many corners and table-tops, and a few colorful birds sat in large floor style cages that stretched several feet higher than his own six-foot-two-inch frame. His eyes extended upward to very high ceilings, light tan in color matching the walls, much like the neighboring desert sands. Several large settees sat across from each other, flanked by several wide armchairs, all decorated in patterned fabrics matching the earthy tones of the room. Lilith sat on one sofa, a cool glass of water on the table just in front of her. Her eyes were red and she wiped her swollen nose with a cloth handkerchief. She stood the minute she realized that he and Simon had entered the room, quickly running into Simon's arms for comfort.

"Oh Simon, whatever am I going to do?"

"Shh…now my Lily, everything will be fine. I'm sorry this happened. But I promise you, I will make sure everything is taken care of at the dig site, and whatever else you might need. You can depend on me."

Lilith grinned, a tad sadly, at his reassuring words. "I know you will darling. I'm just going to miss Father so much. He was all I had in this world; except for you of course; and  our faithful staff over the many years." She grinned and sniffed in Roderick's direction. Bain noticed the man swipe nonchalantly at a stray tear that dared escape. He sniffed, cleared his throat, rounded his shoulders, and stood taller, nodding at Lilith.

"Bain, so good of you to come along. I truly wanted to introduce you to Father. He would have liked you. He enjoyed figuring out puzzles." She smiled at him, setting him at ease a bit in the tad-uncomfortable situation in which he now found himself.

"Thank you, Lilith. I'm sorry I never got the chance to meet him. He must have been a very loved man judging by the somber mood in the house."

Lilith turned to a black and white framed photo of a man on a side table, picking it up and lovingly gazing at it. She smiled slightly. "He was. A very kind and just man to all, no matter their station or position in life. He treated everyone as an equal; his staff included." Lilith turned and handed the photo to Bain.

"This is the most recent photograph we have of him."

"Looks like a strong, handsome man. I can see a great amount of character in his eyes." Bain handed the photo back to her.

"Oh," Lilith expounded. "Father was full of character to be certain!" She laughed at an obvious memory. "Oh goodness, where are my manners, please excuse me. Please, have a seat. Would either of you care for something to drink?"

Simon grinned at her. "Thank you, Lily, water will be fine." He turned to Bain for confirmation, and Bain nodded.

They stayed with her the majority of the afternoon, late into the evening. She took Bain on a tour of the grounds and property, both she and Simon telling him stories as memories surfaced as they walked and talked. The hour grew late, dinner was served, after which they excused themselves to return to the dig site.

Simon asked, "Lilith, are you certain you don't wish me to stay?"

"Yes, thank you darling. I know you have a dig site to tend, and workers to push along. I'll make the final arrangements for Father's services in the morning and hopefully I'll be able to see you after noon. Besides, I'll likely gather most of my things to return to the hotel in Giza for a while. This big old house seems looming without Father's presence to fill it." She kissed Simon on the lips and leaned over to give Bain a kiss on the cheek. "Thank you for coming, Bain. Telling you all about some of mine and Father's adventures has helped to ease the pain of his passing. I believe God sent you to us in a great time of need." She smiled kindly and squeezed his hand. They turned to leave out the door and she stood watching them go, turning to go inside as the large doors closed behind her, diminishing the ethereal glow from within that encompassed her.

After Bain and Simon climbed back in the car, Bain stated, "You're a lucky man, Simon. Lilith seems like a fine, caring, woman."

"Oh I know, Bain. She is the best woman I've ever encountered. A wonderful mix of spirit, playfulness, strength, and kindness. Not to mention she is beautiful beyond compare, inside and out. I thank the Lord often for her. Finding a jewel like that out here in the desert has to be a God-send." Simon smiled tight-lipped.

Bain nodded and they discussed possible plans for Maxwell Cantrell's funeral the next day. Simon said that when the English perished in a foreign land they usually had to be flown out to their homeland to be buried. But since Maxwell Cantrell had been a constant figure here in Egypt for the better part of forty years, he would be laid to rest in the land that he loved so well. Bain never thought of that. *What if something happened to him while here. Where would they send him?* Bain shook the thought from his head as conversation died down and the two of them rode in tired silence for the remainder of the journey to his temporary home, in a tent, on the edge of a great pyramid.

What a strange existence he was living. He'd stepped into a world he didn't know existed. He assumed this God they spoke of was the same as his Creator back on Zanchier. He supposed that every society had some deity they believed in and worshiped. He would make a note to ask Simon about his God tomorrow. He was grateful that his Creator was seemingly taking care of him in this new world. He had everything he needed, including some wonderful new friends.

Bain silently prayed, '*Creator, I know you have a plan for me. I'm unsure what it is, but I trust you, and I appreciate what you've given me here. Just, please take care of Father, Mother, Seadon, Wynne, and Adda.*'

Bain leaned his head back against the seat and drifted off to sleep. He was awakened by Simon a short time later to move into the tents for a more comfortable night's rest. His body was tired from the intense heat of the sun, and the physical exertion he had put into his work that morning. Then, add to that the mental and emotional stress of Lilith's father dying. Bain had had enough death to suit him for the rest of his life. The wars of Zanchier had cost him so many loved ones. Now, just one day into a new land, he was reminded that death was a part of life. He was only nineteen, and life felt so fleeting already. He was so unsure of what the Creator was doing with him. He felt as though the last three-and-a-half years of his life had been lived in utmost turmoil. Was he to live this way for the rest of his life? He certainly hoped not. He was ready for some peace and quiet, and he hoped he could find some wherever it was the Creator would send him to next, unless his life was meant to be lived right here in this strange world of giant pyramids while digging for life and treasures from the past.

# Chapter 3

The next morning, Simon instructed the workers to be given the day off out of respect for the Cantrell family.

Maxwell Cantrell's funeral proceedings the next afternoon were to be held at Heliopolis at the Cantrell Estate. After that, Bain, Simon, Lilith, and Roderick would return to the dig site to hold a small service for the workers who could not travel the hour-long distance. Then Lilith and Roderick would stay in Giza in the Cantrell's flat for purposes of managing the dig.

After the site-side service was over and everyone had their turn to pay their respects to Lilith, Simon took her to the hotel where Lilith's family flat was housed, making certain she made it home securely in her present state of mind. He stayed with her a little while longer then returned to his tent where Bain was waiting.

When he entered the tent, Bain asked him a question.

"So, what will Lilith do now, Simon, with the dig site and her father's company?"

"Lilith will likely either hire someone to handle her father's affairs, or more likely, take them over herself. She knows almost as much about Egyptology as her father. She just doesn't have the university degree to match her knowledge. Even though many of the more powerful men around Cairo will likely try to convince her she isn't fit to take over for her father."

"Why would they do that?"

"Simply because she is a woman."

"I'm not sure I understand that reasoning. Many women where I am from have leadership positions and are brilliantly minded."

"Well, Lad, you must come from a more advanced society than this one."

"I don't know about all that. I'd say we are likely equal in many ways, and very different in others."

Bain looked down at the MAD on his wrist. He had not seen anyone else with the technology nor had anyone here used a matter-arranging-device to travel, so technology here may be at a slight disadvantage to that of Zanchier.

"Yes, well, like most societies I suppose." Simon sat on his cot and kicked off his shoes. "I suggest you get some rest, Bain, morning comes early and so does the workday. Good night."

"Good night, Simon."

Both men drifted off to sleep quickly as the emotional and physical tolls of the day took over their tired bodies and spirits. Because of the day's events, fresh new reminders raced through Bain's thoughts as memories of all the people he had lost recently haunted his dreams and took root in his heart.

It was early, still dark outside when Bain felt Simon rouse him from his sleep.

"Bain, wake up. Are you all right?"

Bain jerked awake, nearly sitting straight up. He hadn't had a nightmare about Raila's death for a month now.

"Yes, Simon. Sorry if I woke you."

"Not a problem, Old Boy, I was just worried about you. You were yelling people's names in your sleep. One in particular was more frequently used."

"Sorry. The funeral yesterday stirred up some old memories and feelings I thought I had gotten under control."

"That's the thing about feelings, they take ever so long to go away, and then the slightest reminder can make them come flooding back. But they are easier to control each time it happens."

Bain sat up and looked out the tent flap as Simon pushed it open.

Simon turned to Bain. "It's still dark out, but nearly sunrise. What do you say to going and getting some nice hot coffee and breakfast."

"I'm game." Bain got up, and the two men got dressed for the day. They went to the same coffee shop Bain had entered to change on his first day here. It seemed as though he had been here for weeks now, but in fact it had only been days.

They had coffee and chatted about things. Mainly about Bain's dreams and fitful sleep, then where Simon was from and how he came to be an archaeologist. Before long, the sun peeked over the horizon and the two men returned to the dig site to get the day started.

The day's work was long and hot, but by that evening the stairway down into the earth beneath the side of the pyramid was cleared enough to reveal the top foot of two large doors.

Simon smiled broadly at the find. "Good work men. Everyone can take an early leave. Tomorrow we'll try and clear away all of the remaining sand and see if we can gain entry into those doors and see where they take us."

Bain leaned upon his shovel handle. He was hot, sweaty, and gritty. Sand felt like it was literally everywhere inside his clothing.

"Simon, I'm going to go get cleaned up."

"You do that, Bain. Then, if you have no further plans, I wonder if you'd like to join my Lilly and I for dinner at her hotel to celebrate this monumental find? My treat of course."

"Sure, thanks. I never turn down a free meal."

"Right then, see you in a bit."

When Bain was finishing getting dressed, Simon came in to do the same. Thirty minutes later the two of them were in Simon's Willy's Jeep headed to Mena House in Giza. They discussed dining at Mena House, then perhaps dancing to the orchestra which played every evening, or maybe even taking a dip in the pool. Mena House was the first hotel to offer an onsite swimming pool and Simon assured Bain that a dip in the refreshing waters was delightful.

Bain didn't know what a swimming pool was. The last time he had gone swimming was three years ago in the Discovery Falls basin in northern Praxtingen back home. That year had been the start of the civil unrest and the wars that likely still plagued his homeland.

They soon reached the hotel, met with Lilith, and enjoyed a night of good food, a little dancing, and even some swimming. The hotel always kept a supply of swimsuits on hand for guests, and

Bain was surprised at the clarity and warmth of the water. After their very late evening of celebrations, he and Simon returned to their tent at the dig site. They fell into their cots and woke early to the morning sun's rays illuminating the fibers of the tent, slightly lighting the interior.

Bain got dressed and walked outside to wait on Simon to wake and emerge. Simon had partaken of much drink last night and Bain figured he would awake to a headache and hangover. Bain looked over the surrounding terrain. Even though Egypt seemed to be made up of mostly sand and desert, the city near the edge of the Nile River was a contrast of beauty; lush, green, and thriving. The amount of people at the hotel was staggering. Simon mentioned that most were tourists. When Bain asked what a tourist was, Simon and Lilith had looked at him as though he had grown two heads. In Zanchier, they never received anyone who traveled from other countries to visit or enjoy the local offerings. The people of Zanchier never knew of any other places other than those within their own borders. There wasn't much to offer visitors either, especially since the Scaithers had taken over.

According to the map that Simon had showed him last night, there was a great, wide world to explore outside of Egypt, which was just one tiny little spot in the entirety of it. It made him wonder how big Zanchier truly was past the White Mountains, the deserts, and the vast body of saltwater he had come across months back. And while searching that same map, they could not find Zanchier anywhere. Perhaps it was such a small place that it wasn't listed, or perhaps it hadn't been discovered. Now, he wished he had asked his father more questions about his time-traveling experience. He had been three years younger when Wilkins and Harper had both returned and he had been happy just to have both of his parents back in his life again. Plus, he was graduating academy and they were all moving and running for their lives from bad men, and at the same time he was trying to start his own life and navigate adulthood.

Simon appeared outside the tent, rubbing his head full of hair then pushed it back and put on his hat. "Morning," he said a tad woefully.

"Good morning, Simon." Bain grinned a bit at Simon's obvious state of having a hangover. "Is there anything I can get you?"

"No thanks. I just need to get myself together and get to work."

They walked the short distance to the dig site, and the work to reveal the doors got underway. Simon had every man he had on the dig down in the staircase shoveling away at the sand. By noon the set of doors were revealed enough to be able to open them while several other men continued clearing away the sand on the steps and walls so the hieroglyphs could be read. Simon skimmed through the images to try and gage who this tomb belonged to, but many of the images were significantly worn away and impossible to make out.

"Perhaps whatever lies behind those doors will give us a better clue as to what or whom we have uncovered." Simon was now smiling broadly, his hangover from this morning now giving him some relief.

They all worked the remainder of the afternoon, carefully brushing, prying, and picking at the seams around the doors trying to gain entry. It was just beginning to get dark when the doors eventually gave way and were able to be pushed open.

Torches were passed down as Simon, followed by Bain and several of the other men walked cautiously into the room. Egyptian temples were known to be booby-trapped, and Simon had no wish for anyone to die on his dig. They scanned the room carefully from the doorway. Simon turned to address the men.

"Good work men. I think we will pull the doors closed for tonight. Two men will stand guard and change out every two hours until we resume work tomorrow. James, the foreman, will give you your time slots. No one goes inside this tomb until I return in the morning. Is that clear to everyone?"

The workers all nodded and went outside with Simon instructing them to pull the doors closed. All the workers went with the foreman to get their placement, then headed to the dinner tent. Simon and Bain stood outside at the top of the steps peering down at the heavy, stone, decorative doors.

Simon sighed. "I just wish Maxwell could have been here to see this. He worked hard the last five years to unearth this discovery." He slapped his sand covered hat against his leg to dislodge the loose particles before plopping it back on his head.

"Well, at least Lilith can come tomorrow to see the inside revealed herself." Bain dusted off his own clothing.

Simon grinned stiffly. "Yes. It will be a bittersweet moment for many of us."

They went off to have dinner with the other men before heading to the tent for another night of rest. Their bodies were bone tired from the digging and excitement of the find. Sleep claimed them both quickly, and they both slept soundly throughout the night.

The next morning, Lilith arrived at the dig site early. She knew they were getting close and she wanted to document the findings on behalf of her father. She had called out photographers, newspaper men, and Egyptian officials to the site for documentation and to establish claim. Everyone was dressed in their finest clothing for the photograph. Simon, Lilith, James, Roderick, and Bain were all on the front row while the workers were all piled in behind them as they all stood in front of the closed, decorative doors. The photographer had stood on top of something to take the picture looking down into the staircase toward the doors.

After the chaos and all the reporters cleared out, Simon's crew got to work exploring the inside of the tomb, Simon promising an exclusive of any findings to the reporter who had ventured to the site this morning. Simon had his own camera, the latest Brownie, with which to take photos of any findings. This task was left to one of the more skilled workers so that Simon could take a hands-on approach to any artifacts they found.

Before anyone was allowed to touch anything, they took photos of the area, then a few of the local men were tasked at checking for booby-traps before anything was officially moved from its current resting place.

Bain looked about the stone tomb. There was pottery, baskets, statues, decorative archways, and other stone tables and monuments. There were places in the walls where torches could be placed to better distribute light throughout the temple's main area. There were several other doorways which led to other yet undiscovered parts of the temple. Dark passages where no one knew what lay beyond. Simon could only speculate as to where they led.

Over the next week, the room was photographed, cataloged, and many pieces were removed to be sent to a museum. Simon, Lilith, James, and Bain explored the long narrow halls accompanied by some of the diggers. Lilith was on site as often as possible and enjoyed exploring with them.

One evening, Simon shared something special with Bain as they cleaned up to get ready for dinner plans with Lilith.

"Well, Bain, tonight is the night I propose to Lilith."

"Congratulations, Simon. I think you will both be very happy together."

"Don't congratulate me just yet. I haven't asked her." Simon nervously pulled the ring case from his pocket. "I took the liberty of obtaining both of our rings so that she wouldn't have to worry about that." Simon smiled proudly as he showed Bain the rings.

"I'm sure she won't turn you down, Simon."

"Yes, I believe she will accept as well. As a matter of fact, I'm surprised Lilith hasn't asked me to marry her herself. She's quite independent you know. My Lilly is a force to be reckoned with."

Bain could hear the admiration in Simon's voice for the woman whom he wished to marry.

"I think I'm going to take one last look at the temple before we leave, just to make sure the night watchmen are on post and that everything is in order."

"I'll walk with you, Simon."

The two men walked the short distance to the stairway that led down beneath the earth. The two guards were on duty, keeping watch so thieves did not chance an opportunity to steal any of the ancient relics from the temple room.

Simon talked to Bain as they walked down the steps. "You know, with a discovery this large, I could retire." He smiled at Bain over the rim of his spectacles. "But I won't. The thrill of the hunt, the dig, and the finding of old relics is just too great a pull."

"Yes, I can see how this could easily get into your blood. It's very interesting to think there are thousands of years of artifacts just lying hidden in these tunnels."

"Yes, and we've barely scratched the surface. This is only the temple room. The Pharaohs were buried with their treasures. There are so many more artifacts to discover down here. Things that will tell us so much about the way they lived, worked, played. Deciphering the hieroglyphs is one of my favorite parts. They teach us so much about past civilizations."

There was a sudden tremor beneath their feet, one that made both of them look to each other with questioning stares.

"Simon, is that normal?" Bain nervously looked around the room.

"I'm not certain. Perhaps it was just a settling tremor from all the digging and excavation. These rooms have been undisturbed for thousands of years. The diggers even believe that they are cursed, and all who disturb the tombs will suffer pain or death." Simon grinned at the superstitious beliefs.

"I don't believe in curses," Bain said, just as another tremor was felt.

"Neither do I, but I suggest we get out of here, just in case."

Simon and Bain began walking toward the double doors and stairway when an earthquake hit the area, making the temple shake violently. The ceiling began to collapse and the torches were snuffed out by the falling debris. Simon Lane and Bain Brinley were quickly buried beneath the falling rubble and sand, deep within the ancient tomb.

# Chapter 4

**Planet of Harilhia, Late evening**

Just as rock, dust, and sand began to pile in around Bain, a bright light opened up and he fell through it as the earth trembled beneath him. When his head cleared and the dust settled, he looked around knowing he was no longer in Egypt. He realized he had fallen through another portal, unlike the one he had walked through, but with the same results. But this time he didn't have anything with him but the clothes on his back. The world he had been adjusting too was gone, along with all of his worldly possessions which were tucked neatly in his backpack in Simon's tent.

Bain stood up, dusted the sand and dirt from his clothing, and looked around. He was on the edge of a wooded area to his one side, and there was a great river and what sounded like a powerful waterfall to his other. He also realized that it seemed to be around the same time of day as when he fell through the portal.

"Simon," Bain yelled, hoping that his friend too had been taken out of harm's way. But unfortunately there was no reply. He now worried that Simon was injured, or worse, and he could do nothing to help him.

Bain walked toward the river's edge to have a look around. When he got closer and rounded the edge of the forest's tree line, a massive, far-off castle up on a hill which overlooked a large city, came into view just above the top of the waterfall. He couldn't really tell how far away it was, but it glistened in the setting sun's light as the pinks, yellows, oranges, and purples of the dusky sky reflected off the taller buildings, sending out shards of colored light in many directions, like the surface of a diamond. It was quite breathtaking and reminded him of his home in Loradin. It too was much like this new city appeared, glass-like in reflection; gleaming in the light. The white stone structure of the castle sat higher up; its buildings free from the traditional walls that often surrounded such structures.

Bain looked back at the flowing water and the powerful churning of the falls. He needed to figure out how to get across the water, but first he would head upstream to the top of the waterfall to see if there was a way to cross there.

Bain realized that his Matter Arranging Device seemed to blip and beep, trying to come alive in this new world. It hadn't worked at all in Egypt, except as a time-telling device. This made him wonder if he was close to home, or at least in the same universe. Well, if his device worked that meant he could use it to cross the river if there was no other way to do so, but he needed to be careful. If there was anyone around, and they saw him vanish into thin air and reappear somewhere else, they may label him as dangerous. He had best save using the MAD for other more important needs. Besides, with a city that size, there had to be a bridge upstream somewhere to allow him passage across the river.

Bain walked along the river's edge finding a narrow path that twisted upward along the side of the waterfall and was quite steep in a few places. Fortunately, the path twisted through the edge of the forest, allowing him to use the trees and bushes to help pull himself along the slope in certain places. By the time Bain reached the top of the falls, darkness had settled over the land, and the city that he inched ever closer to, illuminated the night sky and surrounding area in brightly colored hues of light. There was a stone wall that appeared to be twenty feet in height that surrounded the city, and Bain could see two separate entry gates from his point of view. It appeared that many travelers were going into the city so Bain's arrival may be easier to mask than he thought.

Just ahead of him was indeed a bridge and a road leading off in another direction through the thick forest to his right. Bain merged with the large number of travelers entering the city, drawing a few looks due to his unique style of clothing. These people dressed differently here, and he would have to liberate a cloak or other clothing so as not to attract too much attention. As he moved closer to the city gate, a merchant traveling beside him with a wagon load of cloaks, hats, blankets, and other cloth items happened to pass beside him, and Bain reached out and snagged a cloak to cover himself. Bain wondered as to the amount of traffic and the number of loaded carts entering the city. He looked up at the high walls, noticing the armed guards pacing the top edge along a lower wall. There was a large sign which sat above the gate that was an odd mix of swirls, lines, dashes, and dots above the name Dihendra Rhial, which made him think it was the city's name in a different language. As he walked along with the crowd, he also realized that he could only understand some of what the people were saying, which meant a definite language barrier existed.

He passed through the gate, noticing the thick twelve-foot-wide walls; which probably meant they enclosed stairways leading up to the top level. As he continued into the city, a great fan-fair with ticker-tape, streamers, trumpeters, and other musical instruments lined the streets, and the open areas around each gate entrance. Large creatures adorned with blankets and strands of decorative beads and jewels were led or ridden through the gates and along the streets as people cheered, chattered, and celebrated.

Bain could hear a few of the same words being chanted over and over in excitement; probably the name of whatever celebration or event was taking place. He also noticed the darkly cloaked figure that watched him from a lower interior section around the top of the wall. His years of training with the Loradin Secret Service had given him many skills, one of which was the ability of keen observation and the ability to feel when he was being watched. He saluted the figure that peered down at him, and to his satisfaction, the person blanched, their back stiffening. They quickly turned in a flash of swirling fabric and disappeared.

Bain grinned slyly to himself. This place might be even more interesting than he figured. It was certainly far different from Egypt. His thoughts quickly turned to Simon; he prayed the man was all right, but unless the Creator sent him somewhere else too, he assumed he was buried under a heap of rock, stone, and sand. He shook off the dark feeling and looked around once more at the revelry that was taking place around him.

A massive beast passed by him. It's four dark-green, tree-trunk-like legs were twice as thick and longer than Bain himself. Its long sail like ears in shades of greens stuck out from its head and hung nearly to the ground. The top of its head had three, long, white and green horns, and two long tusks of the same color which protruded forward from either side of its long, thick trunk and they were seated just below large round black eyes. A large platform on the animal's back held several people. One lone boy sat on the creature's head, legs straddling the center horn as he yelled and pointed instructions to the creature, giving the beast an occasional rub and pat.

Bain watched the creature lumber by, the platform on its back swaying slightly from side to side, its passengers happily seated on large, overstuffed pillows as they enjoyed the shade of their covered perch.

"I take it from your expression that you've never seen a Trendelow."

Bain turned toward the voice. The person who had been watching him from the wall earlier now stood before him. She appeared about his age, though the darkness of night and her large hood still camouflaged much of her head and face. She was dressed in leather armor of sorts and carried a sword beneath her robe at her left hip. Her lips curled upward in amusement, likely at his dumbfounded gaze as he watched the happy chaos around them.

"No, I've never seen a Trendelow before."

"Then you must not be from around here. They are a pretty common creature near Dihendra Rhial and the surrounding territories."

Bain avoided the indirect question about where he was from and changed the subject. "So what is this celebration all about?"

She pushed her hood back and looked around at the scene surrounding them. Bain was struck by her appearance. Her hair was the shade of the glistening, light blue, ocean that he had discovered at Ruin City on the other side of the Marshlands back on Zanchier. The color against her olive complexion and straight chin-length style was very becoming. The mix of brown and black leather complimented a trim yet toned physique. Her eyes were most striking in a shade of purplish green which danced in the flickering light of passing torches. He was glad it was her turn to answer him because he was unable to speak at the moment, mesmerized by her awkward beauty.

"It is the Four Moon Festival. Once every three years the four moons of Harilhia generate a banner harvest and the rhial celebrates. People bring their excess into the rhial and Dihendra puts all the excess in storage bins. This excess feeds the poorer people in all the surrounding territories for the harsh winters to follow after the four-moon harvest. People come from all around to join in the celebration and to sell their wares."

"It sounds like Dihendra Rhial is a good and fair place, a just society that helps its people."

"It is." She smiled brightly at his observation, suddenly sticking out her hand in greeting. "Sebena Zentrialle, Captain of the Twelfth Squadron and Protectors of Dihendra."

"Bain Brinley, traveler and explorer."

"Good to meet you, Bain Brinley. What brings you to our fair rhial? I assume it is not the festival since you knew nothing of it."

"Well, I just happened to be passing by and saw the people streaming into the city and decided to follow."

"City? What is a city?"

"It's what we call large places like this."

"Oh, you mean the rhial?" Sebena stated understanding now.

"So rhial means city? And Dihendra is the rhial's name?" Bain asked for clarification on his understanding as well.

"Yes." Sebena stated. "You said you were passing by. Passing from where?"

Bain began to grow a bit nervous. How in the world would he explain where he was from and how he arrived there? "Nowhere really, just exploring and traveling."

"From where did you start your travels?"

Bain simply said, "Zanchier."

A surprised look flew across her features. "So you are from Zanchier?"

This question shook Bain. "You know Zanchier?"

"Why, of course. We studied all about the topography of Harilhia at secondary academy. Zanchier resides on the other side of the planet, but no one I know has ever met anyone from there. You are the first person to ever come out of that place, at least that I know about. We all assumed it to be a wild, untamed place full of evil creatures, or so the stories go."

She looked at him expectantly, her head tilted, a question in her eyes.

Just then another creature lumbered by, though not quite as large as the Trendelow. The beast's long, outstretched neck swayed like the motion of the strikers from Zanchier, and it nearly knocked Bain over. Its elongated head protruded oddly on both the front and back of its neck. The other end of the neck nestled between two protruding shoulder blades which sat above long arms and a thick torso which attached to two strong back legs. A short stub of a tail finished off the beasts odd appearance. He had always thought the creatures of Zanchier to be strange looking, but the beasts here were even more so. The beast was followed by a herd of the same creatures, but in smaller versions. The creature leaned it's long head down in his direction and gazed at Bain briefly.

"I guess you've never seen a Wrotmond either?" Sebena asked, another amused grin tugging at her lips.

Bain looked at her briefly with a slight grin of his own and a shake of his head before his attention was taken again by the odd creatures passing by.

"Well, come along, Bain Brinley, and we can finish this conversation over a pint of barley-wine and a meal."

Bain said, "I could eat, but unfortunately I doubt my currency will be good here."

"It's on me. Besides I plan to bend your ear some more about Zanchier. I've longed to travel and explore myself, but my duties have always been to my homeland."

"Thanks, and I'll answer your questions the best that I can."

As Bain followed her through the maze of revelers, he wasn't at all sure how honest he could be with her about how he came here. Did they know of time-travel here? Was it something that was a possibility? He also had no idea that Zanchier was part of a much larger world on a planet known as Harilhia. Was Earth, Egypt, or the other places he learned about recently anywhere near here or part of Harilhia too? He decided he had better start journaling about the places he had been to and seen, and where they were respectively located. Maybe one day he could make some connections.

He would also ask his own questions of Sebena Zentrialle. Perhaps she could point him in the right direction to get home. He needed to find his parents and let them know he was all right. He only hoped that would be a possibility. When he stepped through the portal in Storm Valley, he was on his way to meet his entire family, who were about to set sail across the ocean for a new life. If they were no longer in Zanchier, where could they be and how would he ever be able to find them? Maybe Sebena could give him some insight about this great big world in which he found himself. He had no idea how to navigate it and when, or if, the next portal would open and send him to a new and strange place.

# Chapter 5

**Dihendra Rhial, Planet of Harilhia, Late Evening.**

Sebena pushed through a mass of people standing on the street in front of what appeared to be a pub and eatery. Bain followed her inside and watched, while she never stopped walking, she nodded at the bartender, raised her hand holding up two fingers, and then made a circular sign in the air. The man nodded, yelled over his shoulder through a window and went back to work. Bain continued to follow Sebena up a flight of steps to the second floor, back across the room, and out on a balcony that overlooked the street where they had just entered the establishment. They sat at a high table giving them unobstructed views of the merry-making below.

Just as they were getting comfortably seated, the man from behind the bar appeared carrying two plates of steaming food, and two large containers of what must have been the barley-wine she mentioned before.

As he sat the items on the table, Sebena said, "Thanks Brecker."

The man nodded and left them alone. Bain looked around at the others who were filing onto the balcony, many that were dressed similarly to Sebena. They must have been more of Dihendra's guards.

Sebena took a large bite of food and watched Bain as he looked around, realizing what question formed in his mind. "This balcony is for use by guards only during celebrations. It helps us to see problems quickly and prevent trouble often before it happens. It is also why we stand upon the wall as people come into the rhial. You're quite observant, Bain Brinley, not many people I meet make such connections."

Bain breathed deep of the fragrant food and took a bite before he answered. "I was employed by a special forces unit back home. My training has served me well."

"Yes, I figured it was something like that. Your build looks strong and lean."

Bain was a bit taken back at her admission to checking him out. "Thanks. I noticed the same about you."

Sebena nodded appreciatively. She was extremely confident and didn't seem to want to play any games; just straight forward speaking.

They quietly and quickly ate their meal, and downed the large mug of barley-wine, which Bain found quite satisfying. The man called Brecker had returned with full mugs once more.

They leaned back in their chairs and continued watching the throngs of people as they chatted.

"So, Bain, you never truly answered my question about what brought you here."

"Well, as I said, I was just traveling and noticed the city above the falls and decided to come check it out."

"Traveling from where? Zanchier is a very good distance from the Dihendran Territories."

"Well, I don't think you'd believe me if I told you."

"Why is that?"

"Have you ever heard of a planet called Earth? Or a place there known as Egypt?"

"No, I don't believe I have. Interplanetary travel is something we have only recently began to explore. Are you telling me you have a ship that you came here on from another planet?"

Bain noticed this seemed to truly pique her interest and she leaned forward as she awaited his answer.

"Not exactly. I've never been on any ship that could travel through space, but I have traveled the sky by way of airships."

"So your airships can travel between planets?"

Bain squirmed in his seat. He wasn't sure he should say more, but she was not going to let up with the questions. He only hoped he didn't regret what he was about to say.

"Sebena, this is going to sound very strange I'm sure. I don't even truly understand how it happens myself, but I can travel through time, between places through a strange light that appears whenever there is a great land-shake."

Her face contorted in confusion and her brow knit together. "I do not understand."

Bain leaned forward and took a deep breath, trying to gauge his next words. "The first time I traveled to another world was through a portal back on Zanchier way up in the mountains. I saw a glowing light in the field and when I went to check it out, I stepped through and found myself somewhere else entirely. When I looked back, the light was gone and I was stuck there. I was only there a few weeks when a land-shake hit, another portal opened, and I fell through and found myself here."

Sebena watched him, her steady gaze never wavering as he told his story. At some point she had sat back in her stool to relax.

She finally leaned forward again and said, "I have an uncanny ability to tell when someone is lying. I find no such untruth in your words, yet I can hardly believe what you say."

"It took me a bit to believe it myself, and I'm living it."

"Why do you think this is happening to you?"

"I wish I knew. Only the Creator knows the answer to that."

Sebena's eyebrows shot up at the mention of the Creator.

"So you too are a believer?"

"Most definitely. I've seen too much not to be."

"I would like to witness this portal, as you call it, for myself."

"Well, if I could show you I would. But I have no control over when it opens. Plus I'm not even sure it will happen again. This is only my second time to travel through one."

"Well, Bain Brinley, you've just earned yourself a permanent companion, for as much as I can do so. I am determined to witness this for myself."

"Since I am new here and have no other options, I'll take you up on that; as long as you don't mind a house guest?"

"Not at all. However, my home is in barracks quarters with the other Twelfth Guard. As Captain, I do have my own room, but you will need to bunk with the others, and I will pass you off as a new trainee for this to be allowed."

"Well, I'm not afraid of hard work."

"Good, because hard is an understatement."

Bain nodded at her as they drained their second glass of barley-wine.

Sebena stood and said, "Well, time to head home. The revelers have all quieted to a small roar and the lower regiment will oversee the night watch. Come along, Bain, I will show you your new home for however long the Creator decides to keep you here."

Bain followed Sebena out of the pub, across the open courtyard and market square toward another side gate like the one he had entered earlier. She hopped onto a vehicle that had no wheels, patting the seat behind her, and starting the engine. Bain had just straddled the mod when she yelled over her shoulder, "Hold on."

Bain barely had the time to grab onto her waist when she took off, causing Sebena to laugh. Bain was shocked to see that the mod actually hovered over the ground a few feet and traveled over any surface like it was flying. They traveled over the land toward the large non-walled castle that Bain had seen above the city earlier when he first appeared in Harilhia.

Sebena steered into the open courtyard of the castle past what appeared to be stables, and into a long stone corridor, stopping inside a room full of the same type of modules. She shut down the engine, the mod sank to the ground, and they dismounted. Bain stepped back in admiration of the module as he looked it over.

"I'm guessing you've never seen an air-rover either."

"No. We have Voyagers back in Zanchier. They had two wheels and traveled upon the ground, not hovering over it like this."

Sebena waved him along, saying, "This way to quarters. It is growing late and we have a very early start in the morning as training begins at first light."

Bain followed her up several flights of stairs and through a few doors to an open area filled with small bunks and hundreds of other guards, many already asleep and others still awake and heavily involved in conversation. When they entered, his presence caught some others attention quickly, and they watched him follow along behind Sebena. Bain nodded to them, but only a few nodded back. Sebena led him to an open bunk on the outer wall beneath a large window. She opened a cabinet nearby and gave him sheets, a blanket, and a pillow.

Bain took them, thanked her, and began to make up the bunk.

Sebena gave him further instructions. "The restroom is around the corner there, along with the showers. You'll find extra supplies in the cabinet located by the sinks." She turned to look at the other men watching them with interest. She then turned to Bain and added, "The guys can be over-bearing to new people, but they are harmless. Just remember you'll have to take your punches like all the rest so try not to take it personally if they give you a hard time for a while."

Bain busied himself with his bunk and nodded looking past her at the men staring him down and laughing amongst themselves. Sebena turned and left, walking through a door a few feet away. Bain, tired from the long day, collapsed upon his bunk to reflect on how different things were between the two worlds. Just this morning he was in Egypt, digging, and cataloging ancient artifacts. Then, that same evening, transported to another world close to his homeland and conscripted into the local guard by a woman who was striking to look at and very outspoken; completely different from any woman he had ever known. Well, maybe she was more like his mother Harper than he cared to admit. His mother had had a hard life over the last ten years, so he completely understood her toughness, forwardness, and hesitation to trust people in general. In this way Sebena seemed different. She seemed to trust him, someone she had just met, but her confidence in herself and abilities was far greater than that of his mother, and of Raila. Raila had been sweet, mild-tempered, easy-going, and quite uncommunicative at times, to the point of not speaking to him for months. But before her death she had wanted to take on the evil that was overtaking Zanchier. She wanted to do more than just hide out with the mothers, children, and the elderly and infirmed. Her lack of military training had been what had gotten her killed. Bain had tried to persuade her to stay behind in the bunker but she had refused.

His thoughts turned back to Sebena. He was curious to see her in action during training in the morning. His thoughts were all over the place tonight so he decided to roll over and try to get some sleep, but not before he noticed the looks and sneers from the other five men across the room from him. Bain exhaled loudly. The last thing he needed was another bunch of bullies like what he had dealt with in academy with Riglan Mortruff and his cronies. But Bain was not a kid anymore. Over the last four years he had dealt with war, his grandfather going to jail, his mother and family being hunted by an insane criminal, war, famine, wild beasts determined to make a meal of him, and more deaths than he cared to acknowledge. These new troubles with overbearing, controlling coworkers should be a breeze; at least he hoped they would. It wasn't long after Bain closed his eyes that sleep overtook his tired mind and body. He slept hard and comfortably for the next five hours, only to be awakened early the next morning to a rather loud alarm that blared throughout the barracks, and men moving quickly to prepare for the morning training. Bain swung his legs from his bed and stood, stretching to alleviate the stiffness in his shoulders as his gaze turned to the door in which Sebena disappeared through the night before. It was closed, and yet he doubted she was still in there.

"Hey," came a voice from the other side of his bunk. Bain turned to see a man watching him. The man stuck out his hand in greeting. "Mercer Rand, but everyone calls me Merk."

"Bain Brinley. Nice to meet you Merk."

"Same here. So, where did you come from?"

"I ran into Sebena in the market square last night, and since I'm new in town and basically all alone with nowhere to go, she gave me a place to stay along with a job."

Mercer snorted at this. "A job huh. It isn't an easy "job" fella'. You'll likely get injured before lunch or die before dinner." Mercer jumped up from his bed, smiled broadly at Bain, and disappeared into the bathroom.

Bain shrugged his shoulders and followed the man, preparing for the day ahead. Mercer showed him where to find bathroom necessities. After, he followed Mercer to the dining hall where they were fed a hearty breakfast, and he also saw Sebena at another table with others who were obviously in charge. She nodded at him and he nodded in return.

"Bain," Mercer said, catching his attention, "trays and utensils go in separate bins. Now we head out to lineup for training. Do you have a weapon?"

"Uh, no. I kind of left that behind before I left home."

"No matter, the captains will likely fit you with an appropriate weapon anyway."

"What do you mean by appropriate?"

"They fit you based on strengths that they look for in training."

Bain nodded his understanding as they, along with many more men and women, filed out into the open courtyard of the training field just as the morning light was beginning to break over the horizon. They all stood an arm's length away in rows of straight lines. Bain grinned at the differences in worlds. In Lillith and Simon's world, women would not fight like they do here.

Bain followed everyone else's gaze as they looked up at a platform which was a story up, where several leaders stood. A loud screech split the air, and a large, winged beast flew up over the edge of the castle wall, and on its back was Sebena Zentrialle.

# Chapter 6

"Huh," Bain muttered as he observed the colorful beast; its scaly skin swirled with reds fading into pinks which then faded into white on its underbelly. The beast seemed to effortlessly take commands from Sebena. Bain wondered if she had the same gift that his sisters had, the ability to speak to other creatures.

Mercer muttered, "I hate rider training. I can't seem to get any of the Baiskreet to cooperate."

Bain asked, "So, this is only one type of Baiskreet?"

"Yeah, there are lots of different breeds. I can't even tell you which one this is. There's a breeder's hatching ground near the castle on the north side."

"Interesting. I'd like to see it."

"You will," Mercer added with a smile. "So, you think you can ride one of those?" He nodded toward the beast and smirked.

"I've ridden some pretty strange creatures, large too, but usually not alone. I was always with one of my sisters, or another LARS telepath."

"LARS Telepath?"

Bain smiled. "Sorry, LARS stands for the Loradin Animal Rescue and Sanctuary. It's an institute where I'm from that aids injured creatures. There are specially gifted kids there that can communicate with the animals."

"Really?" Mercer asked, surprised. "I've never heard of telepathic communication with beasts like this before."

"It's not a common talent, but it's mostly found in younger kids back home."

"Where's home?"

"Zanchier."

"No way! I've never met anyone from there before. You look...normal."

Bain smirked at his reply. "What do you mean?"

"Well, we were always told that crazy, wild, and lawless people, were the only kind who ever came from there."

"Well, I hate to burst your bubble, but there are perfectly normal people in Zanchier. But there is also a large organization of lawless cutthroats who were taking over Zanchier when I left."

"Cool!"

"Not cool." Bain glared at Mercer. "Scaithers are pure evil. The people of Zanchier suffer greatly at their hands."

"Sorry, I didn't mean anything by that. I meant that it was cool that there were normal people there too." Mercer stumbled over his apology, realizing Bain had become agitated.

Bain nodded his understanding, but before he could answer, their attention was taken by the Baiskreet which landed on the ground in front of the lines of trainees. Dust and dirt flew about them from the force of the beast's powerful wings.

"Recruits!" Sebena yelled. "Who wants a turn at learning to command a Lurepture?"

Several people stepped forward as Bain watched a line begin to form in front of the first line of recruits. Bain too stepped forth to take his place in line beside twelve others, several who included the men who had watched him last night when he entered the bunk quarters. One in particular looked at him, smirked unfriendly like, and then returned his attention back to the beast and Sebena.

Sebena watched Bain, surprised that a fresh recruit would be willing to take on a Baiskreet on his first day. *Poor guy*, she thought, *he obviously had no idea what he was getting into. Besides, he had likely never seen a Baiskreet before today either, much like the other creatures of Dihendra.*

Sebena dismounted and  pointed to the tall guy who seemed to be perturbed by Bain's sudden appearance here.

"Guidriun, you're up first."

The man stepped up, saluted Sebena, then confidently took the reins in hand. The Lurepture began to grow nervous as he walked to its side, stepped into the stirrup, and mounted the beast's back. It screeched and danced, unhappy about the unknown invader who so nonchalantly sat upon his back and tugged at the bit in his mouth trying to force discipline.

Sebena smirked at the reaction as Guidriun tried to strong-arm the beast into submission. The Lurepture thrashed and bounced, trying to knock the rider from its back. It turned sharply, slamming into an adjacent building knocking Guidriun off, slamming him into the ground.

Sebena let out a sharp command and the creature calmed. She then walked over to it, placing her hands on both sides of its head and spoke softly to it as she calmed it. She then took the reins in hand once more, led it back to the center of the yard, and turned back to the recruits. She lifted the reins in the air, her eyebrows raised in question.

As Guidriun took his place back in line, Bain stepped forward. Sebena's eyebrows raised even higher as he approached. "You certain about this, Recruit Brinley?"

"As certain as any others who stepped forward."

She nodded and handed him the reins, then stepped away.

Bain stood there, looking into the beast's eyes, and taking in its appearance, listening to its breathing, which had begun to quicken. Bain slowly raised his hand to touch the beast's nose but stopped short, waiting for it to accept the action. The Lurepture breathed heavily for a moment, watched Bain with one golden eye, then cocked its head and leaned into his hand. There was a slight appreciative aww that went around the group. Bain rubbed the creature's nose gently, bonding with it. He stepped slowly to the right, reins slowly slipping through the fingers of his right hand as his left hand followed the length of the creature's neck, never breaking touch with it. Its breathing calmed even more as Bain stopped walking beside the saddle, his hand dropping to the reins in his other hand. He took a deep steadying breath and reached up, grabbing the saddle horn. The Lurepture's head swung around to watch him, giving him a steady look. Bain looked at the beast, as to question if the motion was all right. It turned its head back around and stood steady. Bain stepped into the stirrup slowly climbing up to swing his other leg over and locking his foot into the second stirrup. The Lurepture stood, shook a little, causing its whole body to quiver. Bain held tight to the reins, as the Lurepture turned to look at him, giving him a sinister grin, then quickly stood up on its hind legs as Bain rolled out of the saddle, down its long tail and onto the ground behind it.

Everyone laughed at the motion, including Bain as he looked up at the beast from his place upon the ground. It snorted at him, and Bain could only smile. As he stood to get back into line, the Lurepture nudged him in the back with its head nearly knocking him over once more, snorting again.

Sebena watched the exchange with shocked amusement. "Well, Recruit Brinley, it appears you've made a friend."

"You sure about that?" Bain asked. "It didn't feel too friendly to me."

"A Lurepture Baiskreet is a fiercely loyal beast but can be temperamental. But if they like you, they will turn playful, often annoyingly so. In all the years I've taught Baiskreet training, I've never seen a Lurepture take to someone so quickly. They are often quick to react and extremely stubborn; it can take weeks of daily one on one for a bond to form. Either you have something quite unique about you, or she just really likes you."

"I'm sure it's the latter, Captain."

"We shall see, Brinley. I'll be watching you quite closely with great interest."

Bain nodded, taking his place back in line in the ranks beside Mercer.

"Man, you have got to show me how you did that. I've never even gotten close to any of the Baiskreet, much less climbed on ones back."

"I didn't really do anything, Merk. I just gave her respect, treated her kindly, and took my time with her. You can't show fear either. Animals can sense your feelings, and they react to them with the same emotions. If you're fearful, then they will be too."

"How do you know this stuff?"

"I used to hang out a lot at LARS. I picked up a lot of useful information watching the kids and listening to instruction." Bain didn't mention that it was Raila Orman who had taught him most of what he knew about animals. He didn't feel like explaining about her death and dealing with all the heartfelt apologies. He looked at Sebena once more, realizing she too had glanced his way, nodding at him. He nodded back. Their exchange did not go unnoticed by Guidriun, who watched them both with scrutiny.

The training exercises continued, with each recruit who had stepped forward taking their turn at the Lurepture. None had the success that Bain did, though some came a bit closer as they tried to model Bain's technique.

After ride training was over, the recruits were pitted in battle against one another. Mercer and Bain teamed up, but Mercer, although stocky and strong, was no match for Bain's abilities from his years on the LSS.

This too captured Sebena's attention. Even though Bain had told her some of what his past life had included, she wasn't sure what to expect. His sleek but strong form, over six-foot height, stubbled chin, thick brown hair, brownish green eyes, and laid-back personality made Bain Brinley an all-around attractive man. But she was not in the market for any kind of relationship, she just simply had an appreciation for the man whom she found lost and wandering the streets of Dihendra yesterday. The way he carried and handled himself showed that he had self-control and had led a life that had taught him much. She really wanted to hear more about Bain's life in Zanchier; that wild, untamed land they were taught little about.

Lunch time was called, and as they entered the building, Bain was singled out by many men and women who wanted to get to know this new recruit to the ranks. As each passed by him to introduce themselves, many told him how impressed they were with how he had handled the Lurepture. And with the insights they had learned from watching him, they too had gotten much further with the creature than ever before.

Bain nodded and smiled easily with each person until it finally slowed as they entered the dining room. Bain and Mercer stood in line to receive their trays of food, and Mercer just watched all the admiring glances Bain was receiving from the women in line all around them.

"Man, you sure made an impression today."

"Yeah, but I'm not sure if it was good or bad," Bain answered, completely oblivious to all the staring in his direction.

Mercer laughed. "From all the attention you're getting from all the ladies, I'd say good."

Bain glanced around the line of people at Mercer's words and noticed what he was talking about. Bain crookedly grinned a bit, and nodded at some of the women who were obviously ogling him.

"Ladies," he acknowledged, and they smiled in return. Bain quickly averted his gaze back to the quickly approaching food layout. He and Mercer chose what they wanted, grabbed a couple of drinks, and headed to a two-person table that Bain chose. Not wishing to have any lunch time conversations on how he viewed relationships with strange women.

Mercer said, "Looks like I picked the right guy to talk to. Maybe some of your popularity will fall my way and some of those lovely ladies still checking you out will settle for me."

Bain laughed at his observation. "You can have as many as you like, Merk. I'm not interested in a relationship right now. I have my own set of problems and I don't need to add anything else to it."

"Like what?" Mercer asked, now interested in his new, mysterious friend from the fabled lands of Zanchier.

"You wouldn't believe me if I told you."

Mercer sat up straighter, his interest piqued even more. "Try me. Is it about Zanchier?"

Bain chuckled at the curiosity in his voice and the look of anticipation on his face.

"What is all this mystique around here that surrounds Zanchier? It's just like any other place that I've seen. The same sort of people, creatures, vehicles, trees, water, you know…life."

"No, we don't know. That's just it. I've never known anyone who has ever met anyone from Zanchier."

"Then how do you know it even exists."

"Rumors I guess. We were always taught in academy that there were strange untamed lands to the Northeast that were impossible to reach. No one ever came or went past the vast deserts of the deadly mountain ranges and marshlands that exist surrounding the interior. A few explorers from hundreds of years ago attempted to cross through the marshlands from some of the outer ancient cities, but they never returned or were heard from again. Not many people attempted it after the five previous explorers never came back, especially when their traveling companions who did return told of large voracious beasts near the coast, and how they tried to eat them. They barely escaped with their lives. Since then, the rest of Harilhia would never commission anymore attempts. Historical-house writers just considered it deadly, and people just stop trying for fear of death."

Bain nodded his head as he chewed his food, listening to Mercer.

"Well, those voracious beasts are known as Hungerhounds. Their name says it all. There are lots of other wild creatures too. Huge, flying, fire-breathing, four-legged birds known as Kabihanxu, Pagorinxes which are large black and blue cats that will tear you to shreds, a giant sea-beast known as a Brindelwren. Monshokto which are large hairy beasts that resemble rocks when curled up on the shore but have amazing abilities. There are so many creatures, just like anywhere else I suppose. We don't have Baiskreet there though, or any of the other creatures I saw strolling the streets yesterday."

"Well, what about civilization. Surely you can't live in a place like that. Is that why you left?"

"Believe it or not there are millions of people living in Zanchier. Just like anywhere else, there are the poor, the wealthy, the controlling, the gifted, and the talented. Life in Zanchier was a struggle for the majority of the population as the wealthy lorded over the poor and talentless. Those forced to work the harvest fields and the Rhe Mines because they never showed any sort of gifts or abilities during early academy years. But having said all of that, Zanchier, though wild in many places, was a beautiful place to live. Though I'm sure that now they are overrun with Scaither rule, and the people fight and suffer daily just to survive."

Mercer had sat quietly, listening, and hanging onto every word Bain uttered. By the time Bain finished speaking, Mercer had all but stopped breathing. His spoon tightly gripped in his unmoving left hand; his eyes transfixed on Bain's face.

Mercer cleared his throat, shook his head, and took another bite before responding. "Man, I'd love to see it. If it's so hard to get into the place, how did you get out?"

"That's the part I doubt you'll believe."

"Try me?" Mercer took another bite and chewed, waiting on Bain to explain.

"Through some sort of light portal."

Mercer's expression was one of confusion. "What do you mean?"

"Well, there was a strange, glowing light just hovering at ground level in a valley where I was traveling. Like a tiny sun, yet larger than myself. I went to see what it was, reached into it, then stepped through. It pulled me into another world, like nothing I had ever seen before."

Mercer said, "Are you pulling my leg?"

Bain crossed his arms over his chest and shook his head. "No, I promise, everything I'm telling you is true.

"Okay, so this world, is it here?"

"No. I traveled to another place before falling through another portal and ending up here."

"Can you show me this portal?"

"No, they seem to disappear every time I pass through them. I turned to go back home, but the light was gone. The second time, when I ended up here, was during a land-shake that collapsed an ancient tomb I was in at the time. I fell through and found myself on the outskirts of Dihendra, out by the river on the forest's edge."

"Whew…" Mercer whistled. "Man, you've experienced some strange stuff."

"Well, only you and Sebena know my story, and I would like to keep it that way. So please, don't tell anyone else what I've told you."

"What if people ask where you're from?"

"Just tell them some island on the other side of Harilhia."

Mercer smiled. "I can do that."

The men finished their meals, cleaned up, and prepared for what the day held for them next.

# Chapter 7

**Castle Dihendra, Breeding grounds, Afternoon**

All the recruits were taken to the breeder's Hatching Grounds that afternoon where they were all given orders to interact with and tend to the needs of the Baiskreet that were stabled there. This exercise was to allow the Baiskreet to get used to them being near and in their space. Since Bain's fairly passable interaction this morning, Sebena and the other leaders decided that everyone should try to make hands-on contact with the animals they were interacting with that day.

Mercer, being awkward around the Baiskreet, was given orders to tend to the Nassureptic today; a very laid-back creature. Each were colored in varying shades of blue, green, and yellow, and ranging in sizes from medium to large. The beast was known to be a fast flier after it built up speed, and it could turn invisible along with its rider.

Bain, however, was taken to the pen of a breed that was colored in shades of gold, silver, copper, and bronze.

Sebena told him, "This is the Kriesletrope. They are considered to be the most beautiful of all the Baiskreet; regal in appearance and stature. They grow to be quite large as you can see and they breathe fire. They swim well, although will avoid water if possible. Do you see the soft looking spikes that lay flat along its back?" She pointed for his benefit. "They rise up and stiffen when they feel threatened, and can be thrown, but it can take weeks for them to regrow after. These Baiskreet are characteristically quite snobbish but are also loyal to a fault. They are often the dominate species amongst the Baiskreet, and the largest male is seen as the Alpha."

Bain looked over the majestic looking creatures. "They're quite striking to look at, almost like their scaly skin shimmers in the sunlight."

"Exactly. It's as if they glow when they are content. However, when angered or threatened, the glow disappears and they take on a menacing appearance. Like their scales turn a dark shade and exude what they are feeling. It's quite astonishing to see for the first time."

Bain grinned. "Well let's hope I don't bring out that characteristic today. I'd rather not make any of these creatures angry at me."

Sebena grinned knowing the thoughts going through his mind. "Well, all of the Baiskreet here are bred in captivity so they are quite used to people and new recruits poking about their pens. I'm sure you will be fine."

"Okay, what do I do?" Bain asked, ready to get started.

"Neeanne will instruct you today." Sebena waved to a woman who was pushing a large wheelbarrow across the paddock. She set the barrow on the ground and headed toward them.

"Neeanne, this is Bain. He'll be training with you today."

Neeanne nodded as Sebena left. She then looked at Bain appreciatively.

"Not many first day recruits get to tend to the Kriesletrope."

"Why is that?" He asked.

"Well, they are like royalty. Your abilities and mannerisms with the creatures often lead to where you train. You must have done quite well during introductions this morning."

Bain shrugged. "I suppose. I'm not sure what the normal is during introductions, but I did get to successfully, but uneventfully, mount a Lurepture. That is until it sneakily tossed me to the ground, then looked as though it was laughing at me."

Neeanne laughed at his description. "Yes, the Lurepture can be quite the prankster. But if it allowed you to climb up at all without a fight, it is safe to say that it liked you."

"So I was told."

"Well, let's get you started, Bain. We'll make sure the dens are clean then feed them. You have to watch out for them because with their attitudes, they don't watch for you. So if you want to avoid getting stepped on or squished against the wall you have to pay attention. After, if you survive without being sent to medical," she smiled toothily at him, "we'll see how you interact with them during hands-on time."

"Thanks for the warning. I would rather not be sent to medical, today or any day."

Bain followed Neeanne, grabbed the wheelbarrow for her and followed her into the dens. The structure was like a large, currently vacant cavern dug out of the natural hillside. The odor in the den was a bit over-powering, causing Bain to cough.

Neeanne grinned at his reaction. "It takes some getting used to, especially on the first day. With the Kriesletrope being one of the largest in the Baiskreet lineage, their waste is larger, and smellier, as well. Don't worry, you'll get used to it after a few days."

"Wonderful," Bain eked out as he tried to hold his breath every so often.

Neeanne laughed and smiled each time he let out his air and took in another breath trying to hold it until the job was finished. Bain was glad he didn't have to dodge large stomping feet and the possibility of dropping feces while trying to clean up. They made quick work of the mess and practically ran out of the cavern, with Bain quickly dropping the wheelbarrow and leaning forward, hands on his knees and inhaling deeply of the fresh air. Neeanne couldn't control her laughter at his expense. She slapped him on the shoulder and said, "Come on, wimp."

She grabbed the wheelbarrow and started off across the field. Bain stood up, still clearing his nostrils of the smell, then trotted after her to catch up. They dumped the waste into a pile, then cleaned and stored the tools before heading off toward the aloof Kriesletrope.

The large beasts, one male and one female, walked around with their heads held high, seemingly never looking down, as if the world around them must move out of their way.

Neeanne explained. "You would think they would just smash anything they came close to with how they seem to seldom look down. But believe it or not, they are fairly gentle creatures. They move about with grace and agility and manage to avoid destroying things."

Maybe their peripheral vision is extraordinary?" Bain offered.

Neeanne expression was one of surprised revelation. "Maybe so. That would explain a lot. I wonder why no one else here ever thought of that? You seem to have a thinking head on your shoulders, Bain."

"I do. One of my talents is technology. I used to attend an academy for the gifted in that field."

"Well, you may well move out of animal servicing and training quicker than you think." She smiled at him as they walked to the high fence, and climbed the stairway up several stories to a high walkway that went across a smaller field. Once they were on the top, the Kriesletrope began making their way toward them in a slow, graceful, motion.

Bain could see the entire field dedicated for this breed, and he could make out a nest off under some very thick, tall tree canopies which  held two rather large eggs.

He asked, "So, I notice that even though this is a breeding ground, there aren't a lot of the same types of Baiskreet. What happens with the young?"

"Well, if we kept all the creatures we bred, then we would soon be overrun. Some die of disease or birth defects, others have over-bearing or untrainable traits and we release those into the wilds of Eathreon. It's where the Baiskreet thrive on Harilhia."

"How far is this Eathreon?"

"It's a fair distance. It takes a few days to get there, and the territory is a massive, wild, forested area. Breathtaking to see, but near deadly to visit as the Baiskreet there are wild.  We take the trained beasts for protection to release the untrainable."

"I'd like to see that one day."

"Well, if you stick around long enough, you likely shall."

The Kriesletrope sauntered up to them, both looking over the stranger with what appeared to Bain to be unassuming and aloof attitudes. Bain felt as though they viewed him as no more than a pesky bug on a windshield.

"I assume the larger one is the male," he said.

"Yes."

The male stretched out his neck toward Bain, sniffed the air around him, then snorted out a puff of air, blowing Bain's hair and clothing about.

A low rumble formed in the male's throat, vibrating up and out in another puff of air.

"He's sizing you up," Neeanne told him.

"As what, lunch?" Bain asked, causing another laugh in Neeanne. He watched the large beast stare down at him; each steely, blue-green eye nearly as large as Bain's head. It had to stand at least twenty-feet tall from head to foot and be the same in length; the female was only slightly smaller. The male shook his head causing a tremor to travel the length of his body which also caused his wings to lift and separate. Bain could see another ten feet of length for the tail as it lifted into the air as the beast shook, and the wingspan appeared to be thirty-feet wide. It's beautifully colored, scaly skin, glimmered in the afternoon sun, reflecting small streaks of light in every direction as it moved.

The female soon joined in the display, prancing about them on the ground below. Preening herself like a festive bird. Bain also noticed the spikes on their backs sway softly like feathers with each shake. He couldn't imagine those same spikes turning hard and deadly.

"They are showing off for us." Neeanne smiled brightly as she made clucking and clicking sounds with her mouth as she stretched her hand out in front of her. The male settled down a bit and turned to look at her. He nodded his head as though he were stretching his neck; not wishing to look like he was in a hurry for Neeanne's caressing touch.

The male slowly leaned into Neeanne's hand, pushing at it as she laughed and brought the other hand to rub both sides of his head. The male closed his eyes and made a throaty purring sound.

Neeanne said, "This is Karalis and the female is called Karaliene."

Karalis opened his eyes as one large orb looked at Bain.

Neeanne said, "I think he wants your attention."

"Are you sure about that?" Bain asked, hesitant to touch the beast.

"Pretty sure," Neeanne answered as Bain raised his hand and Karalis leaned in toward Bain as Karaliene stepped toward Neeanne.

Bain could feel the vibration of the creature's breath beneath his skin. Each powerful draw of air into his lungs seemed to cause his body to vibrate. Karalis moved under Bain's touch for the next few moments, then suddenly backed away as if to say, 'I'm done with you now human.' Bain was in awe of the beasts as Karaliene allowed him to touch her as well, lingering a bit longer than the male. They both soon sauntered away to their nest beneath the trees.

"Wow. I have to say that was quite emasculating."

"Yeah, they're pretty amazing creatures. They could squash us easily or eat us in just a few bites. To think they allow us anywhere near them is a testament to how gentle they are in nature. But make one mad and I'm afraid it's over."

Bain turned to look at Neeanne now that the beasts that drew his attention were settling onto their nest. "So, what now?"

"Well, we'll set out their food, then walk around the other paddocks so you can see the other Baiskreet. I'll explain each breed and what they are capable of as we walk. After that, it's back to the barracks for dinner, showers, downtime, then lights out."

"Sounds good."

As Bain and Neeanne finished their chores then walked around the breeding grounds, Sebena and the other leaders watched the new recruits in their duties; her attention drawn more to Bain than anyone else. His way with the creatures, and his fighting skills had impressed them all, but none more than Sebena herself. He had proved to be quite an asset to the guard so far. The man seemed to be good at everything he did, and he was drawing quite a bit of attention from his other peers in the ranks. He also demonstrated some leadership qualities. She just wondered how long he would be staying around. If what he told her was real, then he could just disappear at any point in time, then again, who's to say another portal would ever appear. Sebena was curious to know more about Bain and hoped to get the opportunity to do so soon.

When it was time to return to the barracks for cleanup then dinner, Bain met up with Mercer once more in the dinner-hall, but this time they were called over to a larger table filled with people anxious to meet Bain.

Bain found himself being questioned by eight different people, all clamoring to get their questions answered. He wasn't sure which to answer first so Mercer quieted the table..

"All right everybody, calm down and let the man speak. First question was 'How did you get the Lurepture to accept you?'"

Bain shrugged and said, "Past experience I guess. I just showed it respect. All creatures should be treated with care and respect if you want them to take kindly to you."

Someone said, "Where did you learn to handle creatures? Some of us watched you today with the Kriesletrope. I've never seen anyone touch one on the first day."

"Back home I guess. Besides, it didn't seem too standoffish to me as it just walked up to us. I figured it had more to do with Neeanne being there. The Kriesletrope are used to her."

"Where are you from?" someone else asked.

"Just some island on the other side of Harilhia. I'm sure you've never heard of it."

"Tell us anyway," someone said.

A familiar voice spoke from behind him. "All right you guys. Let the man eat his dinner,"

Bain turned to see Sebena standing there.

Everyone saluted and Sebena nodded for Bain to follow her. He grabbed his tray, slapped Mercer on the back, and followed Sebena out to a balcony where it appeared that the only people there were the leaders.

She set her own tray on a private table and sat down. Bain did the same.

They smiled at one another and ate their dinner, after which, Sebena set in with her own questions.

"So, is this animal control part of your training from Zanchier?"

"Not really. I'm just used to being around strange, large, creatures. I guess working near the animals at the rescue back home taught me more than I thought."

"Well, Bain, you're turning out to be quite interesting to watch. It seems you're good at everything."

"Probably just my years of training with the LSS."

Sebena nodded and grinned.

Bain asked, "So will tomorrow be the same as today?"

"Yes, pretty much. But if Karalis or Karaliene will let you mount one of them, we'll try flying."

"Creature flying I've done, but not on anything quite as large as Karalis."

They smiled at one another, made small talk for the next twenty minutes, and then everyone retired to the barracks for downtime before lights out by ten p.m.

# Chapter 8

The next morning the recruits were up early once more to do the day over again. During introductions, the recruits were given the chance to mount another Baiskreet breed.

Sebena explained. "This, most of you know by now, is a Copasedrom. It's colors are in shades of purple, gold, and gray. When they are young, like this one, the colors are softer, but as they age they become very vivid and bold. They are typically of average size, though some have been known to grow to be quite large, although not like that of the Kriesletrope. The Copasedrom have a sleek, powerful build, and are made for speed. They fly faster than any other of the Baiskreet, are quite agile in the air, especially if it catches an upstream, and its screech can disorient its prey or enemy allowing it ample time to attack. Now, who's first?"

Many stepped up this time, anxious to try out their newly found tactics on the beast to be the first to ride it.

Several people went, trying their best to mount the creature, but only a few got onto the beast's back before being thrown to the ground. Bain watched as the creature looked as though it wasn't engaged with the activity at all. He could tell it wanted to be somewhere else entirely as it often looked up at the sky each time it became agitated by the people trying to climb upon its back.

It was Bain's turn with the Copasedrom. The creature was quite agitated by now after a dozen or so tries. He walked up to it and stopped in front of the beast. He slowly reached his hand out to it and the creature stopped moving and looked down at him. Bain waited, unmoving, until the beast leaned down to sniff his hand. Realizing that he was not going to hurt it, the beast pushed at his hand with its nose, and Bain began to pet the creature with both hands as he spoke to it.

"There we go, that isn't so bad is it? I bet you want to go flying."

The Copasedrom bobbed its head up and down as though it understood him. So he tried one more question.

"If you let me on your back we can take a little trip around Dihendra. How does that sound?"

Once again, the beast bobbed its head up and down, eyeing Bain.

"Sebena," Bain said, "does this creature have a name yet?"

"Yes, we call him Corpse."

Bain slid around the creature's side, slowly and gently climbed up into the saddle, and said, "Corpse huh?"

"Yes," she said with a toothy smile as she watched Bain tighten the reins around his hands. "Because he is so wild that he just might make one of whomever dares ride him."

"And you brought him to introduction training?" Bain asked a bit nervously as Corpse grew excited and began to flap his powerful wings as the two of them lifted off the ground.

"Corpse," Bain yelled to the beast, "don't kill me!"

They both took off like a shot as Bain screamed in terror and excitement. He had flown before, but with his sister Wynne. He had never been the one in control of the creature he was riding, and yet the beasts all seemed to take to him for whatever reason.

Corpse flew high very quickly, taking Bain up to the clouds as they soared over the territory of Dihendra. The land before them stretched for hundreds of miles in three directions, but to the east Bain could see a vast body of water. It had to be the ocean, or a large lake. Bain could feel the dampness of the clouds on his skin, then the warmth of the rising sun as they emerged from the mist. The air smelled crisp and clean, and had a little bite to it, causing Bain to shiver, although he wasn't sure if the shiver was from the chill in the air, or the thrill of the ride.

Corpse turned to fly over the water, diving down close to the smooth surface. Bain leaned forward, sticking his hand down and feeling the water break against his fingers as he trailed them through it. Corpse, sensing Bain's joy, leaned slightly left so his hand would go deeper into the water. Bain smiled, feeling the bond already forming with the creature. Bain sat upright in the saddle, and patted the beast on its long, smooth, scaly neck.

"All right Corpse, we best fly back or else the others might think you've run away with me."

Corpse let out a small screech and turned abruptly to the right, taking a wide radius to return to the land. Corpse suddenly reached down into the water with its right foot and plucked out a fish with its sharp talons. It threw the fish in the air and caught it with its mouth, gobbling it up in just a few bites.

"So, you like fish. Good to know."

Bain laughed as the creature shook its head in answer and looked back at Bain with one eye. He couldn't believe that these beasts could understand him. He couldn't speak to them like Wynne and Adda could, but it appeared that they could understand him. Maybe, he could one day fly one of these creatures to Zanchier to find his family and bring them all to Dihendra. Of course, when he disappeared, they were all about to board ships and sail across the ocean to find a better life, so they likely were not back on Zanchier. He never thought he would be so close to finding them when he found himself on Harilhia, the planet on which Zanchier existed. Perhaps the Creator was finally leading him home.

As Bain and Corpse flew back toward land, another creature had taken notice of them. Wren, the Brindelwren which they had discovered in the waters of Zanchier, in the underground, bioluminescent world beneath the Marshlands, and that had bonded with Bain's youngest sister Adda, trembled with excitement as it popped its head above the water to watch the two fly away.

She snorted excitedly and slung her kelpy mane back and forth. She had sensed a familiarity that she had not felt in months since leaving Zanchier when the rider's hand had touched the water. Wren knew him and sensed his presence. She decided to cloak herself and follow the flying beast and the human she knew as Bain toward the land. She would wait to see if she could reach him without revealing herself to others. Not all humans had been friendly to her, and even some that knew her had still feared her, afraid to get too close without the aid of the telepaths. She had been forced back to the sea, alone once again in the vast, dark, deep ocean. A new den to call home was not something she had been able to find yet. Perhaps she could find one near Bain, and maybe even find Adda and Wynne as well.

Corpse returned to the training grounds and landed just where it had taken flight. Everyone there cheered loudly at Bain's success, even Guidriun reluctantly clapped for him.

Sebena walked over and took the reins Bain handed her as he jumped down.

"Well," she said, "another victorious connection, Bain, and you even made it back alive. As you can see, everyone is quite impressed with your ability to connect with the Baiskreet."

"I'm not sure why it's easier for me than anyone else. Though, I do feel they can understand me when I speak to them."

"I'm certain they do. The Baiskreet are intelligent creatures, as are many of the other beasts of Dihendra. I've just never seen such a connection to the creature world as what you have. Our tactics have been more of a dominating stance; not cruel, just controlling. Perhaps we need to change our tactics. The other leaders and I have been discussing your triumphs in the two days you've been here. We feel you need to lead introduction classes for the other recruits."

"Me?" Bain asked incredulously. "I have no idea what to teach them, because I have no idea what it is I do that makes me successful, other than trying to give the animal the time and connection it needs."

"Teach them that. Patience, understanding, feeling what the beast may need." Sebena thought for a moment. "You offered to take Corpse flying if he allowed you to ride him. That's not a tactic we've ever tried. We know they can understand us to a degree, but you speak to them as though they truly understand every word you say. That is what we want you to teach."

"Well, I'll give it a try. You don't think there will be any hard feelings with me taking over classes?"

"If there are, we'll deal with them as they arise. Now, Recruit Brinley, if you please, lead the others in your skilled assessments of the Baiskreet so we can get this lot of recruits trained to ride well. And rest assured, we leaders will be taking notes as well. Although we already ride any beast we wish, we do not have bonds like the one you've displayed. It will serve us well to learn your techniques."

"Yes ma'am."

Bain exhaled heavily as the others all waited patiently for instruction from the gifted newcomer.

Wren swam the shoreline around the area where Bain had flown, looking for a waterway inland. She soon came across one and followed the flying beast that carried Bain on its back. The river cut in many directions and a few times she lost sight of them. But she soon caught the direction they flew from Bain's scent which still lingered on the air. As Wren got further inland, the river, which occasionally emptied into small lakes, grew more narrow, winding uphill, through waterfalls, and upwards even more until Wren found herself near stone walls, in a narrow channel. She could sense and smell so many humans and other beasts, however, the strongest scent was Bain's.

The long day of training recruits and taking care of the breeding grounds was finally over. Bain walked the grounds of Castle Dihendra as a few other people milled about in the cool night air. He thought about the day and the many successes had with the trainees who listened intently to what Bain had said, putting his instruction into practice. Corpse had gotten to fly many times that morning, even Guidriun had managed a ride. The look of sheer joy and exhilaration on his face when he returned showed he was very pleased. He even nodded at Bain with a slight grin of appreciation.

Sebena watched Bain roaming the grounds below. She decided to go have a chat with the man who seemed to be turning their strictly structured world on end; but in a good way. He fascinated her, and he was good looking to boot. Sebena left her chamber and went to catch up with him.

Bain walked the quiet grounds, breathing in the cool air. There was a little breeze and Bain could hear a low moan sift by. He stopped in his tracks, the moan felt familiar somehow. He shook it off, figuring it was one of the Baiskreet, yet it didn't sound like anything he had heard any of them make in the past two days. He continued his walking looking up at the four moons visible in the night sky. He had never seen four moons from Zanchier's boundaries. Only one was constantly visible, though scientists that taught at academy did say that every third year a portion of a small planet was visible past the moon. They must have been witnessing one of the other three Harilhian moons.

Bain stopped, hearing the haunting moan again. It was definitely familiar. Where had he heard that sound before? Then it struck him like a bolt of lightning. Wren! It sounded like the Brindelwren. Could she be here somewhere? He traced the sound of the low moans, trying to remember the layout of the castle from his earlier flight. Were there waterways to the castle? There had to be something somewhere for the castle to have running water and waste systems.

Sebena noticed that Bain had stopped and was listening intently. She also heard the mournful sound of a low moan on the night air, and oddly enough he seemed in a hurry to find where the sound was coming from. She quickly and quietly followed him, hoping not to be seen until she wanted to be.

"Wren?" Bain whispered loudly, knowing the beast probably shouldn't be seen by anyone, but hoping she could hear him.

There, the sound was different than before. "Wren?" he whispered again.

He heard it again. It was Wren, and she was calling to him. He found the channel for the out-going waterways and followed them outside the outer castle buildings, still lowly calling for Wren as he went. About three hundred feet from the last building was a small lake, likely where the waste emptied. If Wren were there, she couldn't stay there long without getting ill.

Just as Bain walked to the edge of the lake, Wren uncloaked and excitedly thrashed in the water. Bain chuckled at her as she nuzzled him affectionately.

"Hey there, girl, it's so good to see you too."

Wren was so excited she made cooing and throaty gurgling sounds. Bain tried to calm her to quieten her down before someone heard or saw her.

"You're a long way from home, Wren."

She shook her head up and down.

"Do you know where the others who left Zanchier went?"

She shook her head up and down again.

"Could you show me?"

Before she could reply, she went transparent and Sebena stepped out of the shadows into the brightness of the four moon's light.

"What on Harilhia is that creature?"

Bain was a bit nervous. He wasn't sure what to tell her or how she would react.

"Bain, it obviously has a cloaking ability like that of the Vurcransu, but I have never seen anything like it here before."

"She's not to be taken for studies or training. She is a free beast that belongs in the oceans."

"Yes, I understand, but you still haven't told me what she is."

"Wren?" Bain looked up, knowing she hadn't gone far.

Wren slowly revealed herself and Sebena gasped in awe.

"She is a breed known as a Brindelwren. The old-timers back home called her a sea-beast. For years they thought her to be dangerous, but she bonded with my youngest sister Adda many months back and she became one of the many animal protectors of the Zanchier people. My father told me she helped hundreds escape Zanchier and the Scaither's cruelty."

Sebena never took her eyes off Wren. "She's magnificent. May I touch her?"

"That's up to Wren."

"So it is these types of creatures where you learned your patience and appreciation for beasts; and why they respect you so?"

"Her and many others."

"There are more like her?"

"No, not like her, just other wild beasts with which the telepaths back home have bonded. I was just lucky enough to be a family member of two of those remarkable people. Because of them, I became a part of the animal brigade and got to meet and learn about Wren here."

Sebena slowly walked toward the water's edge and held her hand out to Wren. Wren sniffed the air, tilted her head, and looked at Sebena quizzically. She then lowered her towering head down toward Sebena.

# Chapter 9

Sebena smiled broadly at the large, gentle beast in front of her. Wren allowed Sebena to brush her hands all along her head and down her neck as far as she could reach without falling into the water. Wren's hard, steady, breathing washed over Sebena with each deep exhale, and throaty, vibrating purr.

"She is a beautiful creature. And you say she is from Zanchier?"

"Yes. Though why she is this far from home is beyond me. Didn't you say that Zanchier is on the other side of Harilhia?"

"Yes. According to the stories and legends it is very far. Though I've never traveled there or even tried to reach it myself. It was always sort of taboo. Though now, after seeing her," she smiled up at Wren, "and what you are capable of, I think I might try a visit one day."

"Well, true it isn't as wild and unattainable as people might believe, but it is very dangerous and the Scaithers are no joke. They are ruthless and their reach was growing and had grown to unbelievable heights when I left. I can't even imagine what it's like there now. So I truly advise you against a visit."

"Unless I had someone with me who knew how things went?" She looked at him with questioning brows.

Bain smiled at her. She was definitely not afraid of anything.

"Perhaps, if finding my family leads me back there, I'll take you along."

"I'm in! No question's asked." Sebena oohed and awed over Wren, obviously infatuated with her. "How long is she? I'm obviously only seeing a small part of her."

"About forty feet. And her tail has spikes that are deadly poisonous, so avoid that area if possible."

"Does she have other abilities?"

"Not that I've seen. Besides, she's large enough to inflict any damage needed to win a battle."

"Yes, this I can see. But she seems lonely. Her moans are hauntingly sad and mournful."

"She must be growing home-sick, and probably missing Adda and Wynne. That must be why she tracked me down, thinking they were with me. I figure Wren followed the travelers she aided in crossing the Marshland waterways as the sailing ships and air ships left Zanchier to find new homes. Maybe the ships stopped somewhere and Wren left for whatever reason. But I'm sure that if my sisters were with the ships, she would have stayed with them. She seemed awfully happy to see me, like she's been alone for a long time. You know, the last time I saw her she actually saved my life. I was being chased by three Hungerhounds and she took them all down. I'd be dead if not for her."

"Hungerhounds sound menacing."

"You have no idea, and there are other things just as bad if not worse that will snatch you up for a meal faster than you can blink."

Wren suddenly vanished, cloaking herself against something she sensed nearby. This action caught Bain and Sebena's attention.

Then, a voice rang out in the mist covered night.

"Who's out there?"

"I am here, Captain Nigel," Sebena said irritably.

"Oh, Captain Zentrialle, Recruit Brinley, I didn't realize it was you two."

"Now you do. All is well, Captain, you can go back to night watch."

Captain Nigel hesitated a moment, then asked, "Did either of you see something in the water?"

"Only the moonlight on the mist," Sebena replied.

"I was certain I saw something quite large."

Sebena continued, "You know how the four-moon's light can play tricks on the eyes during this season, Captain. I assure you, there is nothing there, as you can see for yourself." Sebena gestured out over the water as the rolling mist moved in shadowy patterns across the surface.

Captain Nigel nodded, accepting that his eyes were likely playing tricks on him, but then stopped and asked, "What are you two doing out here anyway?"

Sebena grabbed Bain around the arm and said, "Having a romantic walk along the water, out of the sight of prying eyes." She glanced at him knowingly.

"Oh, sorry Captain. Brinley." He grinned crookedly at them before turning around and walking back toward the castle.

Bain smiled at her. "Good cover story."

She smiled back at him. "Who said it was a story?"

Bain's smile softened to a grin, just before his and Sebena's lips met in a soft, slow, kiss.

Bain reluctantly pulled back and took a deep breath to steady his pounding heart. "Are you sure you want to start a relationship with me? You know I could vanish at any time. Besides, what would the other captains and recruits think?"

"Well, as far as everyone else, no one needs to know anything. We will just have to be very careful."

"What about Captain Nigel?"

"I'll handle him when we go back. Now, as far as you disappearing, then don't."

"I haven't been able to control that yet, Sebena."

"We'll deal with that if it happens. Let's just enjoy getting to know each other more."

"Deal," Bain said, leaning down to kiss her once more before breaking apart.

Bain turned to say goodbye to Wren, promising to visit her in the morning out near the ocean so she could get away from the waste pool. He would wake early and take Corpse for a ride. Sebena agreed to go with him.

Sebena and Bain walked back to the castle appearing as just two friends out for a stroll. Sebena made a bee-line for Captain Nigel to make certain he knew to keep quiet about what he thought he witnessed. They did not need problems in the ranks with Bain being so new to the recruits. Plus, her commanders may not agree with her decision to form a relationship with a recruit. But Bain was no ordinary recruit. So far he had displayed extraordinary abilities, strength, and from what she could see already, character as well. He deeply cared and worried for his people in Zanchier. That was a rare thing to find in anyone, much less a younger man.

Bain watched Sebena turn to go find Captain Nigel and he turned in another direction toward the barracks. He soon crawled onto his bed to think about the evening's events, the kiss from Sebena and the possibility of finding his family. The only reason he didn't leave with Wren tonight was that he needed to know just how far Zanchier was first before he just took off, and then there was Sebena to consider. She was such a different type of woman from what he was used to. But getting involved with her could mean leaving the chance to find his family behind, and Bain wasn't willing to do that, not yet.

Bain had a hard time getting to sleep and so slept very little. Sebena appeared from her door and she and Bain slunk from the barracks as quickly and quietly as possible, but not without being followed by Guidriun.

Guidriun wasn't sure what they were up to so early, but he was going to find out.

Sebena rode the Lurepture from day one while Bain mounted Corpse. They soon took off toward the Dihendran coast.

Guidriun coaxed another Baiskreet; a Nassureptic; which allowed him to ride it, and quietly followed them from a safe distance. The coast was a short flight, and Guidriun watched from his perch on the top of the cliff that overlooked the secluded part of the shoreline. The mouth of the rivers merged here and emptied into the ocean.

A massive creature emerged from the water and wobbled onto the sand. Bain and Sebena had to calm their Baiskreet due to the animal's reactions to the large beast. When their creature's lurched in fear, so did Guidriun's, giving his spying position away. Sebena waved him down from the hilltop, a stern look on her face.

"Recruit Guidriun, what on Harilhia do you think you are doing following a captain about?"

"Sorry Ma'am, I guess my curiosity got the better of me," he said, staring at the beast that towered over them by at least twenty feet. And that did not include its length of body that stretched out behind it. He looked at the large fins and smooth bluish-green skin, the seahorse shaped head, and long eel-like body.

"Guidriun!" he heard Sebena forcefully say.

"Ma'am?" He stood at attention, his gaze back on the forceful woman who stood directly in front of him now, anger set on her features.

"I could have you severely punished for insubordination, Recruit."

"Yes Ma'am," he replied unflinchingly.

"Now that you've seen Wren here, I have to figure out what to do about you."

"How do you mean, Ma'am?"

Bain stepped up. "Perhaps we can trust Guidriun to keep my secret?" Bain looked the man in the eyes.

Guidriun then cut his gaze to the large creature known as Wren, then back to Sebena, and then Bain.

"What's the secret? Isn't it just another creature from Dihendra, just one we've never seen yet?"

"No. She is a Brindelwren, from my home in Zanchier."

Guidriun's eyes grew wide for a moment, then he relaxed again.

"Still, why the secrecy?"

"Those higher up the line may try to capture her to study, especially since Zanchier is such a mystery. Not to mention the fear associated with Zanchier and the creatures there. I'm trying to find my family, Guidriun. We were all separated many months ago. Wren knows where they are, and she only just found me last night."

"So you're leaving Dihendra?"

"I'm not sure when or how that will happen, but yes. There is a lot to consider."

Sebena stated, "If anything happens to that creature, I'll assume it was you, whether it was or not and I will deal with you myself."

"Neither of you need to worry, your secret is safe with me."

Sebena looked at him threateningly, then said, "At ease."

Guidriun relaxed, then asked, "Is she dangerous?"

"She can be if she doesn't like you," Bain replied.

"How do you know if she doesn't like you?"

"She'll either squash you or eat you."

Guidriun gulped hard, then gathered up the courage to put what Bain had taught him into practice. He stretched out his hand high in the air and waited.

Wren glanced over at Bain who nodded. She then leaned way down toward Guidriun who flinched just a little when her massive head came close to him. She sensed his fear and stopped moving, blowing a puff of air at his head, ruffling his hair and clothing. She didn't move until he opened his eyes and looked up at the large head dangling over him, her long, kelpy mane hung down around her face, some nearly dragging the ground around him. Her nose brushed his hand gently, nudging him to assure him she would not be eating him today.

Guidriun relaxed, grinned slightly, and patted her nose and face. She then pulled back and stood tall and regal as the morning sunlight began to bathe the area in yellow and orange. Wren then quickly cloaked herself and slid back into the water that lapped quietly at the shoreline.

"Did I do something wrong?" Guidriun asked.

"No, she must have sensed something," Bain answered.

Just then, several boats rounded the coastline, flying across the water, passing where they stood on the beach.

They watched them pass, then Bain yelled, "Wren, I'll come back tonight during downtime."

They heard the huff of her breath, and a low growl to signify she understood him. Then there was a splash in the water as she obviously dove beneath the surface and disappeared.

Sebena said, "We best be getting back if you two want breakfast before our day begins."

"I can eat." Bain smiled.

"Me too," Guidriun put in, then added, "can I come back with you tonight?"

Bain said, "As long as all of us taking off together doesn't cause questions."

Guidriun nodded. "I'll say that I'm going into the village for something and I'll take an air-rover and meet you out past the dunes on the north side. It's pretty secluded there. You can pick me up and give me a lift on Corpse."

"Sure, but how do WE get away, Sebena?"

"I'll inform the other captains that I am speed training our most promising recruit on flying to better train the other recruits."

Bain said, "All right, sounds good. I guess we need to get back, but we'll have to either go in from different directions or give each other time between returns."

Sebena said, "Guidriun and I will fly back and enter at separate gates. Then you can follow ten minutes later. That should be enough time to not draw any attention to the fact that all three of us was out riding early."

Guidriun said, "I'll go in from the south near the breeding grounds. I'll hide the saddle and put it away later. I'll sneak the Nassureptic in through the back gate of its paddock. If anyone asks I'll just say I wanted to check him out because I noticed something strange with him last night."

Bain asked, "But won't the other captains question my taking a Baiskreet without permission?"

"Possibly," Sebena replied. "You'd better return with me. I'll just tell them what we agreed upon earlier, about the speed training. So that means we can all return now, but Guidriun you'll have to fly out and around to the other side. See you at breakfast."

They all mounted their Baiskreet and headed back to Castle Dihendra with Guidriun taking a wide berth toward the southern gates.

# Chapter 10

**Castle Dihendra, Recruit Introduction Training, Day 3**

Each morning the recruits were introduced to a different Baiskreet from the Breeding grounds, and this morning's was a large rotund beast called a Brundwedim.

Sebena began. "The Brundwedim is a very large breed that likes to burrow by nature and can even dig through softer types of rock. They are not very fast and need a running start to take flight due to their size and weight. Their skin is very thick and tough and they tend to slam into adversaries to knock them over. They are known bullies with a deep, loud, reverberating, roar. Recruit Brinley, let's see if you can master this one as quickly as you have the others."

Bain reluctantly stepped forward, only because he wasn't used to being in a teaching position or being the center of attention. He walked slowly up to the Brundwedim and stood still, just watching it for a minute.

The Brundwedim watched him closely. Bain walked back and forth in front of the beast and noticed it tracked his every movement. When Bain moved too quickly the Brundwedim would growl lowly. He wasn't sure if it was an excited or irritated growl so he decided to experiment. He watched the rest of the beast's body language as he moved about, realizing that it was merely getting excited, like it wanted to play. He took one of the sparring sticks lying against a nearby wall. He held it out in front of the Brundwedim.

"You want the stick, boy?"

It grew even more excited and began to growl lowly, panting like a dog in between throaty growls. Bain spun the stick around a few times as the beast grew more excited before Bain threw it to him. The Brundwedim caught the stick and shook it around before crunching down and splintering the wood into many pieces. It then picked up the broken pieces and did the same.

Bain noticed its tail wagged slowly in happiness as it continued to crunch the wood to bits. Bain slowly walked up to the beast and patted it as it continued its work. He slowly walked to its side, keeping contact with it, and put his foot in the stirrup to climb up. The Brundwedim suddenly stopped playing and turned its chunky, thick neck to watch Bain with one large eye. It narrowed its gaze and growled. That growl was definitely different from the one before it.

"Okay," Bain said, holding up his hand and starting to back away, but he wasn't quick enough. The Brundwedim stepped left and bumped Bain with its thick side knocking him backward and onto the ground.

Bain coughed and sputtered, totally unprepared for what had happened. The Brundwedim busied itself again with the sticks, which now were little more than a pile of toothpicks. The Brundwedim continued to much the stick until all the pieces were eaten.

Sebena went to give Bain a hands up, pulling him to his feet as he held his stomach, trying to catch the breath knocked from his lungs at impact.

"You do know that was a tiny, playful, tap." Sebena smiled and gave Bain an amused look.

"So what you're saying is he likes me?" Bain managed to say through garbled breath.

"Yes, I think so," Sebena said with uncertainty.

"Well, then I'll have to make sure to be very cautious around this breed in the future."

Sebena stepped back as Bain walked around the front of the Brundwedim and said, "I think you're going to take a bit more convincing, big fella."

The Brundwedim snorted at him and shook his head violently causing a ripple to continue throughout his body to the tip of his tail. Bain noticed how the saddle on his back shook from side to side which caused the beast to moan, then turn and bite at the saddle.

Bain walked back to the saddle as the Brundwedim watched him again, snorting indignantly. Bain uncinched the strap which held the saddle in place. He followed where the strap lay against the beast's skin looking over every inch until he came to a place on his side close to his upper back that  appeared to have a few loose scales. Bain looked under the scales, lifting them slightly until the beast growled again.

"Sebena, come look at this. Could this be a sore or boil of some kind?"

Sebena walked over to look at the area in question.

"Why yes, it looks like it is. Captain Merchon," she yelled, "take this Brundwedim back to the breeding grounds and see that it receives medical attention." She then turned back to Bain. "Good eye, Recruit Brinley."

She then turned to the recruits and said, "Recruit Brinley found a sore on the Brundwedim, simply by paying attention and watching the beast's body language. As future and current riders we all must be aware and more perceptive of what our creatures need. Since the Brundwedim is injured, hands-on is complete for today. Instead of sparring, we will head to the breeding grounds and spend time watching and learning about the creatures with which you are matched. Each recruit will be expected to give an account or record of what you observed about your creatures today."

Everyone turned and headed to the breeding grounds to spend the morning in observation. After lunch, half the recruits gave their observation statements while the other half were given reprieve until after dinner. Everyone returned to the breeding grounds to continue care of the Baiskreet pens. The Brundwedim was checked over and his wound treated once again. Mercer just happened to be one of the recruits who was paired with the Brundwedim breed, and he was tending to the creature's wounds when Bain came into the den.

"Merk, how's it going?" Bain asked, stepping up to the creature's side and looking at the ooze coming from under the scales.

"Hey Bain. Good I suppose. I mean, it's only been half a day since we discovered his sore spot, but I am trying to make sure it's kept clean, medicated, and bandaged. Brutus doesn't seem to mind me messing with it, so that's good. What are you doing here?"

"Oh, I am officially assigned to all the pens until hands-on training is over. I have to take each day at a different paddock, and today it's here. So, Brutus huh? Is that the name given to him at birth or one you came up with?" Bain smiled at him.

"After this morning's display, I came up with it." Mercer laughed. "The Baiskreet are seldom named at birth. We often wait to see if personality will reveal it. Believe it or not, Brutus here is only a year old."

"Really, I figured he was older considering his size."

"Nope. And he will get a lot bigger in the years to come. Brundwedim often get nearly as large as a one-story home, and almost as rotund." Mercer laughed at the look on Bain's face and the mental picture his description must have created. Then he asked, "Where did you take off too so early this morning? I woke about four a.m. and you were gone."

Bain wasn't sure if he should tell Mercer about Wren. Too many people knowing about her may draw unnecessary attention their way. Besides, he knew Mercer would want to tag along, and since Guidriun was already becoming a constant presence, he just didn't want anyone else around.

"I couldn't sleep. I guess it's all the added pressure of sort of being the new trainer for hands-on time, plus I just have a lot on my mind."

Bain wasn't lying about that. The responsibility of having first touch training as a recruit with the Baiskreet was daunting, and then there was this budding relationship with Sebena to consider, and how all of this would affect his future and that of his family.

"I can understand that," Mercer said. "How about after dinner, we take some down time and head into the city for a few drinks and fun?"

"That would normally sound great Merk, but I already have something important that I need to tend to. Maybe another time."

"Sure," Mercer said, a little put out, and curious as to what Bain had to do that was so important. But if Bain didn't want to tell him then he didn't feel like he had the right to ask.

Bain and Mercer tended to the Brundwedim in the pen, cleaned the den, fed the group, and sat observing them until it was dinnertime.

In the dining hall, Bain grabbed a wrapped sandwich and a few pieces of fruit, and quickly disappeared. The action captured Mercer's attention and he decided that Bain was acting strangely and that made him concerned for his friend. So, he did the same and followed after Bain as quickly as possible, trying very hard to catch up to him. He wasn't entirely sure where he went so he walked the outside grounds searching for him. Growing tired of searching, he was just about to go inside with everyone else and have a proper dinner when he saw a shadow cross the ground. He looked up to see Bain riding on the Copasedrom known as Corpse, headed toward the east.

"What are you up to friend?" Mercer wondered if he could get one of the Brundwedim to allow him to mount them so that he could follow Bain. "Well, it's worth a try."

He set out toward the breeding grounds as he finished gobbling down the sandwiches, apple, and fruit he brought. He arrived at the Brundwedim den, looked over all the larger creatures before his gaze returned to Brutus.

"Well, little fella', are you up for a flying lesson with me?" Mercer looked at his injury. It was better. Not really oozing like it had been, and the scales looked as though they were tightening back up and sealing off the wound, but he didn't want to further injure him. So, he turned to one of the larger, older creatures, hoping that they wouldn't get agitated and crush him against one of the stone walls. He gingerly approached one of the larger females, but soon found himself running out of the den, headed for safe ground as she chased after him, snorting and grinding her teeth.

"Fine!" Mercer yelled as he clamored through the door of the tall metal fence. The fence couldn't hold them if they actually wanted to get out, but it had taught the Baiskreet hatchlings boundaries. The fencing was an inaccessible area unless allowed out of the paddocks by their handlers.

Mercer ran his hands across his face and head in frustration. He looked in the direction in which Bain had flown. "Now what?" A thought crossed his mind and he went to the parking area where the Air-Rovers were kept. He hopped on one, started it up, and sped off across the castle grounds and out of the gate headed in the direction he saw Bain fly. He didn't know what he was up to, but he sure hoped he could find him. Mercer traveled toward the coast until he came to the cliff's overlooking the shoreline. He traveled the cliff's edge north until he came to where the river met the ocean. There on the beach below were Bain, Sebena, and Guidriun.

"What is he doing out here with them?" He mumbled, perturbed that he wasn't invited but it appeared that Guidriun had been.

Then he saw a creature emerge from the water and head straight for them. His friend's backs were to the ocean. That thing might eat them. Mercer sprang into action, riding the cliffs quickly while screaming their names.

They looked up to see someone on an Air-Rover coming their way. Bain panicked.

"Wren, go back!"

But Wren was too excited to see her friend once more.

Then Bain noticed who it was, as did Sebena and Guidriun.

Sebena was agitated once more at yet another spying recruit.

When Mercer's Air-Rover appeared on the beach next to them, he jumped from the vehicle, and ran to them sputtering wildly and pointing to the water.

"There's a creature, you're in danger!"

"Merk, calm down," Bain said to the man.

"Recruit Rand!"

Mercer stopped in his tracks. "Ma'am." He saluted, watching the beast in the water which stared down at them, inching ever closer.

"What are you doing here, Recruit Rand?"

"I was just worried about my friend Bain, Ma'am."

"Does Recruit Brinley look to be in harm's way?"

"Yes Ma'am, I mean no Ma'am. Th…th…there's a beast Ma'am."

"Do you really think us to be so ignorant as to not know about the massively large creature just behind us in the water?"

"Yes Ma'am, I mean, no Ma'am. Sorry, I don't know what I'm saying Ma'am."

"Obviously there is a lot you don't understand, Recruit Rand."

Sebena looked at Mercer then at Guidriun. "It appears we've been lax in our training. Our recruits feel as though they can just take off whenever they feel like it." Sebena noticed that she had lost Mercer's attention as his gaze shifted upward as Wren loomed directly behind them.

Mercer gulped hard.

Bain stepped over to him. "Merk, this is Wren."

Mercer looked at Bain sideways, not willing to take his eyes off the odd-looking creature in front of him.

"Wren huh?"

"Yes, and she is gentle, for the time being."

That caught his attention. "What are the time's when she's not?"

Bain chuckled lightly. "When threatened, like any other creature. She's an old friend of mine from Zanchier."

Mercer watched Wren watching him.

Sebena realized Mercer was still at attention. "At ease, Recruit Rand."

Mercer's stance relaxed some, yet stiffened a bit as Wren's large head came ever closer to him.

"She won't hurt you, Merk," Bain reassured the man.

"Okay," Mercer eked out. "Nice Wren," he stuttered as she nudged him with her nose, making him take a few steps back to steady himself. He raised his hand to pat her head, noting the feel of her wet, smooth, thick, skin.

Sebena said, "We have to do better when sneaking around or else we'll soon have the entire castle following us about; especially with your newly found fame, Recruit Brinley."

Bain smiled at her observation, then his demeanor turned serious. "True. I'll have to figure out a way to see her where others won't. Maybe it's time we leave. I do need to find my family."

"Leave?" They all three said in unison.

Bain looked at Guidriun, then Mercer, then Sebena.

"I don't know what life is going to throw at me next. With portal travel being so unexpected and uncontrollable I never know when or where I'll go next. While I'm able to get to my home, I need to try to find my family before I'm whisked away to someplace new."

His friends looked at him in understanding, all except Guidriun who asked, "What are you talking about? What's portal travel?"

# Chapter 11

**Dihendra, Cliffside, Eastern Shoreline**

Bain and Sebena looked at each other, Guidriun's unanswered question hanging in the air. Mercer saw the tension between them, understanding what the looks meant, and went to explain to Guidriun while Bain and Sebena spoke.

Sebena walked up to Bain so their conversation would be more private. "So you're leaving then?"

"I need to, Sebena. As much as I like it here, as much as I've come to care for you, I have to find my family."

"I understand, Bain, truly I do. I just wish you could stay."

Bain was quiet for a moment before he said, "You could always come with me."

Sebena was surprised by his statement. "As much as I'd like to, I also have a life here. A family of my own. One I'd hoped to introduce you to one day soon."

Bain and Sebena looked at one another. Sadness and understanding in both of their eyes. Sebena stepped up to Bain and placed a kiss on his lips. This action caught the attention of the two men who were talking just thirty feet away, halting their conversation.

Bain and Sebena embraced for a moment longer, before splitting apart.

Sebena said, over her shoulder, toward Mercer and Guidriun, "Not a word from either of you." Then she turned to Bain. "You'll need supplies before you take off."

Bain answered, "That would be nice since I arrived here with nothing."

Sebena smiled slightly at the memory. "I will return to the Castle, gather what you need, and bring it back to you here within the hour."

"Thank you, Sebena." Bain's words were pained yet grateful.

"I'll go with Sebena," Guidriun stated stepping up to Bain. "I'll send back some things she might not think about."

"Thank you Guidriun," Bain said, shaking the man's hand.

"Good luck, Bain. I hope you find what you're looking for." Guidriun turned and  walked over to Corpse, mounted him, and took off. Sebena mounted her Baiskreet and took flight, while Mercer stood there with Bain.

Mercer said, "Man, I'm going to miss you. You're the only real friend I have here."

"I'll always be your friend Merk, no matter where the Creator takes me next."

"Likewise buddy," Mercer stated, shaking Bain's hand. His attention then returned to the beast known as Wren. "So how are you going to ride her? Can you breathe underwater too?"

Bain laughed. "Unfortunately no. Wren is an air breather. She can also cloak herself and her rider so we will be undetectable to others. She may have to dive underwater a few times to wet her coat depending on how far we have to travel, but with the warmer weather at least I won't freeze."

"Well, good luck to you, Bain. I sure hope to see you again one day."

"Me too, Merk."

"So, where to after you find your family?"

"I'm not sure I will go anywhere else. I've only been here three days. The first, and last time I traveled I went to a place called Egypt for several weeks, which apparently is on a different plane, realm, or planet."

"I didn't even know that was possible."

"Neither did I until it happened to me less than three weeks ago."

"Three weeks? That's all?"

"Yeah, yet it feels like it's been months already. A lot has happened to me, even before I left Zanchier. My world has been one of unrest, struggle, war, and work; though I've had peace since I began time-traveling, but I've also had sadness and uncertainty."

"I could go with you, Bain," Mercer offered.

"As much as I'd like that, Merk, I'm unsure what to expect myself. I don't want to drag you into a life of uncertainty."

"I don't have anyone keeping me here. My relatives are all on the other side of Zanchier. I left home at an early age to try and make something of myself. That's why I joined the Dihendran Guard."

"The last friend that was with me when I jumped here may be dead. If he couldn't come with me, I fear no one else can either. Besides, your future is here, Merk. Maybe one day I'll return to find you're a captain."

"Maybe so." Mercer smiled, adjusting his stance, and standing taller. He then asked, "So, you and Captain Zentrialle?"

Bain chuckled. "Yeah."

Mercer smiled. "Well, I guess I'd best be heading back to the castle. Good luck, Bain. May the Creator guide you in the right direction."

"Thanks, Mercer, you as well."

They shook hands once more before Mercer climbed on the Air-Rover and disappeared over the cliffs. Bain then turned to Wren who had curled up on the beach waiting on him.

"Well, girl, it looks like it's just you and me. As soon as Sebena returns with provisions we'll head out. I'm sure you know where my family is."

Wren bobbed her head up and down as if answering him. Perhaps she was. Bain often wished he could truly speak to the creatures the way Wynne and Adda could.

Bain and Wren sat in the quiet of the evening, on the deserted coastline as the waves washed in against the shore, the rhythmic sound and motion soothing Bain's soul.

Sebena, good to her word, returned an hour later with a backpack full of clothing, weapons, toiletries, and food. She and Bain embraced one last time, holding on to one another for a few precious moments. She kissed him gently before she quickly mounted her Baiskreet and flew away. Bain slipped the backpack on and climbed on Wren's back as he watched Sebena's form grow smaller by the second. Wren slid into the water and swam off into the growing darkness of night. Both excitement and sadness filled Bain. How could so much emotion inhabit a body all at once? The turmoil of whether to stay here and build a new life or to go find his family tore at him. The later won out of course, but Bain hoped to one day return, and perhaps sooner rather than later.

Sebena turned in her saddle to watch Bain and Wren disappear into the horizon. To her surprise, silent tears streaked her cheeks. She had never felt so deeply for a man before. How could she have fallen for someone so quickly? Bain would be hard to forget. She turned back and urged her Baiskreet ever faster, hoping the wind would dry her tears and blow the melancholy feeling from her breaking heart.

Wren swam for the better part of the night as Bain drowsily dozed on and off in the early hours of morning. She found a remote, deserted island and slithered out of the water onto the dry sand. Bain groggily slid from her back onto the ground beside her and fell fast asleep with Wren curled up around him. She cloaked herself and Bain before falling fast asleep as well.

When the sunrise broke over the horizon a few hours later, Bain and Wren both awoke to the brightly streaming sunlight on their faces. Bain stood to stretch the soreness from his muscles as Wren did the same. He sat and ate breakfast from the supplies provided by Sebena while he watched Wren chase down her breakfast from the sea.

The two were soon back to gliding through the water headed south from what Bain could tell. He had no idea in which direction Wren had traveled last night. Bain held on and just tried to make mental notes of markers when he could see one. A few hours later they began seeing a string of small islands dotting the horizon, one in particular to which Wren swam. The closer they got, Bain could begin to make out shapes: buildings, life, and people. The nerves in his stomach began to flutter with excitement.

"Is this it, Wren? Is my family here?"

Wren snorted and shook her head in reply. She swam to a small alcove where a sea cave opened out into the inlet. There was no one here and she would not be detected. It was a safe place to drop Bain and quickly hide herself. She swam up to an outcropping of rocks and let Bain climb off her back. He then turned to her.

"Thank you, Wren. I'll return here later tonight to see you, girl."

Wren snorted and disappeared into the water as Bain walked the slippery rocks toward the other end of the cave which opened onto the shoreline. He had to wade through the water a bit to reach the land but he was slightly wet already after the long ride across the ocean. Bain walked back in the direction which he had seen life, soon coming to a coastal city. The buildings were older looking, and some in need of paint and repair, but still in decent shape. People milled about the shoreline and docks that stretched out into the water. Several boats were returning with nets full of fish. People moved crates of fish to a market that Bain could see up a side street. He looked up at a large worn, wooden sign which stretched across the street from one side to the other, positioned on thick poles which were securely anchored to the ground. The sign read Phiorellia; apparently the cities name. As he entered the area no one paid him much mind, only nodding in a brief hello.

*Strangers must not be a big deal here,* he thought.

Perhaps this is a popular port of travel like the ones that Simon and Lilith had often told him about when speaking about their travels. Bain had no experience with travel outside of Zanchier until just a few weeks ago.

He walked the busy market streets lined with booths and people selling goods or services. Bain couldn't help but smile at all the activity and life. It reminded him of the Praxtingen market back home, and his old friend Silus Aerser. The Raisedback Vindaper vendor had been a tough, kind, old man who had lived a full life. He had fought in the early wars of Zanchier with his old troops and had many victories, but the Three Army War most recently had taken him from Bain; along with Raila, Kreelie, Nan Trea, and so many of his friends at the LSS. Bain shook off the painful memories and tried to enjoy the teeming life all around him. The beauty of the island was breathtaking as well. Tall palm trees swayed in the constant ocean breeze. Flowering trees and plants which bloomed fully in bright colors lined the streets and grassy areas. Multiple story homes with balconies that overlooked the area stretched side by side on both sides of the winding streets. People hung from the railings, yelling out to people below in friendly fashion. The atmosphere here felt light and congenial, like no one had a care in the world. Bain noticed a coffee shop with quaint little tables lining the sidewalk just outside the wide, open double-door. He walked inside, and asked if his currency from Dihendra that Sebena had thoughtfully placed in his pack was usable. Getting a yes, he ordered some coffee and a wonderful smelling bread with spices and nuts, paid for his items, and took them outside to one of the tables.

Bain sat watching everyone as he ate the wonderful tasting confection and drank the strong yet satisfying hot liquid. He had yet to have a cup of coffee as strong as it was back on Zanchier, but he was beginning to enjoy the different flavors that each place brought that he had been. He had so much for which to be thankful. He had always been sort of restless growing up, wanting to do more and be more than his technical talent was going to allow with government placements. Bain thought about his life so far, and all the things he had experienced up till now. He definitely had been given a life of adventure. He had not sat in a building, stuck in a room creating new technology and barely seeing the light of day. Bain was grateful for his technological abilities, like those of his mother Harper, but he was also grateful that his grandfather Aaric had given him the chance to be a field agent with the LSS. That experience had taught him many useful skills, which over the last month had served him well. Bain realized that the Creator had been preparing him for the life he now led. He had lost so many people, but he gained new friends everywhere he went. He just wasn't sure what it was he was supposed to be doing with this traveling through time thing. Perhaps it was merely coincidental that he walked between worlds. Perhaps it won't happen again. Maybe he was meant to be here. Was he meant to find a new life outside of Zanchier for the benefit of those that were still trapped there? He would try to keep tabs on his travels and make notes and maps of where he had been and all he had learned about each place.

Bain looked around the area finding a shop just across the street. He finished his coffee and cake, then walked over to browse the shop for a book in which he could record his life's adventures. The shop was filled with different items ranging from furniture to paper goods. Bain found a shelf full of wonderful, old, leather-bound books. He was fortunate enough to find a book on Harilhia's geography which he picked up, along with a blank, leather-bound journal full of natural, unlined paper. The book was large, thick, had a leather wrap which bound the book closed with a twisting latch that secured the strap. Bain looked at the price of the two books in hand. They were expensive, but both were needed. He took the purchases to the counter, paid for them, then returned to the table where he had sat drinking his coffee. He walked inside for another cup and pastry, then sat for the next several hours as he wrote down his adventures since leaving Zanchier. He drew maps, sketched pictures of all the things he saw and the people he met along the way. The sketches of people were rough to say the least as he was not skilled in that area, but Cartography was something he did well.

# Chapter 12



Before Bain realized what time it was the noon hour had passed and he had filled about twenty pages of his journal with tales of his adventures and images to go along with them.

In his journal he also drew images of his family. His parents, siblings, and grandparents, hoping to be able to show people the rough sketches and see if anyone knew them. But, his images were basic at best, which caused him to hope that someone might recall their names.

Bain grabbed lunch, something portable from the shop where he had taken up their table for the entire morning and set out into the streets showing people the pictures. He asked everyone if they knew Aaric or Neitha Brinley, Gracelynn Fenore, or his parents, siblings, or Uncle Finn and Aunt Paisley. No one had yet said they knew or recognized any of them. He spent the rest of the day walking all over Phiorellia Rhial searching for them. Wren said they were here, but how long ago had that been? All in all, it could have only been a few weeks to a month since that was how long it had been since he had disappeared. It had likely taken them a few days to cross the ocean and settle here. Come to think of it, there had been several airships that had crossed with the boats too. Surely someone will remember those. Perhaps that was the question he should be asking? Bain excitedly began asking people if they had seen the airships. He then retraced his steps asking those he had already spoken with if they had seen the airships. Several people did remember them, and one man in particular told him the conversation he had had with a man from one of the boats that traveled with the airships.

"I do remember them, it's been a while ago though, but I told a man that the island of Phiorellia was too small and congested for the airships to land here, but that they could possibly set the ships down on an adjacent island to the west, on the other side of

Phiorellia. There should have been plenty of room for the airships to land over there. Several of the islands are inhabited, but it is minimal, so it should have been possible."

Bain excitedly said, "Thank you very much, sir."

The man nodded and smiled as Bain left. He busied himself walking around the island some more, taking in the sights and sounds of the coastal life while he waited for evening to come. Then he would meet Wren back at the cave and then go to the other islands.

Bain sketched some more while he sat watching people and their activities. As night began to fall the air began to fill with music, and Bain could see people gathering in a beach front establishment while a group of musicians played for the enjoyment of the customers. This life on this island seemed one of completely carefree living. This was something Bain could maybe get used to. It seemed his whole life since leaving academy had been filled with danger, war, strife, running from bad people and worrying about his loved ones. Then, the constant changes in scenery, which he had to admit he didn't totally dislike; but to live in a place like this just might be pure bliss. Unless of course he got bored without any excitement in his life, which would likely occur. Bain laughed at his mind's wonderings. He had to admit, he liked the action and adventure his new life afforded, he just wanted to make sure his family was safe, then he would happily travel anywhere the Creator decided to send him.

Bain walked the few miles to the watery cavern, waded out to where Wren had dropped him earlier that day, and waited for her to appear. It wasn't long before she did just that, breaking through the surface of the water, apparently excited to see someone she knew on a regular basis. She must have been very lonely on her own.

"Hey girl. We have to travel to another one of the islands on the other side. I hope everyone is still there."

Bain climbed onto Wren's back telling her where to turn as they followed the coast around the island to the other side, several miles away. When they reached the other side of the island of

Phiorellia, it was so dark they couldn't make out which direction to go.

"Surely there is some light to be seen from the islands. Maybe they are so far away that we can't see it. The man I spoke to earlier did say the islands were populated, though very little." Bain spoke to Wren as though she would answer, and sometimes she did in her own way, but this wasn't a question she likely would or could answer.

Wren set off across the ocean, and Bain hoped she knew where she was going. An hour later, Wren was swimming up to the shoreline of another island, but Bain could see no light whatsoever.

"Are you sure about this Wren? It doesn't look inhabited."

Wren snorted and nodded as she slid onto the dry sand to let Bain off. She then cloaked herself to make certain she wasn't seen by anyone who might happen to pass by.

"I'll try to be back soon girl, though I'm not sure what I'll find. You stay here and stay out of sight."

Bain heard her snort at him again which made him smile. Never did he think he would be talking to creatures, let alone count one amongst his closest friends. Just knowing Wren could understand him even though he couldn't telepathically communicate with her, made him feel special somehow; probably another provision from the Creator. He looked up at the starry heavens and thanked the one who made it all.

He sighed heavily and said, "Right. Let's see if I can find life out here." He opened his pack, pulled out a torchlight, again thanking his friends in Dihendra for their forethought, and set out into the dense underbrush of trees and plants searching for any clues that would lead him to finding his family. Bain walked around for an hour with no success at finding any signs of life. He decided it would be much easier to search during the daylight hours and headed back to the beach where he would curl up with Wren for the night. But as he turned around to head back, he was taken by surprise by someone who had sneaked up behind him and struck him on the head. Before he could react, Bain went limp as everything went completely black.

Bain awoke hours later, the darkness of night still evident. He could hear sounds coming from somewhere outside as he took in his surroundings. He could feel that his hands were tied together and lashed to another rope which encircled his ankles. His head ached, especially where he had been hit, and he tried to look around the room he was in, searching for his backpack. He could make out a light through small cracks in the walls of the shack. He scooted closer to the wall and peered out a crack searching for the source of light. Just about fifty-feet from the shack where a fire crackled, and something turned on a spit just above it, sat one lone girl. Was that who had hit him? She didn't look big enough or strong enough to knock out a fully grown man. But if Bain had learned anything over the years, it was to not take people for granted. He had seen the smallest and youngest do mighty things during war time. This girl, whomever she was, might not be at war but it appeared she might be alone, at least for now. And since he was still alive she apparently wasn't interested in killing him. Bain thought about his size compared to hers. There must be someone else with her, or else how did she ever drag him here. He didn't figure she did it alone. Bain sat observing the scene before him, trying to learn whatever he could from the situation he was in, to try and find a way out of it. It wasn't long before some of his questions were answered when a rather large creature lumbered out of the jungle just on the other side of the fire. The beast was covered in short fluffy hair that looked gray in the firelight and was dotted with nearly perfect spots in a darker color. It was large; taller than Bain stood anyway, had four legs, and a large head with massive, powerful-looking jowls. The girl pulled a large piece of meat and bone from the spit and tossed it to the beast who snatched it out of the air and happily laid down beside her to chew at its dinner. The girl patted the beast as they quietly sat eating.

Bain worked at the ropes around his hands and feet. She fortunately had not thought to search him because she missed the small knife he kept on a strap around his leg hidden by his pant leg and boots. He managed to get the knife out and began sawing at the ropes which held him. After a few minutes of working the knife, he freed himself. He continued to watch the girl and the creature through the cracks in the walls, noticing that she had his backpack. After she finished eating, she picked up his journal, and leafed through his writings and images. She suddenly stopped, as though she recognized something she saw. She looked toward the shack, laid the book down and stood up, walking his way. Bain stepped back, not wishing to frighten her when she realized he was no longer tied up.

The shack door swung open as she searched the interior for Bain, finding him standing near the front wall. Seemingly unsurprised that he had freed himself from the ropes.

"Are you Bain Brinley?" she asked.

"Yes." He was confused, but a little excited too. Maybe she knew his family.

"What are you doing here?"

"Looking for my family. I assume you know them since you know who I am?"

"You don't remember me do you?"

Bain was confused. Surely if he knew her he would remember her. He hadn't been gone that long. "I'm not sure."

"I'm Jilian Porter, Jilly, from LARS."

Bain was confused. "Weren't you thirteen the last time I saw you?"

"Yes," she said, confused at his question.

"You don't look thirteen to me. How is that possible?"

"Well, it has been a long time since I last saw you."

"It was only a few months ago when I left Loradin after the wars."

"No, Bain, it wasn't. It's been years since we all sailed away from Ruin City and the Forgotten Coast."

"That's not possible."

Dot looked at Bain and went back to chewing on the carcass of whatever animal they had cooked for dinner.

Jilly looked at Bain, realizing what she had done.

"Sorry for hitting you, but since the pirate attack last year, I'm pretty leery of people, and since I haven't seen you in five years, and with the beard you have, I didn't recognize you."

"I understand Jilly," he said, rubbing his head and the knot that stuck up slightly.

"Are "I don't know where you've been, Bain, but five years have passed."

Bain leaned against the wall of the shack, totally shaken by what he had learned.

"Five years? How is that even possible?"

"I don't know where you've been where you would think that only a month has passed, but here, we've lived years."

"Where is everyone else? My family?"

"We were all separated when the pirates came. Some of us managed to escape and stay hidden on the island, but many of the young were taken, some of the older people were killed. You're grandfather, grandmothers, Finn and Paisley, Captain Donner, and Doctor Barrister all managed to escape. I don't know where they are as I haven't seen anyone since then. That was about a year ago."

"What about my parents? Wynne, Seadon, and Adda?"

"They never left Zanchier with us."

"What do you mean?"

"They went to look for you in the Xantifal Mountains. Wynne said her parents wouldn't leave without you, so they all went to find you. Your grandfather received a com-call from your father telling him that they thought they knew where you had gone, and that they were going to look for you, and to leave without them."

"No. Surely they didn't go through the portal." Bain said, thinking out loud.

"What portal?"

"Never mind, Jilly, it isn't important. Are you all alone here?"

"Yes. I haven't seen anyone else in nearly a year. Not since the pirates."

"I'm sorry. It has to have been lonely for you."

"Yes, except for Dot."

"Is that the creature outside?"

"Yes. He is native to the island I think; although I have never seen another one like him."

Bain and Jilly walked outside the shack to sit around the fire to chat. Dot raised his head and growled.

"It's all right Dot. This is Bain, he is a friend."

you hungry?" she asked, leaning over the spit, and pulling a leg from the meat and offering it to him.

"Sure, I can eat, thanks." Bain took the offered meat and sat beside the fire, realizing Wren was back on the beach. "Jilly, do you have any idea what time it is?"

"Probably around midnight."

"Do you always stay up this late?" Bain asked around bites.

"No, I had a stranger as a prisoner. I was a little too worried to sleep." She grinned sheepishly at him.

Bain smiled at her. "I see. Well, how far are we from the eastern shoreline?"

"Maybe a mile or so."

"Wren is waiting for me on the beach. I don't want her to wait too long."

"Wren is back?" Jilly asked excitedly. "I'm so glad. I haven't seen her for years, not since some locals tried catching her. It was awful. We weren't even sure she survived the attacks. They were shooting large harpoons at her."

"Who would do that?"

"I'm not sure who they were. Just some fishermen from the large island of Phiorellia." She suddenly became frightened. "No one else has seen her have they?"

"I don't think so. At least I hope not after what you've told me. She was awfully careful to stay hidden."

"Good. We should go back to the beach then and bring her here so she isn't alone. Poor thing has missed Wynne and Adda, but mostly Adda since she was her bond mate."

"Yeah, she was pretty excited to find me."

"How did she find you?"

"I was in Dihendra Rhial working with the castle guard when she just showed up."

This news seemed to make Jilly very nervous.

"Jilly, what's wrong?"

"The Dihendran guards were some of the people I heard the pirates talking about when they raided our island. They said the castle guards would pay high dollar for the children they took."

"You must be mistaken. I was there for several days and I never saw or heard anything that would make me think they were buying slaves."

"All I know is what I heard, Bain."

Bain sat, his brow now furrowed in thoughtful confusion as he tried to think about everything that he had heard and saw while he was working at Castle Dihendra. Nothing Jilly was saying matched what he remembered.

# Chapter 13

**Outer Phiorellian Islands, Midnight, Day 4**

Bain and Jilly walked back to the beach where he had left Wren. Bain called to her as they approached.

"Wren, where are you?"

They waited patiently, knowing she was likely sleeping.

Jilly asked, "You don't think she went for a midnight snack do you?"

Bain grinned. "Anything is possible."

"Wren," they both called.

They heard a snort, and as Wren uncloaked, she stretched her long body and yawned, a small growl rumbling up from her throat. Dot yipped in fright, backed up, then held his ground, coming to stand beside Jilly, the hair on his back raised, yet ready to defend his friend.

Jilly laughed at the creature. "Dot, it's all right, this is Wren, she is an old friend of mine."

Dot whimpered and whined again, then looked at Jilly.

She replied, "No, Wren won't eat you. She likes fish."

Bain was taken aback some, suddenly remembering that he was in the presence of a telepath once more. It had just been a while since he had seen anyone actually speaking with creatures, reminding Bain that most life was intelligent, even if we can't hear them speak. He turned to Wren.

"Wren, if you like, you can come to the island interior with us until morning."

Wren shook her head no and growled in answer.

Bain looked at Jilly. "What did she say?"

"She said she will stay by the sea since she will need to enter the water soon anyway. It's been hours since she fell asleep here on the sand, and the winds and heat dry her skin out more so than if she were in a sea-cave."

Bain said thoughtfully, "Makes sense. I knew she needed water, but I also remember finding her asleep in the cave under the Marshlands back home."

Bain and Jilly spent a little time with Wren before she dove back into the water for a while, then they returned to Jilly's camp. They bedded down for the remainder of the night, catching whatever sleep they could before dawn broke over the trees and filtered into the shacks cracks and crevices, casting shadows and light here and there.

Bain woke, stood, and stepped outside the shack. In the morning light and the cool breeze of the island, he stretched his back as he looked at his surroundings. Jilly had very little in the way of supplies. It amazed him to think she had lived here alone for nearly a year, well except for Dot, whatever sort of creature he was. Bain smiled at the memory of Dot's earlier reaction to Wren. He had been frightened, but he loyally stood by Jilly willing to fight to protect her, even though his mind had told him to run. This brought back memories of the creatures of Zanchier that had fought in a war that was not their own, bravely flying and running into battle beside their bond-mates. Bain had seen and known true loyalty not only from the creatures, but from his friends and family, many who had fought and died in the Three Army Wars.

Jilly walked out of the shack, squinting against the morning light. "Good morning. If you're hungry, we can go fishing or hunting."

Bain smiled at her. "How about we just grab something from my bag?"

Jilly smiled. "An easy breakfast would be nice for a change."

Bain grabbed his bag, handed Jilly one of the travel meal packs that Sebena had put in there, and they sat and chatted while they ate. Afterward they made a plan on what to do next.

"Jilly, I have to try to find my family. You did say that my grandparents were here on the island."

"They were, but I haven't seen anyone for a while. But I don't travel far from home either." She nodded toward her shack.

"Surely you don't want to stay here alone forever?"

"No. Not really."

"Do you and Dot want to come with me to look for the others?"

"Yes. I've been alone long enough." She looked at her companion for the last year. "No offense, Dot, but human companionship is a little different."

Dot snorted, and to Bain it seemed he was a little indignant at her words.

Bain said, "Well then, gather up whatever you want to take with you, and keep in mind, you likely won't be returning."

"Okay." Jilly set about the shack, packing what she could into a self-made bag, looked around outside for any tools or weapons she could carry, and then took one last look around. She then looked at Bain and said, "I'm ready to go."

"All right then, first we'll go back to the beach to inform Wren that we'll be looking inland around the island. If we don't find anyone, we can return in about a week to meet her again."

"Bain, I can just telepathically communicate all that to her. Our abilities reach a good distance. Unless you just want to tell her goodbye?"

Bain had forgotten the telepaths could communicate over great distances. "No, that's fine, Jilly. Will you just tell her goodbye and thank you for me, and that we hope to see her again soon?"

"Sure thing, Bain." Jilly was quiet for a minute as she closed her eyes and searched telepathically for Wren. Bain saw her smile briefly and then she nodded and opened her eyes. "All done. Oh and Wren said to say that she'll miss you."

Bain nodded thoughtfully, then grinned at Jilly. He nodded for her to follow and they set off toward the interior of the island.

Bain asked, "When was the last time you saw anyone?"

"Like I said before, it's been nearly a year."

"Where was that exactly?"

"Well, back toward the beach where Wren dropped you, but much further south. There is, or was, a small village there where everyone had settled down, you know, made new homes, and formed relationships. But then the pirates came and everyone who wasn't captured scattered."

"How do you know who was taken and who escaped?" He didn't ask her about those who were killed.

"I watched from my hiding place and am grateful they never found me. When they left, I went looking for people, that's when I saw the dead. I knew they took the kids because of the conversation I overheard, and the fact that I saw them loading kids onto the ships. Plus, I saw your grandparents, the Mobleys, and the Donners sneaking behind buildings as they ran for cover, trying to grab whoever they could help in the process."

"I can't believe they took off without helping, especially grandfather and Uncle Finn," Bain said, surprised by her words.

"You don't understand, Bain. There was nothing anyone could do. There were so many pirates, and they didn't care who lived or died. A few of the village men tried to stand up to them, but they were shot before they even took two steps. Running and hiding was all anyone could do, and those were the lucky ones. Your grandparents, being elderly, would have likely been killed on sight. I'm sure your grandfather and Finn were thinking about the rest of your family, and Captain James about his wife and children."

Bain looked at her with understanding this time. "You're right. Besides, I've been there and have no room to judge anyone."

He then asked, "So, You've been on this island for five years?"

"Well, almost."

"Have you looked around much or explored the area?"

"Not really. We were trying to settle in, everyone making a place for themselves or their family to live. All of the LARS students who left with Dr. Barrister, well Donner now, and whose family was either dead or decided to return to Zanchier from Ruin City, lived with her. When she and Captain James married, most of us were old enough to handle living on our own. They kept watch over us, but naturally they wanted their own space, but so did those of us who were coming of age."

"So, did the other kids live with you as well?"

"Well, Jerod was old enough to have his own place being sixteen, and so was Oudree. She turned sixteen shortly after we arrived, and she found some friends here her age and they all moved in together. Matteo was nearly fifteen, but still a bit immature, so he, Kasin, me, and little Naphin, and Eckshum all lived with Dr. Barrister. Naphin and Eckshum stayed with her after the wedding because they were still too young. Kasin and I stayed in the old house together. She was like a sister to me. The pirates took them all you know."

"All of them?"

"Yes, even Jerod and Oudree. I'm not sure about Matteo, he always talked big, but he was a little cowardly at times, especially if his bond-creature wasn't around."

"Yeah, I remember him, never satisfied with what he had. Always wanting something more grand, someone else's bond-creature. He never really liked the Raisedback Vindaper with which he was paired."

"Yes, he always resented Wynne because she was several years younger than him and was bonded to the firebird, Roamey. She was the first of all of us to make a true connection. We all knew we could communicate with creatures, but Wynne was without fear of any of them."

"Yeah, she always was a headstrong, fearless little girl." Mention of his sister made him wonder where they were. "Jilly, you said you heard they went after me. Was that when they went to the Xantifal Mountains to the treehouse?"

"No. Your father already knew you were there. They went there using the MADs to get you and bring you back to the ships before we left. Your father said, once they were already there that you were gone, and they were going to find you."

Bain exhaled loudly, realization setting in. "So they likely went into the portal after me."

"Portal?" Jilly asked, a confused look on her face.

"A time-portal, Jilly. That's where I've been for the last five years. Although, for me it was only a little more than three weeks."

Her brow knitted together in thought. "How is that possible? Where did you go if you went through a time-portal?"

"Several different places, I just don't understand how it works."

"So those were all the places you talked about in your journal. The place called Egypt with the tall triangular buildings. And then the castle at Dihendra."

"Yes, which is where Wren found me."

"You've certainly had many adventures in such a short time period. All I've done is sit near my shack, look for food, and try to survive while staying hidden from the pirates who returned a few times."

"Do you know why they came back?"

"I suppose to look for more kids to sell as slaves. I'm sure they knew that some of us escaped."

"How long has it been since you last saw them?"

"Probably six months or so. I think they've finally given up and moved on."

"Well, hopefully we can find my family, then maybe do something about getting everyone back that the pirates took."

Jilly looked at Bain with a questioning uncertainty. She doubted he knew just what he was getting into. But Jilly had always seen Wynne's big brother Bain as the strong, adventurous type. She even had a crush on him during the wars, but he had been with Raila, who was more age appropriate for him at the time. Bain was much too old for her then. Now, all Jilly wanted was to find her family and friends, like he did. She was tired of being alone, even though she had Dot. She looked over her shoulder at the creature she had found wounded a year ago. He had been her constant companion since. Dot trudged along behind them, sniffing the air for any signs of danger, her ever-constant protector.

Bain and Jilly walked in silence for the next several hours, only speaking when necessary. They marched across the interior of the island and up to the peak of the mountain in the center. Bain looked closely at anything that might be a cave, or somewhere people could hide. He also looked up into the trees, remembering full well Treetop Village back home. The entire village had been built in the massive tree branches of the Carpasian Mountains. Although the trees here were nowhere near as large as many were back in Zanchier. Bain soon found an area with some fallen trees which they could use to sit and rest for a while.

"You want to take a break and eat some lunch?" Bain asked.

"Sure. I am a bit thirsty." Jilly removed her backpack and other items, setting them on the ground. She then plopped down on an obliging log to rest and eat.

Bain handed her another ready meal pack from his backpack and the two of them ate in silence. Bain could hear the call of birds chirping through the trees overhead. They sounded as though they were speaking to each other. There was something so familiar about the calls.

Then the sound of a gun clicked, and a voice from behind, one he recognized well asked, "Who are you?"

Bain smiled but moved slowly. "Bain Brinley. How are you Captain Donner?"

"Bain?" The Captain lowered his weapon and smiled. "Where have you been all this time?"

Bain smiled. "I guess you could say traveling."

James looked at Jilly and smiled broadly, pulling the girl into a hug. "Jilly, I am very pleased to see you. We thought you were taken with the others. Where have you been?"

"Living near the coast by myself."

"For a year?"

"Yeah. Well, I had Dot."

"Who's Dot?"

"He went off in search of food. He'll be back soon. He's a creature I found shortly after I ran away from the pirate attack."

James nodded, the memory of the dark day casting shadows across his features. "Well, let's get you two to the hideout. Your grandparents and Finn are going to be thrilled to see you, Bain."

"No more than I will be to see them." Bain smiled as they picked up their supplies and followed James Donner through the thick underbrush. Jilly called to Dot who finally found them.

James pointed his gun at whatever was breaking through the underbrush in their direction.

"Captain, it's only Dot." Jilly assured him.

When Dot appeared, James was slightly taken aback by his size. He wasn't a massive creature, but he was nearly as tall as himself and thick through the shoulders.

"You're certain he's friendly?"

"Yes, why?" Jilly asked.

"From the size of his jowls, I figure one or two bites would be all he needs to finish me off otherwise."

Jilly giggled. "Yes, his head is rather large, but his heart is larger." She fondly snuggled the beast who pushed and purred at her in returned affection.

"Good," James smiled. "We're not far from camp. It won't be long before you two are reunited with everyone."

# Chapter 14

**Afternoon, Day 5**

The hideout was undetectable from the outside, the tunnel opening covered with vines that hung over it so thickly it was bound together like a thick carpet. James had lifted one side and slid beneath. Bain, Jilly, and Dot followed after him.

They walked a little ways into the cavern before James yelled, "Everyone, I have a surprise for all of you." They entered a large opening on the other side of the long tunnel they had just walked through.

Everyone's eyes were on them as Bain, Jilly, and Dot appeared.

Bain heard an audible gasp flit through the room just before they were descended upon by people, all talking excitedly and pulling him and Jilly into forceful hugs. Then Bain came face to face with Aaric.

"Grandfather," Bain said fondly.

"Oh, my Boy, where have you been?" Aaric said as he grabbed Bain, pulling him into a hug. His grandmother Neitha and his maternal grandmother Gracelynn both joined in, all wrapping around him in a tearful reunion. Next was Finn and Paisley.

Bain noticed Gracelynn looking past them through the tunnel, a questioning look on her face. "Grandmother, there's no one else with us."

Gracelynn looked back to him. "Your parents and siblings never found you?"

Bain hung his head in sadness and shook his head no. "I had no idea they had even followed me into the portal."

Aaric said, "We can discuss this a bit later. Let's get you and Jilly here a proper lunch and settled in so we can catch up. A lot has happened since we last saw you."

"So I've heard. But my experience is much different."

After getting their packs put into a bedding area, and some hot food and cool drinks into their stomachs, Bain took his journal from his pack and sat at the long, roughly hewn, wooden, communal table showing them what he had seen and done in the last nearly four weeks. They were all shocked to think that for Bain, he had only been gone a short time, but it had been five years for the rest of them.

Aaric asked, "Bain, you're scientifically minded like you mother, why do you think time changed for you, but when your father Wilkins experienced time-travel before, time stayed the same for him?"

"I don't know, Grandfather. I can't understand it either. Unless time plays out differently in the places I went. Or perhaps I just traveled to a later time here then when I left."

"Extraordinary. You look the same, except for the beard and mustache. It took me a minute to recognize you when you came in, except for the fact that you look just like your father when he was your age."

"Yeah, I need to shave. All the running around, and training with Dihendran guard has kept me busy. It took Wren and me nearly two days to find anyone we knew. That's when Jilly here stumbled upon me."

"Knocked you out you mean." Jilly winced at the memory. "Sorry again." She gave him a pained grin.

Bain smiled at her and chuckled slightly at her discomfort. He then looked around the interior of the cavern at the people there. Many he recognized from Zanchier, but there were still so many missing.

"Grandfather," he said, "do you and the others plan to live out your days here in this cavern?"

Aaric looked at Bain. "Well, I guess we never thought about it. We've been safe here, but now that you ask, it isn't really living is it."

Bain shook his head no. "You could leave here, find another place to live."

"Perhaps. We do have two working airships, and a few of the other sailing vessels that are still in good order."

"The pirates didn't destroy them?"

"No, fortunately. We had them stored on the back side of the island. The airships are cloaked by a device that Maubrey and Kamsten, created."

Bain thought about his two friends from the LSS technology department and looked around. They were obviously not there. He didn't want to ask if they had perished, so he simply waited on a reply.

Aaric noticed Bain search the faces in the cave. "They too were taken by the pirates."

"But they aren't kids." Bain said confused.

Aaric explained. "No, but when the pirates realized they were highly intelligent, they figured they could get a good price for them as well."

Bain sighed. "Well, at least they're still alive. Now, what are we going to do about these kidnappings?"

"What do you mean?" James asked.

Aaric answered, "He means, why haven't we gone after them already?"

"Exactly," Bain said, with a questioning look at his grandfather.

"It isn't all that simple, Bain. We have very little weapons, and many of the people here are not fighters."

"Grandfather, you ran a spy organization for years before leaving Zanchier. I can't believe you can't organize a rescue."

"I also don't have all the technology and resources available to me that I had back on Zanchier either."

"No, but now you have Jilly. She can communicate with the creatures and call them here. They would be a great help."

"True, but we have no idea where they took the children."

Jilly said, "I heard the pirates talking about Dihendran guards paying top dollar for the kids they took."

This surprised Aaric, Finn, and James. Finn said, "I'll admit we've only been around for five years, but I've only heard good things about Dihendra Rhial."

James offered, "Perhaps it is all a ruse. Maybe there is deceit and treachery at its heart?"

Bain shook his head. "No, I was there for nearly three days. I never saw anything like that from the guard. There must be another explanation."

"Well," Aaric said, "I'm game for a rescue mission. But how do we go about it?"

Bain said, "I know a little about the castle grounds, and some of the area from my short time there, but not much about Dihendra Rhial. I do have friends there who might help us."

"How would you get in touch with them?"

"I'd have to go back."

Gracelynn quickly added, "But you only just got here. Can't all this wait for a little while?"

Bain looked at his grandmother. "It can't. We don't know why the kids were taken or what they are going through. It's already been a year."

Gracelynn nodded her understanding.

"Right then, people," Aaric said, "let's form a plan to get our people back."

Everyone sat around the table making a plan to venture to Dihendra Rhial, figure out what was going on, and see about finding those that were taken by force and possibly sold to the Dihendran Guard.

As Jilly called to the few creatures that inhabited the island and the sea around them, the others made plans for the search for those taken by the pirates. They made the trip to the backside of the island where the three airships were, two of which were still in working order. While checking them over they found that the cannons still worked as well, but not truly certain as they were unable to test them on land for fear of setting everything on fire. Last year after the pirates had left, many people returned to the coastal city to search for survivors. They salvaged everything they could along with the few sailing vessels that survived the pirate attack. They then sailed them around the coast and anchored them in a sea cave on the back side of the island to hide them from the pirates.

While the men set about making small, needed repairs, and checking equipment, the women hauled supplies onto the ships for the journey. The airships held less people than the sailing ships, so thirty people were selected for each of the airships and given a crash course in operations and weaponry. The same was given to those on the sailing ships. Many of the crew, the able-bodied men, and women, who had tried to fight against the pirates, had lost their lives. So others were needed to be trained to replace them. They all knew it was going to be a learning experience while they sailed away from the island. Fortunately, nearly every person who had escaped Zanchier had also held a weapon and had fought in the wars, so teaching them to fight was not needed.

Jilly introduced the creatures around so that people wouldn't fear them. Wren also made a reappearance and the people of Zanchier cheered and welcomed her, happy that she was still alive. When everything was ready, and everyone loaded onto the ships since no one wanted to stay behind, they set sail.

Aaric decided to sail to the main island to inquire about purchasing some weapons before making the long journey to recover their people. After securing weapons, food, and medical supplies for several hundred people, they set sail, heading northeast. Bain wasn't certain as to the coordinates, but they followed Wren who swam out in front and led the way.

Bain asked the airship captain, "Captain Easton, are you certain the airships can make the journey on what fuel they have?"

"Well, they got us to the islands from Zanchier, and it was nearly a two-day journey."

"From what I remember, Dihendra was a day and a half's journey by water. Wren did find a small, uninhabited island on which to land so we could sleep for a while."

"Perhaps she will lead us there again. We will need to land for rest as well. Flying for that long can be dangerous."

"Also Captain, won't we need to test the weapon's system at some point before engaging in battle?"

"Yes. When we get further out to sea, we'll do that. I don't want to take any chances at alerting anyone to our presence. Plus, Jilly will have to make certain that Wren knows what we are doing so she won't be frightened."

"I'll com-call James and let him know about the island and to tell Jilly to alert Wren. Maybe we can test them on the island either before we land or before we resume our journey tomorrow."

"That sounds like a good plan. Then you and Jilly can be with Wren to keep her calm. I'm afraid she may be shell-shocked after her last encounter with men, boats, and weapons."

Bain nodded his understanding. Bain com-called James to inform him of their conversation. James, Dr. Patrice, and Jilly were on the lead of the three sailing ships.

Aaric, Neitha, and Gracelynn were on the lead airship with Bain, along with Finn and Paisley.

"Bain," Aaric asked, "What all do you know about the weaponry capabilities of Dihendra?"

"Not much I'm afraid. I was only there for three days, training with the Baiskreet mostly."

"Those are the creatures you were telling me about?"

"Yes sir."

"Do you think Jilly will be able to communicate with and control them?"

"I don't know. Besides, I'm hoping to find allies at the castle. I never saw anything happening there like what you all heard the pirates say. I don't believe the Castle Guard to be involved in anything like that."

"Three days is little time to gauge what business goes on in a place, unless you're looking for it of course."

"True. But grandfather, the people I met seemed very genuine."

"Perhaps they are oblivious to what the upper command is involved in. Many soldiers just simply fight and take orders without knowing what they are fighting for."

"Yes, like the Martanzian and Bakrisian military from the Three Army Wars on Zanchier. None of the leaders knew how corrupt Commander Raif Martray was at that point. Kreelie had fought because he thought he fought for the right side." Bain remembered his life-long friend who had perished in the war, but he had turned and had been fighting for the right side when he died with honor, protecting the people of Everly Sound and Martanzia from the evil Scaither regime.

"Maybe these people you know were once children themselves who were taken and raised as soldiers?"

"I don't believe so, Sir. I understood all the people who were training with me to be new recruits."

"Still they could have come from a place where they were all raised together?"

"Well, perhaps, but Mercer I know for sure had joined himself, leaving his family to do so. And Sebena, I think she had family as well. I really didn't get to know people well in such a short time, but I will say, there is no way that the Protectors of Dihendra in the Twelfth Squadron would have anything to do with kidnapping. Or that it is a city-wide thing. Sebena was adamant about Dihendra being a just city, and I noticed that myself while there. People flocked to the city for the Four-Moon Festival to help pack the food storage bins with their excess for the hard winter they were expecting. I can't imagine a city that does all that being into kidnapping."

"Perhaps they aren't, but they may be unknowingly purchasing kidnapped children for purposes unknown."

"Surely one of the kidnapped would say something. There's no way they could be oblivious as to where they came from." Bain said incredulously.

"There are many ways to keep a slave quiet such as fear, threats, and drugs. They may not even remember who they are themselves to even complain."

"When we return to Dihendra, I will seek out my friends before we do anything. My training with the LSS should allow me to tell if any of the others are lying."

"Yes," Aaric said, "perhaps they heard or saw something that didn't make sense at the time, but with new information, it can lend understanding to an otherwise useless memory."

"Let's hope so, Grandfather. If there is anything sinister going on in Dihendra I'm  certain that my friends in the Twelfth Guard will help us in finding out."

# Chapter 15

**Day 6**

The trip across the ocean was uneventful, except for a small storm that had passed over them while anchored on the small island Bain and Wren had visited on their way to Phiorellia. It was closer to the southern islands than that of Dihendra Rhial, but they went ahead and took the time to check the weapons systems of the air and sailing ships before proceeding. The long ride to Dihendra's coast would take all day, and finding a place to set down inland, or anchor offshore without being seen was something Bain would have to figure out.

Bain made the second part of the journey on the sailing ships so that when they got close to land, he could mount Wren and they could scout where to tell the others to put into shore.

Bain, Jilly, and Wren rode the eastern shores of Dihendra looking for an undetectable spot. It had grown very dark, so it was hard for Bain to see. However the benefit of having Jilly around was so that communications with Wren were open. When Wren turned inland swimming between tall spires of rock extending from the ocean floor  he looked a Jilly.

"Where's she going?"

"She says there are some open caverns just through these jagged rocks."

Bain said, "The sailing ships will have to be cautious when navigating through here."

Jilly replied, "The airships as well, but the opening looks tall enough for them to fly through. Let's hope the cavern's interior will accommodate the airships."

"Let's hope, but even if they fit through, where would they land?" Bain answered.

As Wren swam through the treacherous, rocky waters and into the cavern, it was even darker with the moons light now extinguished. Wren, understanding Jilly's thoughts turned on her bioluminescence and with being so large a creature, she glowed powerfully enough to make out the caverns interior as they passed along through the waters.

Bain and Jilly smiled broadly at each other, giving Wren a good rub for her ingenious thought and abilities.

Bain remarked, "I didn't know she had luminescent abilities. I don't think I've ever seen her use them."

"Well, creatures don't reveal everything about themselves because, unlike humans, they aren't cocky, or self-absorbed, prancing about for all to see. They only use their abilities when needed. There may be so many other things about our creatures that we haven't discovered yet. The right situation may reveal something entirely new."

"That's true, Jilly. It seems you've learned a lot from Dr. Barrister."

"Dr. Donner you mean." Jilly smiled.

"Yes, I forgot she and James are now married."

They took in the size of the cavern, noticing a dim light ahead of them which seemed to illuminate a large grassy area which also had some trees and plants growing.

Bain said, "That area where the light is coming through must be a hole in the top of the cavern ceiling. That would account for the life that seems to have taken root down here. The sparse trees and grass must get sunlight and rain. Meaning, that hole way up there has to be much larger than it appears."

"Then the airships should be able to hide down here instead of having to use the cloaking devices," Jilly stated.

"Maybe so."

As they got closer, they could make out that the hole was indeed quite large, and the ground where the grass, trees, and shrubs grew seemed hard and stable.

Bain said, "Jilly, ask Wren to make sure that the waterways are passable for the sailing ships. They are heavier and sit much deeper in the water than she does."

"Sure thing." Jilly turned to Wren and communicated the question without words. Wren snorted in indignation before diving below the surface.

Bain sensed that she was perturbed about something and asked, "Is something wrong with Wren?"

"Yes. She's aggravated with you because you no longer speak to her yourself."

Bain looked confused as he stared at Jilly trying to decipher her meaning.

"Oh. That's right. She understands me even though I can't hear her."

"Yes, and she feels like you don't like speaking to her. It has hurt her feelings."

Bain grinned at Jilly's understanding. "I'll apologize once she returns."

"Good." Jilly stated, then something struck her memory. "Bain, Jerod and Wynne once tried an exercise with one of the workers at LARS who wanted so badly to speak to the creatures himself. I saw Wynne place the fingers of one hand on his temple and then do the same with her other hand on her own. After about a minute of telepathic communication, the man could hear and communicate with many of the creatures at LARS."

"So, you think this would work for me?"

"I'm not sure. Perhaps the man had hidden telepathic abilities and we just brought them out. Or, perhaps somehow, doing that opened a section of the man's mind that he had never used."

"I'm game. I would love to be able to speak with the creatures the way you all do."

"All right." Jilly stepped up to Bain, standing directly in front of him. She placed her fingers on both their temples. "Now," she said, "close your eyes and concentrate on me. Try to read what I'm thinking."

Bain and Jilly stood in the quiet dark cavern, illuminated by the moonlight streaming through the giant hole far overhead.

Bain smiled. "I think I can sense you."

"Shush...use only your thoughts, not your words."

Bain concentrated, realizing Jilly was calling his name.

*'Bain, can you hear me?'*

*'Yes. Can you hear me?'*

*'Of course I can, I'm telepathic.'* Jilly giggled audibly, breaking their concentration, and causing Bain to open his eyes and look at her.

"Okay, ask me something telepathically," Bain excitedly said.

"All right." Jilly thought for a moment and communicated to him with, *'Try talking to Wren now.'*

Bain smiled. "Did you ask me to speak to Wren?"

"Yes." Jilly smiled as broadly as Bain did.

Bain turned to look at the water and with his mind communicated, *'Wren, is the water passable for the ships?'*

Wren understood the difference between how she heard from Bain before and how she was hearing from him now. She surfaced and jumped into the air, splashing back down into the water, her excitement evident that Bain's communication worked.

*'Yes, clear all the way, as long as they follow close.'*

Bain smiled even broader as he received her communication. Bain turned to Jilly and grabbed her, pulling her into a big, grateful, hug. "Thank you Jilly. This is amazing."

Jilly giggled at his excitement. "You're welcome."

"Why doesn't everyone ask to do this?"

"Well, it can be hard to control at times, especially when there is a lot going on. You'll have to learn to block people out when you don't want them reading your thoughts, or you don't want to read theirs."

"Wait, I can actually read other people's thoughts?"

"Well, I'm unsure about how much. Each telepath is different. Some have stronger abilities than others, but it could be a possibility."

"I never considered that. Have you all been able to read others minds all these years?"

"No. Not always. It is something that I've developed over the last few years, but being separated from people for nearly a year has made me a tad rusty. And it usually only happened when people were under extreme duress."

"I can see how that could become a real problem. Probably the reason there aren't many people with the gift."

"Yes, and if everyone could speak to the creatures as we do, we Telepaths wouldn't be needed anymore. You know, that vain, self-absorbed thing we humans do that makes us feel important or necessary."

Bain grinned at her in understanding. He had to admit, it was nice being the one everyone respected or wanted to be like back at Castle Dihendra.

Wren returned soon, and the three of them went back out the where the ships waited. They communicated about the large open cavern and the immense hole where the airships could navigate to the ground safely and put down on the island in the cavern. The ships followed Wren through the treacherous waters as the airships floated just above the land, looking for the large opening to stay safely hidden until Bain could scout the area, find his friends at the castle, and see if anyone knew about the pirates selling slaves to the Dihendran Guard.

What Bain didn't know was there was one lone rider on the back of a Baiskreet staring off into the ocean waters, suddenly surprised to see a very small fleet of air and sailing ships disappearing into the coast several miles to the south. An investigation into who it was that was trying to hide along the coast was something worth checking out.

Once the last airship had floated into place on the ground, and the last of the sailing ships had safely navigated the narrow, rocky, cavern pass, Bain, and Jilly rode on Dot's back, along the shoreline and up over the cliff edges to the grassy hilltops above, headed toward Castle Dihendra. Bain was positive that there were no local creatures that looked like Dot, and therefore did not want the animal to be taken and studied any more than he had wanted the same for Wren. So, as they got close to the castle, Bain sent Jilly and Dot back to the cavern.

"Can you find your way back on your own?"

"Yes. Dot doesn't get lost, it's something in his genetic makeup."

"All right, then you two get going."

"What about you, Bain? How will you get back?"

"I'll take one of the air-rovers, or maybe a Baiskreet."

"I'm not sure I like leaving you all alone," Jilly protested.

"Jilly, I've been alone for weeks now. Except for the people I've met along the way. I will be just fine. Besides, I have friends here, remember?"

Jilly sighed heavily, before turning Dot around and sprinting back across the hilly, grassy land toward the coast. As Dot and Jilly entered the cavern, they could see a figure slinking around in the edges of darkness just in front of them. They approached with caution as Dot sneaked up behind the cloaked and hooded figure. Dot was standing nearly directly over the person when his hot, ragged breath, and a low growl emanated from his mouth. The cloaked figure froze in place, not sure whether to move. When no attack came, they slowly turned to see what was behind them. Jilly watched as the hood slid backward from the strangers head when they looked up at the strange beast looming dangerously over them.

Jilly was struck with recollection, mainly from Bain's journal. His description of her was spot on. She was definitely exactly as he stated.

"Are you Sebena Zentrialle?"

Sebena's stance became rigid, surprised by this girl knowing who she was. "Who's asking?"

"Sorry," Jilly said, patting Dot and saying, "It's all right Dot, she's friendly." She then slid from Dot's back to the ground. "My name is Jilian. I'm a friend of Bain Brinley."

Sebena was shocked. "Bain's back? Where?"

Sebena turned toward the ships and began walking away.

"Not here I'm afraid. I just dropped him at Castle Dihendra. He went looking for his friends."

"Well, then I shall go find him."

Sebena zipped past Jilian, not waiting for any further explanations. She was soon flying on her Baiskreet, which had been cloaked just outside the cavern entrance, and was speeding toward the castle, hoping to soon find Bain. But why all the secrecy and hiding? Why had he not returned straight away to the castle? Something very peculiar was going on, and she wanted to know what that was. Bain had the answers, and she would soon find out what those answers were.

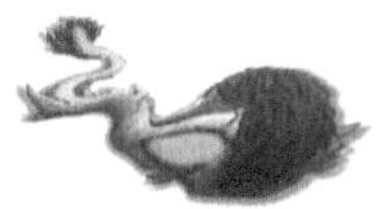

Bain walked through the castle grounds, no one paying him much mind except for the few who recognized him and said hello or waved. One woman in particular asked where he'd been the last several days.

"Just some family matters to tend to," Bain replied.

She nodded and smiled at him, gave him a wink, and said, "Well, I'm glad you're back."

Bain nodded and gave a stiff grin. He only hoped he would get that sort of welcome from Sebena. He rounded the corner and nearly bumped into Captain Nigel.

"Recruit Brinley? Sebena told us you left."

"I did, Sir. I had something to tend to and now I've returned."

"Odd, Sebena made it sound as though you wouldn't be returning."

"You must have just misunderstood."

"Perhaps. Carry on Brinley."

"Sir," Bain nodded and walked off. He went to the barracks where he peered inside scanning the room for Mercer, catching the attention of a surprised Guidriun in the process. Bain nodded and Guidriun excused himself from his group of friends and left the barracks to speak with Bain who was waiting just outside the doorway.

"Bain, what are you doing here? I thought you left for good."

"Well, I thought I had left for good as well."

"Did you find your family?"

"Some of them, but not my parents and siblings."

"So why are you here then?"

"I've discovered something distressing. I need to speak to Sebena before anyone else. Have you seen her around?"

"No, not since the breeding grounds."

"Bain?" Came his name from just behind him. He turned to see Mercer smiling broadly and walking toward him. He grabbed Bain and gave him a hug. "I can't believe you're back already. We all figured your leaving was permanent."

"Well, I didn't expect to return so soon. Have you seen Sebena, I'll explain everything when I find her."

"Well, I saw her take a Baiskreet and fly east after dinner," Mercer answered.

"Okay, I have to go find her." Bain turned and left for the breeding grounds.

Mercer and Guidriun looked at each other, shrugged, and took off after Bain with Mercer yelling, "You're not leaving us behind!"

# Chapter 16

Sebena landed in the courtyard of the castle, jumped from her Baiskreet, and hurried to the dining hall, but Bain wasn't there. As she walked the halls toward the barracks she saw him; followed closely by Guidriun and Mercer. She stopped walking and stood looking at him; Bain doing the same. She wanted to run to him, jump into his arms, but knowing they would draw way too much attention, she nodded for him to follow her outside to a more private area.

They followed Sebena outside and around a corner, and when Bain stopped in front of her she just stood there looking at him. Before he could speak, she launched herself at him, locking lips with him. Bain leaned into the kiss.

Guidriun and Mercer tried to avert their eyes and look at anything else but them.

Sebena broke the contact and said, "I didn't think I would ever see you again, much less days later."

"It wasn't planned, sorry."

"What do you mean? And who are all the people in the sea cave?"

"How do you know about the sea cave?"

"I was out riding when I saw the airships disappear into the ground. So naturally I went to find out who was hiding out beneath Dihendran soil."

Bain nodded, knowing she would have done so. "Okay, now, listen, I need you all to be honest with me," Bain said, looking around at everyone. "Do the Dihendran Guard purchase slaves from pirates?"

"What!?" Sebena asked perturbed by his question. "Why would you ask that?"

"I found some of my family and friends, but many were taken by force by pirates a year ago, who said that the Dihendran Guard would pay well for the slaves they stole."

"I don't know who told you that, but I assure you the guard does NOT buy slaves. Dihendra is a peaceable nation, one which helps its people. It doesn't buy stolen children." Sebena protested strongly.

"Sebena, I'm sorry to say things that upset you, but maybe there is an organization here in Dihendra posing as the guard then?"

"Bain, I've lived and worked for the guard for seven years. I've never seen or heard of such a thing. And as the guard, we should know if such an organization exists."

Mercer and Guidriun looked at each other and shrugged shaking their heads. Mercer added, "We haven't either."

"Well, someone has them, a lot of them, and the pirates killed many more who they considered useless. I have to find my friends, and the words overheard from the pirates are all we have to go by."

Sebena thought for a moment. "Surely one of the other captains would know if such an organization exists. I'll ask around."

"Sebena," Bain said, "be careful. It may not be a well-known topic or one that someone wants to be found out."

Mercer asked, "But what could someone want with a bunch of kids?"

"Not just kids," Bain said. "They took a couple of technological geniuses as well. Both are much older."

"Still, what would they want with the kids?" Guidriun asked.

"Well, if they knew about the special abilities of some of the kids they took, then I can understand why."

"Like what?" Sebena asked.

"Some of the kids from Zanchier can speak to creatures."

Sebena said, "I remember you telling me that. And that girl, the one called Jilian, she spoke to that beast she rode, the one called Dot, as though it could understand her."

"Because she can. Jilian is a telepath. She was able to hide and escape capture. My grandfather and our people are here to free our friends. We just need to know who we are fighting. Since you say that it isn't the guard, why do you think the pirates would say it was?"

Guidriun offered, "Perhaps someone wants people to believe the guard is corrupt."

"But why?" Sebena asked. "What good could come from discrediting the castle guards?"

Bain shook his head. "I don't know, but we need to be careful. I wouldn't just go around asking outright about this, Sebena. You need to be cautious when searching for answers."

"Yes, I see your point. Surely there is a mistake or misunderstanding. I will see what I can find out, but you have to be wrong about this. I refuse to believe the guard is entangled in this in any way."

Mercer said, "We can all split up and search for answers."

Bain replied, "Fine. Let's meet back here in two hours with whatever reports we find. I'll take the second level of the castle."

Guidriun said, "I'll take the main level. Mercer can have the level below ground."

"Right, give me the dark, dank dungeon to search, that's great."

They all smiled at him.

Sebena said, "I'll search the upper levels. None of you would be allowed up there anyway. There are areas we aren't allowed either. Now I question why that is."

They all looked at each other one more time, checked their watches, and split up, all going in separate directions.

Bain walked the long narrow hallways of the castle interior checking through any doors that were unlocked. Any that were, Bain would knock and listen for any noise from within. He had found nothing so far. He hoped the others were having better luck.

Guidriun did the same as Bain, walking and searching any unlocked doors, but Guidriun had another talent, he could pick locks and spent a little more time looking behind such doors, but still came up empty handed.

Mercer had to use a light to search the dim, dusty, damp rooms of the castle's lower level. He hadn't found any signs of people, but he did come across more than a few gutter grints. Their beady little eyes shining in the light of his torch. Mercer shuttered. He could handle big beasts like the Baiskreet, but he hated things that scurried about in the dark. He continued his search, though he was ready to run if necessary.

Sebena made her way to the upper levels of the castle; particularly the one where captains weren't allowed. As she walked the halls peering into open doorways and trying to open locked ones, she suddenly heard talking come from somewhere behind her. She ducked into an obliging archway recession and into the shadows it offered. She listened, hoping to be able to recognize the voices.

"Yes sir, Commander."

"Now, I'm depending on you to keep this quiet, Captain. If you mess this up, it'll be the end of all our careers."

"You don't have to worry about me, Sir. I can handle the situation."

"You'd better. We can't have any more of them trying to escape. No one can know about this."

"I understand Sir."

Sebena couldn't believe her ears, but she had definitely stumbled onto something. She followed the men, slinking quietly through the hallways. She recognized them both to be superiors with the First and Second Squadrons of the guard.

The men walked to a securely locked section of the castle, unlocked the doors, and walked through them. Sebena quickly ran to the door and grabbed the edge before it closed, hoping to squelch any squeaking of old hinges. She waited just a few seconds before pulling it slightly open to peer inside.

The interior was several separate hallways leading in different directions, lined with small doorways with slide-bolt locks. The two men disappeared down another long hallway and through another door on the other side.

She slid into the room, blocking the door open with a leather pouch, just in case it locked when it closed. She then slid up to the first bolted door and peered inside through a small slit near the center. Nothing. She then peered into another one. Still nothing, then she heard a small whimper coming from somewhere. She continued her search of the bolted doors until she stopped abruptly when she saw someone sitting inside one of the small cells.

She watched the child who couldn't have been more than eight years old rub her eyes and sniff. She huddled in the corner of the room on the small cot, a blanket wrapped tightly around her. Sebena could make out her shivering, and the sound of sniffling coming from her small, frail body.

Sebena turned away, her back to the door. She was growing angry and confused, afraid that her temper would soon overtake her if she didn't get a handle on it. She looked at the door the other men went through and peered into the other rooms, being careful not to be seen as she walked by, noting that several were occupied by young people. Questions reeled in her head as to why the First and Second Squadrons were holding kids prisoner. She had to find out more about what was going on here. She walked to the door, opened it carefully, and peered inside. The room was lined with machines, and tables with straps. What on Harilhia would a room like this be used for? She waited for signs of the two men to appear to see what happened here, but realized her time was running out. She needed to get back to the others and tell them what she found. Then they needed to go to her superiors and inform them of the treachery as well.

She left as quietly as she arrived, taking note of exactly where she was in the castle. The castle was a massive building which housed fifteen Squadrons of approximately one hundred recruits each. And that did not include the three captains, the single commander per squad or the General in charge of all the guards. All in all the castle held approximately sixteen hundred people, which included all the kitchen and cleaning staff.

Sebena went to meet up with the others outside as agreed, being the first to arrive. She paced back and forth, her mind reeling over her discovery. She couldn't believe that General Garth knew about any of this. But as a general, how could he not? Wasn't it his job to keep tabs on everything that happened under his command?

Did that mean he did know about it and was involved? Who was she supposed to go to? Who could they trust? She stopped pacing, a thought forming in her mind. She knew that several commanders had had issues over the years with the way General Garth handled certain situations. Perhaps they would have some allies by taking her findings to them?

Bain suddenly appeared, followed by Guidriun.

Sebena filled them in on her discovery, and her plan to take her findings to two particular commanders for help. Just as they were finishing up their conversation, Mercer appeared.

"Well, anybody find anything?" Mercer asked.

"We'll fill you in as we walk," Bain said.

"Sounds like we have a problem."

"Sebena found some kids being held in the upper levels of the castle. Now we just have to figure out how to set them free."

Mercer let out a puff of air. "Right. Time for action."

Guidriun looked at him seriously. "Yet, against some of our own."

The seriousness of the situation fell hard upon their shoulders. The men and women who trained alongside them every day could soon be the very people they were fighting against.

Bain com-called Aaric to inform him that someone had found some kids, but he wasn't certain who they were. He would let them know the plan as soon as he could, but to be ready to go into battle at any moment.

Aaric informed all the captains of the situation. The only problem was the fight was inland and the sailing ships wouldn't be of any help. But, if for some reason the battle extended out this far, they would be ready.

The airships prepared for battle, ready to lift up out of the hole in the ground, under the cover of night, and set out toward the castle. They would put down where Sebena had instructed Bain to tell them to go. They waited anxiously on Bain's call to action. The four sailing ships would then set sail back out into the open waters near the coast and hide behind some of the large rocks that they had sailed past into the cave. They would be ready to help should the need arise.

Bain wasn't sure how to tell the airships to attack. They wouldn't know the difference between the people they fought against or with. Hopefully Sebena's plan to speak to the upper command would squelch any fighting before it started. But either way, Bain would free his friends; he only hoped they were the ones being held prisoner here.

Sebena, Bain, Guidriun, and Mercer all walked the steps up to the commander's quarters.

Sebena said, "They often will retire to the commander's lounge at this hour. We should find Commanders Bridger and Vertrite there. You three stay here. The commanders will not take kindly to recruits being up here." They stood at the end of the hall waiting on Sebena to speak to those in command.

She walked up to the entryway into the open room. She had only ever seen this room once before when she had a problem with one of the other captains. The room had a large fireplace on an interior wall which went the height of the castle and serviced rooms on every floor. Comfortable leather chairs sat neatly in front of it. One wall was lined with a bar, full of whatever liquor the commanders desired. There were bookshelves lined with books of different genres; many on battle strategies. Maps of Harilhia and discovered territories were woven into large tapestries that hung from poles that lined the edges of the ceiling. Sporting tables encircled by chairs sat scattered about the room, and in the center of the room were several seating areas.

Sebena stepped into the room and gave the gong a good knock, then stood at attention.

All the commanders in the room gave her their attention. Many looking at her with raised eyebrows.

"Captain Zentrialle, how can we help you?" Commander Bridger stood and walked toward her.

"I request to speak to Commander Bridger and Commander Vertrite."

Commander Bridger looked about the room. "Well, it appears there is only me. Commander Vertrite does not appear to be available."

"Fine, Sir."

"Shall we speak here then?"

"No sir, it is a delicate matter sir, best held in private."

"Well, Captain, follow me then." Commander Bridger left the room and Sebena followed, stopping him just outside.

"Commander, my friends wish to join us." Sebena nodded over her shoulder at the others who stood at attention at the end of the hall.

Commander Bridger looked at them then gave Sebena an unsatisfactory glance before waving them forward to follow. Once inside his private quarters, he sat behind his desk as the four of them lined up in front of it.

"At ease Captain, Recruits."

"Thank you, sir," Sebena stated.

"Now, what is all of this unorthodox, urgent, matter we needed to discuss in private, Captain Zentrialle."

"Sir, we have proof that someone in the guard is holding prisoners on the highest level of the castle grounds. And not just any prisoners sir, most are children."

"These are serious accusations Captain. What proof do you have?"

"I've seen them with my own eyes sir."

"And what possessed you to go into the General's area without permission. You know those floors are off-limits to lesser ranks."

Bain stepped forward, "May I speak, Sir?"

Commander Bridger was slightly agitated by Bain's interruption but allowed him to speak with a curt nod of his head.

"Sebena was doing so as a favor to me. You see sir, it is my friends and family who were taken by pirates and sold to Dihendran Guards."

"Those are some very lofty accusations recruit!"

"We understand that sir, but true none the less."

Commander Bridger sighed heavily, deep in thought. "Where are these prisoners being held, Captain?"

"In a room full of small cells on the southwest side of the level sir. It is locked."

"We'll see about this," he said.

"All of you follow me."

Commander Bridger then grabbed his com-call. "Commander Vertrite, Lieutenant Commander Bridger here, stand by to engage O.C."

"Yes Commander," came the voice over the com-call.

"Now, let's go see about these allegations of yours." Commander Bridger grabbed a large keyring full of keys from a drawer in his desk and they quickly left his office.

132

# Chapter 17

As they walked hurriedly up the castle steps to the highest level, Sebena asked, "Commander Bridger, may I ask what O.C. means?"

"If your accusations are correct, you'll find out soon enough."

Sebena nodded and they followed quickly and as closely as they could, soon coming upon the door in question.

"Is this the door Captain Zentrialle?"

"Yes Sir."

Commander Bridger took the keys, trying each one in the lock. "It appears I have no key for this lock; which is suspicious in itself since all commanders are to have access to any room on any floor, except the General's personal quarters."

Guidriun stepped forth. "Sir, if I may, I can pick the lock."

"Where on Harilhia did you learn that, Recruit?"

"Let's just say I had an interesting upbringing Sir, before joining the guard of course, Sir."

Commander Bridger stepped aside and waved him over to the lock. "Have at it Recruit Brunzfeld."

Guidriun knelt in front of the lock, pulled his tools from a small pocket at his waistband and went to work.

"I'd best not find you using your unique abilities, Recruit Brunzfeld, to enter any off-limit rooms in the future."

"No Sir, I would never Sir," Guidriun answered calmly as he stealthily worked.

There was a click, and the door handle turned, allowing them entry.

Commander Bridger was surprised by what lay inside. They had never sanctioned a prisoner ward to be held on this level of the castle. All cells were in the underground section.

"Check every door and open them if anyone is inside." Bridger commanded as he walked to the other end of the hallway toward another door. This one was locked as well. Sebena, Bain, and Mercer all went to work freeing the imprisoned.

"Recruit Brunzfeld, your services are needed once more."

"Guidriun hurried to the door, opening it in record time. The Commander stepped inside surprised yet again by what looked to be some sort of torture chamber. He was even more surprised by the number of children filling the hallways behind him as the cell doors were unbolted.

Bain hugged several of those that he knew, two of them being Kamsten Whitsler and Maubrey Vanderpol.

"Bain," Maubrey said, "am I ever glad to see you. But what are you doing here of all places?"

"I'll explain later." Bain pulled Maubrey in front of Commander Bridger. "Commander, this is Maubrey Vanderpol. He is an old friend and can likely explain why they are here."

Commander Bridger said, "No time for that now. There has been a serious protocol breech here, and the unsanctioned holding of people against their will in non-war times. We especially do not sanction the holding of children."

Commander Bridger used his com to call Commander Vertrite once more. "Commander Vertrite, Lieutenant Commander Bridger. Are we a go for O.C.?"

"Yes commander" came a voice across the com. "O.C. is prepped and ready Commander."

"Good, commence with O.C. You know for whom we are searching, Commander."

"O.C. is engaged, Lieutenant Commander."

An alert was heard throughout the grounds as people could be seen shuffling about below from the high windows.

Bridger commanded Guidriun and Mercer, "Take these people down the main stairs and into the commander's lounge for now. They should be safe there. Stay with them until I return. I'll send more recruits in from the seventh squadron to help guard them while we go in search of the guilty parties."

"Yes sir." Both men saluted and led everyone away.

"Sebena, do you know who it was that you followed into the room?" Commander Bridger asked.

"One of the captains and commanders from the first and second squadrons, Sir."

Bain asked, "Sir, if it was one of the commanders, will my friends be safe in the commander's lounge?"

"Absolutely. After the alarm sounded, they were all to vacate and go to ground level to await further orders."

"Won't General Garth be curious as to why an alert was called without his knowledge, Sir?"

"Yes, he likely will. But, as Lieutenant Commander, I have certain responsibilities that come with my position. One of which is to hold the General accountable. Now, less chit-chat. We have criminals to catch."

They all raced down the stairway with Commander Bridger calling orders in every direction to every captain and commander that crossed his path. He turned to Sebena and Bain.

"Captain Zentrialle, take the Twelfth squadron to the air. It seems as though reports are coming in of the first and Second squadron mounting Baiskreet."

"Yes sir." Sebena and Bain raced to the training field where all recruits stood at attention waiting on orders from their captains.

Sebena raced up the platform steps to address the troops and other captains. "Recruits, it appears we have dissention and treason in the guard. Our orders are to take to the air and defend against the first and second squadrons! Prisoners are to be taken if possible. Now, to the breeding grounds and your Baiskreet!"

The Twelfth Squadron along with the other sky rider squads, thirteen through fifteen, took off to the breeding grounds. They found once there that some of the Baiskreet had already been mounted and were flying about, shooting at them as they tried to mount their own.

Bain sensed someone calling him.

*'Enlightened one, come ride with me against this tyranny.'*

Bain stopped running, looking around wildly for the bearer of the voice.

*'It is I, Karalis, king of the Baiskreet who calls you.'*

Bain was shocked but took off at full speed. The Kriesletrope paddock was the last in the long line of dens as theirs was the largest. When Bain arrived, slightly out of breath, Karalis was waiting on him. The creature was standing at the cross over bridge.

Bain ran up the steps and across the bridge where he could drop down onto Karalises' back.

Bain asked, "Are you sure about this?"

Karalis stretched his neck and roared in agitation as a grumbling voice filled Bain's head.

*'I would not have offered human if I did not wish it.'*

Bain nodded and jumped onto Karalises' back. The massive Baiskreet took easily to the air, his powerful wings stirring up dust, dirt, and fallen leaves as they lifted into the sky. Bain could see his mate Karaliene settled upon her nest, watching anxiously as the two of them flew off to battle against their own. Bain wasn't certain how they were supposed to make out who to fight against in the dark, when a sudden storm appeared on the horizon. Lightning filled the sky, illuminating scenes of battle already taking place. Squadrons fought one another from the backs of Baiskreet, the creatures each doing the bidding of their commanding riders. Bain watched as ground troops fought with weapons: guns, bows and arrows, and swords, trying hard not to kill the recruits from the first and second squadron. The first and second were severely outnumbered, with the remaining thirteen squadrons bearing down on them, and Bain figured their revolt was merely a ploy to distract everyone from the leaders of the operation and allow them to get away.

Bain thought for a moment. He had no idea for whom they were searching.

*'I know them. I know them all.'* Karalis communicated to him.

Bain said audibly, "Then let's go find them and end this before too many people die."

The storm rolled in as lightning continued to fill the sky and large drops of rain began to sting Bain's exposed skin. Streaks of fire, ice, and light filled the night sky as well, as the Baiskreet battled against one another. Bain recognized that the first squadron's uniforms were yellow, and the seconds were green. He supposed that was how they could differentiate who to fight against.

Karalis sailed through the sky searching below him for the traitors, not a worry in the world, as no Baiskreet would dare to attack the king of them all. As Karalis flew over, many Baiskreet below fled in fear, quickly darting  away, their hunters giving chase.

*'There are your traitors.'* Karalis said to Bain, looking below and circling around the area in question; a secluded section of the castle where no one fought held figures scurrying about.

Bain could barely make out five figures below who were climbing onto air-rovers in an attempt to flee. As they started to take off, he could see two other figures jumping onto air-rovers and giving chase. Several more followed them. As Karalis flew over, Bain watched the chase below as those fleeing turned to shoot at their pursuers. Gunfire opened in both directions, and brief streaks of light sliced through the night air. The rain had stopped at some point during the chase, and Bain was glad of it, because he was certain he saw a portal open in the sky not far from where he and Karalis were flying.

Karalis flapped his powerful wings, gaining ground out in front of those that fled capture. Karlis turned back toward the air-rovers, diving toward the ground in the process, landing hard, and causing the earth to shake. A few of the air-rovers came to an abrupt halt as their drivers were taken by surprise. Several others broke off in opposite directions as those behind gave chase, soon catching up to them. General Garth stood transfixed, as Karalises' massive head focused on him and his cohort commander, bending low to where his hot breath washed over them, their hair and clothing effectively blowing about with each exhale. Karalis smiled wickedly, knowing how his presence caused unimaginable fear in the men. He could feel it coursing through their veins with each rapid heartbeat. He chuckled wickedly, releasing a small puff of smoke from his nostrils, watching it circle around the terrified men.

Bain could sense the joy that Karalis was feeling at the intense fear his presence caused, and that made Bain a bit nervous. Karalis knew he was powerful, and that power, left unchecked, could be deadly.

*'Don't worry, Enlightened one. I feel your concern for my eternal soul. We Kriesletrope mate for life and will protect our females with all that we have in us, for they are our ground. They keep us in check, otherwise we are capable of terrible things.'*

*Bain said, "Let's hope Karaliene out lives you then."*

*'Yes, let's.' Karalis turned his head slightly to grin at Bain, his eyebrows raised in haughtiness.*

Commander Bridger and several others who helped in the pursuit, soon returned with their captives. They rounded up the insurgents, lashed them all together with rope, and Karalis and Bain lifted the lot of them off the ground to transport them back to the castle to be locked away until charges and punishment could be brought against them. The others followed on the air-rovers and would send some recruits back for the abandoned machinery they had to leave behind.

Upon returning to the castle, all the recruits from the first and second squadrons were rounded up and encircled by the other squads, guarding them until Lieutenant Commander Bridger could return.

Many recruits were wounded and taken to medical to be checked over, discovering that all recruits in both squadrons had been chipped with some sort of technology in their necks along the spinal column, making them extremely submissive to their direct superiors. Kamsten and Maubrey were the ones who had been forced to design the technology, so when it came time to remove it, they knew how.

The use of the kidnapped children was to try to extract their telepathic abilities and inject it into the recruits from the first and second squadrons hoping for a superior soldier, though nothing ever came from it other than illness and some covered up deaths of recruits from failed attempts. The purpose, they found in some paperwork belonging to the General and the corrupt commanders, cited a plan to overthrow the Dihendran government and set upon a new rule, one where they would enslave all of Dihendra's citizens.

Bain and Karalis returned to the paddock, and Bain climbed off the beast's back. Karalis gave a mighty shake starting at his head and ending at his long tail. Water flew everywhere, and Bain felt as though he had been rained on all over again, having already been dry from the flight back to the castle.

Bain said, "Thank you for your help Karalis. It is greatly appreciated."

*'Yes, I know. The happenings of the human world affect the happenings of our own. So as the king of the Baiskreet, it is my duty to not only protect your world, but also mine and the future of the Baiskreet. So you see, it wasn't only for your kind. We Baiskreet can be quite selfish creatures.'*

Bain smiled at the honest answer of the beast before him. He turned to leave but Karalis had more to say.

*'Good luck on your journeys Enlightened one.'*

"Why do you call me that?"

*'Since returning from your recent journey, I could sense a change in you. I knew your mind had been opened to our tongue.'*

Bain nodded in understanding, realizing he had said something else. "You also said good luck on my journeys. How do you know I've been traveling?"

*'We know many things. Things past, things present, and things yet to come, although we cannot see the end, only parts of the journey.'*

"And you see me on this journey?"

*'Yes, we see all who stand before us, and you have many more journeys to make, and several paths from which to choose.'*

"Can you tell me when I might possibly make the next one?"

*'No. Again, your choices will affect your journeys. Such as choosing to fight instead of fleeing through the portal you saw earlier.'* Karalis let out a mighty yawn and turned to walk away toward his mate and their nest. *'Farewell Enlightened one.'*

Bain nodded, knowing the beast could care less whether he returned the sentiment. Many thoughts ran through his mind as he walked the distance back to the castle grounds. Much was still happening as clean-up was underway, recruits were marched to medical, some to the cells below the ground, and others were walking their Baiskreet back to the breeding grounds to tend to their needs.

Bain com-called his grandfather and told them about the events and finding the stolen children. He then told them all to settle in for the night and that he would contact him again in the morning. He then returned to the commander's lounge and found everyone still there, having been fed and their immediate needs tended to by the staff of the castle. Guidriun and Mercer had seen to the details.

"Thank you, Guidriun, Mercer," Bain said, shaking the men's hands.

"Of course," Guidriun answered.

"Yeah, some of them were looking a bit run down," Mercer said, thumbing over his shoulder to a very young girl and boy. Bain thought he recognized them as LARS students but they were five years older now, and very pale from their year in captivity. Probably the most recent victims of blood being drawn in an archaic attempt to try to extract their abilities.

When those who remembered him recognized Bain, they all jumped up in excitement, clapping and rushing toward him to extend hugs. Bain was overwhelmed by it all.

Kamsten kissed him on the cheek. "Our hero!" she said ecstatically. "Your parents would be so proud of you."

Bain turned serious. "Speaking of, have either of you heard from them?"

Maubrey said, "No. Not since they followed you into that portal. I assume that's where they went since that is what your father told your grandfather on that last call."

"Yeah, Grandfather mentioned that."

"So, you haven't seen them either?"

"No. Apparently they went through to somewhere else entirely. I was in my last world for weeks with no contact. Maubrey, your mind is more technologically advanced than my own. What do you think happened? I mean, how is all of this even possible?"

"Wait, you said weeks. Not years?"

"No, in my time I've only been gone nearly four weeks. Here, it's been five years."

"Hmm…" Maubrey thought about Bain's words. "Perhaps upon returning here, you arrived at a later time. Time is infinite you know. We don't know where we ourselves are in the space-time continuum. There could be hundreds, even thousands of years ahead of us. I'd say that you have the unique perspective of finding out, Bain."

"Yeah, but I never know where I'll end up or even when I'll leave."

"Well, how have you been traveling?"

"The first time was through a glowing portal in Storm Valley during winter. The second was through an earthshake that hit where I was and I just appeared here. But then, during the storm earlier this evening, I did see a portal generate in the air, not far from where I was at the time."

"It sounds as though maybe you're mode of travel will be through storms that are strong enough to open portals to other places. Oh, how I wish I could go with you!" Maubrey excitedly said.

"Hey," Kamsten protested.

"Oh, sorry my love, we. I wish WE could go with you."

Bain smiled at them. When he had left Zanchier, their relationship was just a budding possibility. A lot had changed in five years.

"Grandfather and the others will be here in the morning. I need to go find someone. I'll let you get some rest and see you all tomorrow."

They waved as Bain left the room, nearly running over Sebena who was coming to find him.

Sebena reached up, grabbed his face, and planted a long kiss on his lips. Bain wrapped her in his arms, realizing that he didn't want to go traveling anymore. Dihendra was feeling more and more like home.

When they parted, Bain said, "You're making it really hard for me to want to leave again."

"That's the idea." She smiled. "Seriously, Bain, I don't want you to go, but if you do, I'm going with you."

Bain was shocked by her profession of loyalty.

"Sebena, I don't know if or when I'll ever be able to return here."

"All the more reason to go with you."

"I also don't know when I'll be pulled into a portal. Who's to say we'll even be together when it happens."

"I don't have all the answers, Bain. I just know that I want to be with you. Wherever that is."

They embraced once more for another long kiss and a promise of a future together, Creator willing.

# Chapter 18

**Castle Dihendra, Day 7**

The next morning Commander Bridger gave Bain explicit orders to com-call his grandfather to have them all come to the castle. Large transports were sent to the coast to collect the people from the ships, and a few recruits stayed behind to watch over the ships while everyone was away. Wren stayed with the ships at the shoreline while Dot and the other creatures stayed on-board, the recruits that guarded them were a tad nervous around unknown beasts. Jilly assured them they were safe, as long as the creatures didn't feel threatened. The airships sailed to the castle and put down just outside the gates. The three airships flying over Dihendra Rhial drew much attention, and so many people flocked to see who it was traveling to and setting down near their rhial in such a strange transport.

The night before, when the corrupt officials were captured, Commander Bridger called a court martial for the next morning. All the dignitaries from Dihendra Rhial and surrounding areas were there, as well as many of the rhial's citizens who flocked to the castle, curious as to the happenings.

As people filed onto the castle grounds, Bain's family and friends from the ships were reunited with their taken friends and family, and all of them were given front row seats for the trial. Commander Bridger stood on one of the platforms that overlooked the large courtyards to address the crowd and begin with the proceedings.

"Leaders, and people of Dihendra, yesterday a great injustice to the name of our fair and beautiful city was uncovered. These five men and women bound behind me participated in treason, treachery, plots to overthrow our government, and the instigating and kidnapping of innocent children and people, their actions ultimately resulting in the cover up of past murders of some of our own guard."

A loud gasp emanated around the yard, and murmurings began.

Bridger continued. "For their treacherous deeds, they will be stripped of their titles and rankings, and placed into holding cells for the next ten years. After which, they will serve Dihendra in whatever capacity is seen fit for the remainder of their lives."

The crowds cheered.

"Seated before you are the afflicted. These men and women came here the night before last to claim what was rightfully theirs; their family and friends, who were kidnapped from their homeland by pirates sanctioned by the accused. Only a few hundred men, women, and beast's which they command, prepared themselves to take on an entire city —need be— to free their loved ones. We just last night, discovered that thirty children and adults had been kidnapped by pirates and sold to the corrupt officials behind me. These kidnapped people have been held in prison and tortured for nearly a year. As Lieutenant Commander, second in command under General Garth, I and Commander Vertrite have known something to be corrupt, but knew not what that was. This slight on our Guard, the brave men and women who guard Dihendra Rhial and all surrounding territories is a travesty. Four brave souls, under the guard command, uncovered the truth and bravely came to me to make the accusations and to set in motion the capture of all the guilty, uncovering a heinous plot to enslave all of Dihendra, and discovering the horrid treatment of the people imprisoned."

Commander Bridger turned to wave them up to the platform.

"I would like to introduce to you your saviors. Captain Sebena Zentrialle, Recruit Bain Brinley, Recruit Guidriun Brunzfeld, and Recruit Mercer Rand."

As the four of them walked up the platform to stand at attention, the entire courtyard erupted in praise. Whistling, clapping, and shouting rumbled for the next several minutes until Commander Bridger settled the crowds down.

"These four are a small part of the brave men and women who serve in your guard. Many fought last night, and many were captured or injured. And they did so bravely and under extreme duress against their own friends and comrades here at the castle. The recruits of the First and Second Squadrons are not at fault for their part in the treachery of the accused, as they were all under the control of the accused by way of mind controlling devices. The First and Second Squadrons will be given time off to recover their mental and physical abilities to the full extent, and then will incur rehabilitation if needed before resuming their guard duties."

Again people cheered and clapped as all the guard stood off to the sides at attention, unmoving, and unflinching.

"Please, people of Dihendra, give a hearty thank you to the people who serve your fair city, and welcome and make comfortable our guests as we begin a new day with renewed confidence in the security of Dihendra Rhial's superb Castle Guard."

Clapping and celebration erupted as the accused were led away in cuffs, down to the dark dungeons below. The people of Dihendra congratulated and saluted the guard as they passed by in formation to be given the day off for relaxation and celebration.

The First and Second Squadrons were all given a month's leave and counselors, if requested; to help them sort through what had happened to them. They marched by the other guards all standing at attention and saluting them as they passed, to assure them there were no hard feelings.

Sebena, Bain, Guidriun, and Mercer were congratulated throughout the morning by all the people milling about as they walked around the grounds. And all of Bain's family and friends were given quarters by the dignitaries of Dihendra, free of charge for the next several days, on the edges of the ocean in one of Dihendra's most beautiful and exclusive hotels. They were given the best medical attention for those who had been wronged, and the city even offered to compensate them for their time imprisoned, setting all thirty people up with land, homes, or monetary compensation.

All the people of Zanchier were overcome by the welcome and treatment given them by the Dihendran Council. Aaric spoke to Bain and the other leaders of their people about what to do next.

"I'm in awe of how this rhial treats its people," Aaric stated, still shocked by their more than kind offers.

Bain nodded. "I told you I couldn't believe that the Dihendran Guard would be so corrupt as to be involved with the kidnappings."

"Technically they were," Finn Mobley added.

"True," Aaric stated, "but the few bad apples were removed so that the whole barrel wasn't ruined."

Bain said, "Amazing how greed, lust, and selfishness can truly corrupt a man's soul."

Sebena added, "Yes. I was truly shocked to discover that what Bain told us was true. I am glad that we found your people, and that they are all in decent health. The Dihendran Dignitaries and Council members will see that every one of them gets compensated for the crimes done to them."

Aaric smiled at her. "I truly believe they will. Now, we must decide whether to stay here, or find somewhere else to inhabit."

"Why not stay here?" Sebena stated. "Dihendra has many territories and vast amounts of land. The government here also takes care of each and every citizen. Everyone works together here. Besides, many of your people may already be staying, depending on which offer they accept as recompense."

"True," Aaric stated. "We'll have to speak to the others before we make any decisions. Today I think we will just rejoice in the return of our people and take full advantage of the beautiful accommodations which your government has offered to us. Once we can gather everyone together, we will decide what to do."

James added, "Besides, no matter how wonderful this place is, those that were held and tortured here may not want to stay."

Aaric nodded, "Yes, very true, James."

Bain said, "Well, what do we do about the ships moored out by the shoreline?"

Sebena said, "General Bridger commanded that they be brought back here and tied up at the docks near the hotel where your people will be staying."

"General Bridger?" Bain asked a bit surprised.

"Yes, naturally." Sebena smiled. "He was second in command, so he has already been sworn in with the title of General by the

Dihendran Council. And commander Vertrite has been promoted to the position of Lieutenant Commander."

Bain nodded and grinned in appreciation. Sebena then added, "I was also offered a position as Twelfth Squadron Commander."

Bain said, "That's great, Sebena. But why don't you look happy about it?"

She shrugged. "I told them I'd have to think about it. I'm not sure where I'll be in the next few days." She looked Bain in the eyes, her meaning not lost on him.

"Take the position, Sebena. I told you, I never know when I'm going to be called to leave, if ever."

"I know, but I'll still give it a few days before confirming either way."

Aaric asked, "What do you mean, Bain? Surely you aren't going to go looking for your parents?"

"Grandfather, I need to find them. They are only out there, who knows where, because they are looking for me. I need to return the favor and put in the same effort for their sakes. Besides, we've all been through enough over the last eight years, don't you think?"

Aaric nodded and patted Bain's shoulder. "Yes, son, I agree. And if I didn't have Neitha, and Gracelynn to worry about, I'd be right beside you looking as well."

Bain and Aaric embraced, and Aaric pulled away, a stray tear in his eye. "Now, let's get this party started shall we?"

Everyone chuckled and they joined the rest of Dihendra in merry making and revelry as the visitors were transported through the streets and to their rather comfortable accommodations by the sea.

Bain and Sebena tagged along with them to make sure everyone was tended to and made comfortable, especially those who suffered at the guards hands. Then, they went out on the docks to see the creatures and spend some time with Wren before heading back to Castle Dihendra and their duties to the guard.

The celebration was still ongoing, with many of the guards quite enjoying the day's festivities when Bain and Sebena slipped away to find somewhere to be alone.

Sebena said, "I know somewhere we can go. I've been wanting to show you this place anyway."

They hopped on an air-rover, with Sebena driving of course since Bain knew so little of the territory, taking off across the land headed toward the heavy-ladened forest. Sebena cut through the sparse underbrush of the large trees, sunlight streaking through the canopy making shadows across the forest floor. Bain held tightly to Sebena for no other reason than the fact that he could. His life felt strange and fleeting. Only a month ago he had disappeared into a portal from Storm Valley in the Xantifal Mountains, leaving behind everything and everyone he ever knew. Raila Orman came to his mind, the first girl he truly ever liked. He had even begun to fall in love with her right before she died. Now, here he was, riding across a strange and foreign land with a woman who had fully captured his heart nearly from the moment he laid eyes on her. They were vastly different women, yet both held a special place in his heart. Bain thanked the Creator above for bringing him to Dihendra Rhial.

Then his thoughts turned a bit dark, wondering when, or if, he would be called to leave. Dihendra itself had quickly become a very special place for him, and the more he came to know and see, the more it felt like home, even more than Zanchier. There had been struggles, wars, and evil men, far worse than a ship full of pirates. The people of Zanchier unfortunately still had to deal with the Scaithers. He couldn't do anything about that, except pray that the Creator would end their suffering.

Sebena steered the air-rover over and around hills, and fallen trees and rocks, until they broke into a clearing with a magnificent waterfall unlike any Bain had ever seen, and Zanchier had some pretty spectacular ones. She pulled the air-rover to a stop and they both climbed off. Bain stood transfixed by what he saw.

The waterfall had to be two-hundred foot high, and nearly as wide. The water was clear, and sparkled like jewels in the sunlight as it fell and splashed against the rocks that split and broke its path all the way down. The massive basin beneath looked deep and refreshing, the water so clear you could see the rocks and fish beneath. The sunlight played and danced on the surface of the water, sparkling, and flashing brilliantly every so often. Bain finally found his voice to speak.

"I've never seen anything like this before."

"My friends and I from academy call this place Jewel Falls."

Sebena smiled and giggled at his expression as she grabbed his hand and pulled him closer to where they could sit and enjoy the view. They sat quietly for a while, just watching the falls.

Bain suddenly realized there was no outlet for the water. He looked around for the river the falls fed but found none.

"Where does the water go?"

Sebena smiled brightly. "There is an overflow ledge nearly all the way around the basin. The excess water rises and falls onto the ledge into an underground cavern. Come, I'll show you."

Sebena stripped off the outer layer of her clothing, where she only had on a t-strap undershirt and a tight pair of shorts that stopped just to the top of her thighs. Bain had not seen this much of Sebena before and he greatly appreciated her toned physique. Bain followed her example, knowing they were about to go into the water. Bain stripped down to his pants and dove into the water behind her.

The coolness of the water was a bit of a shock, but the clarity below the surface was astounding. Bain watched as the rocks on the basin floor shimmered and gleamed in the sunlight that filtered down. He swam down to inspect the rocks, curious as to what they were. Sebena motioned for him to follow her as they swam back up to the surface, breaking through the water and taking in a large lungful of air.

She smiled at Bain's expression as the two of them laughed together.

She said, "Now take a big gulp of air. We have a bit of a swim."

"All right," Bain agreed, and the two of them sunk down into the water again. Sebena led him to where the falls fell into the basin, down and around some rocks, and back up into a glistening pool which sat behind the falls. They climbed from the water, and Bain took in the magnificence of their surroundings. The walls glistened and shimmered from the dappled sunlight that managed to filter through the powerful falls.

"This is amazing, Sebena."

"This isn't what I want to show you."

She grabbed his hand and pulled him through a stair-step, tunnel-like area which spiraled downward. As they walked, a large underground cavern opened up, and before he knew it, he was walking in water again, only this time it was only about waist deep.

Bain Marveled at the flow of water which entered the underground cavern, as light and water spilled over the ledge that encircled the front and two sides of the basin. The light that broke through glistened and danced on the shimmering rocks that lay along the ceiling of the cavern, illuminating the entire cavern in a pale glittering light. The water ran slowly down a narrow river that seemed to snake off in several directions beneath the falls above them, giving the constant flow of water someplace to go.

Sebena watched the emotions that flitted across Bain's face.

"It's breathtaking isn't it?"

"I don't think even that describes it. How did you ever find this place?"

"I grew up near here. I used to come swimming and exploring here all the time as a kid. Some of my friends and I found this place when in secondary academy. I make it a habit to come at least once a month. You're the only other person I've ever brought here."

Bain turned to look at Sebena. They locked eyes and soon were in each other's arms, the events of yesterday and today, the excitement of being together again, and the majesty, beauty, and solitude of their surroundings fueling their uncontrollable emotions.

# Chapter 19

**Jewel Falls, Late Evening, Day 8 on Harilhia**

Bain and Sebena swam back up to the surface after exploring the underground cave and river and laid beside the basin's bank staring up at the night sky. They watched as the four moons of Harilhia slowly diminished to where within the next week, the only two constantly visible would be the two largest, and those would wane from month to month. The sky was filled with glistening stars that twinkled like the ceiling of the cavern below. A shower of meteors streaked the heavens zipping across the sky, some disappearing in the ethereal moonlight.

Bain was once again in awe. "I've never quite seen anything so spectacular."

Sebena grinned. "You've never just laid outside at night as a child and gazed at the night sky?"

Bain shrugged. "I guess I did, to some extent, but I've never seen anything like this before."

"Perhaps it is because of the four moons. Many spectacular things take place during this time. The meteor showers, for one, happen every year as the festival ends and the moons begin to align once again."

"I guess our view from Zanchier was either very limited, or we were always just so wrapped up in the happenings of daily life and struggles that we just never bothered to really look up much." Bain smiled down at her. "Of course, when I was in the Xantifal Mountains right before I walked into that portal, I had a lot of time to just think and take in my surroundings. Of course, it was winter while I was there and everything was blanketed in blue snow, but when I did look up, the sky was definitely clear. But, again, I was lost in grief, pain, and loneliness; although the last affliction was of my own choosing."

"Well, you won't be lonely anymore. I'll see to that." Sebena smiled brightly at him.

Bain smiled back and brought their clasped fingers to his lips, brushing the back of her hand with a kiss. They fell asleep in each other's arms, blanketed by the warmth of their intertwined bodies.

Bain's eyes were closed tightly against the morning sun when he felt something wet on his face.

"Sebena, what are you doing? Why are you licking my face?" Bain rolled over to avoid another draw of the scratchy tongue on his cheek. He opened his eyes, startled by the large beast standing over him; its tongue thoroughly enjoying the taste of his skin. Bain screamed and pushed away from the four-legged, flop-eared, hairy, rotund creature.

It snorted in excitement at his quick movements, and its whole body wiggled as it watched him enthusiastically.

Sebena came rushing out of the forest, stopping short and laughing at his situation.

"Don't worry," she yelled as she walked closer. "It's only a hobbling."

"A what?"

"Hobbling. They kind of hobble about as they walk. Their long torso's and happy attitudes make them wiggle incessantly." Sebena laughed as the creature wiggled even harder as it had yet another person to give it attention.

"Is that really its scientific name?" Bain asked, skeptically.

Sebena looked at him and shrugged. "I don't know, it's just what we've always called them growing up. I've never heard them called otherwise. Many farmers keep them as they make great plow pullers." She stepped up to the beast and gave it a big hug and patted it happily. The Hobbling wiggled harder, its breath coming out in snort-like gasps like it was having an asthma attack. Sebena giggled hard and rubbed the beasts chest in the center, which seemed to give it some relief from the breathing issue.

Bain bent over the water's edge and splashed the cool liquid on his face to clean the slobber from his skin, watching Sebena as she plucked a branch full of leaves from an obliging tree and gave the tender stem to the Hobbling. It happily took the stick and wiggled some more, as if to say thanks, before it bounded away into the forest with its mouthful of tree limb; it's long shaggy tail wiggling as it disappeared into the underbrush.

Sebena watched the creature with delight, and Bain watched her with the same feeling of contentment the Hobbling likely experienced with the branch. She had fully captured his heart in a very short time.

They soon climbed back onto the air-rover and sped across the forest floor toward Dihendra Rhial and a new day in their positions at the guard.

Bain wondered if Sebena would take the Commander position offered to her.

Sebena thought about the day ahead, wondering if the commander position was one she should accept. If she took it, she would be the youngest ever to make commander. She thought about her age, realizing she had no idea how old Bain was.

"Bain," she yelled back to him, "How old are you?"

Bain smiled. "Nearly twenty."

His answer surprised her. He seemed much more mature than twenty. Of course, the life he had described back on Zanchier likely made all the kids grow up much faster than the rest of Harilhia.

"You?" he asked her, waiting for an answer.

Sebena turned to look at him briefly, a large smile on her face. "Twenty-four."

"Ooh..." Bain smiled brightly. "I've got myself an older woman."

He watched her over her shoulder as she smiled brightly, love evident on her face.

She threw over her shoulder, "That you do sir, and you have me completely."

Bain clasped onto her waist even tighter, his soul happier than it had been in a long time.

The edges of Dihendra Rhial came into view, and it wasn't long before they rode through the rhial gates toward the coast and the hotel to see Bain's family. They arrived just in time to sit down with his grandparents for breakfast.

"Good morning you two," Aaric and Neitha chimed together.

"Good morning," they both replied.

Aaric asked, "So what are your plans for the day?"

Bain answered, "Just get back to work I suppose. Sebena has a meeting with the General to decide on taking a promotional position."

Aaric nodded approvingly. "Congratulations, young lady."

Sebena grinned. "Thank you, but I'm unsure whether to take it."

Neitha questioned, "Why is that?"

"Well, I don't wish to take a position where I may not be there for very long. With Bain's uncertainty to when he will be called to time-travel again, I want to be able to be near him and go with him."

Aaric was surprised by this. "Are you certain you want to take on that sort of life? The uncertainty of where you'll go, how you will survive, or even if you will find that for which you are searching." Aaric looked at Bain with his last statement.

Bain and Sebena looked at one another. She added, "I'll go wherever and whenever he is called. Bain is my life now. I will help him, comfort him, and be his steady for as long as the Creator wills it of me."

Everyone smiled at her answer, and the four of them ate their breakfast and chatted between bites.

Aaric was impressed with her drive, determination, and loyalty. Although he wasn't at all sure they knew what they were getting into. Even though Bain had time-traveled a few times already, they had no idea the extent of the universe, worlds, or type of people they would encounter. It seemed as though, so far, he had been fortunate to find friends along the way, but Aaric knew, with the laws of probability, that wouldn't last forever. They had been born into, and escaped from, a world of treachery, deceit, lies, and brutality. He supposed that Bain was prepared for whatever his travels threw at him because of his upbringing. Aaric just hoped he would find his parents and siblings sooner rather than later and be able to return to Harilhia with them. But Aaric also worried that he would never see his grandson, or his own son and the rest of his family again. They would have to figure out how to navigate the dimensions and planes in order for Bain and Sebena to be able to return here. Who knew how long something like that would take. Bain had a brilliant mind, no doubt, but was it enough? Aaric's thoughts were interrupted just then by Maubrey and Kamsten approaching the table.

Maubrey nodded. "Good morning everyone. May we join you?"

Neitha waved her hand in a dismissive manner. "Of course, no need to ask, you know that."

"Yes, well, with the finding of young Bain here, I thought perhaps you all needed time to visit."

Aaric said, "Yes, but you are family too Maubrey. There's nothing we can discuss that you can't hear."

Maubrey and Kamsten sat down at the table. "Thank you, Aaric. So, what were you all discussing?" Maubrey asked. Kamsten nudged him in the ribs with her elbow, causing him to look at her questioningly.

They all smiled at the man, and Bain answered. "Mine and Sebena's futures. She has been given a promotion and may not take it. She wants to be ready to go with me should a portal open."

Maubrey and Kamsten looked at one another and Maubrey cleared his throat before continuing. "About that, Kam and I would like to go with you as well."

Everyone looked at him with shocked stares.

Bain asked, "Maubrey, are you sure. I can't say it will be safe traveling."

"Yes, quite sure. Kam and I have discussed it quite thoroughly since you released us from the castle prison. We are quite certain we would like to see and experience this time-travel for ourselves. And, not to downplay your own skills Bain or to sound conceited,

Kam and I are both quite brilliant, and our cognitive and mechanical abilities may well serve you on your travels. Plus, with the new-found home situation of our friends and family from Zanchier, Kam and I feel as though we have exceeded our usefulness here."

Bain said, "Well, Maubrey, I can't exactly stop you. You have your own mind and will, plus you're right, I could use your and Kamsten's skills, but I can't promise we'll be together when a portal opens. I'm not even sure how to gauge when one will appear."

"Well, my friend, we shall be stuck to you like glue until then; or perhaps we can figure out how to tell when one will open. You did say that you think they happen during storms, correct?"

"Yes, except for the one in Storm Valley in Zanchier."

"Yes, but, relate the name of the valley with what we know."

"True, Storm Valley's name likely isn't just merely coincidental."

"Definitely not," Maubrey stated excitedly. He turned to Kamsten and smiled. "My dear, I think we have some significant research ahead of us."

Kamsten smiled back. "Wonderful. I'm ready for a new challenge."

"Then let's see if General Bridger will grant us access to that lab where we were forced to make the chip inserts. Perhaps the equipment there will allow us to design a few useful tools."

Sebena put in, "I can speak to the General for you. After breakfast, Bain and I are going to the castle. Would you two like to tag along?"

Maubrey smiled brightly. "Absolutely, Miss Zentrialle, thank you."

"Just call me Sebena."

"I shall try, but my strict upbringing may cause me to stumble, so please don't take offense if I revert back to Miss Zentrialle, Sebena."

"Of course I won't, Maubrey."

Bain said, "Maubrey, my MAD started working again once I arrived on Harilhia. It didn't work at all except as a clock in the last world I visited. Maybe we could take a trip back to Zanchier to check out the energy fields that exist in Storm Valley?"

"Hmm, perhaps, but I'm not at all sure it would work to travel quite that far. Besides, Kamsten's and mine were taken when we were kidnapped. The pirates figured they would be worth something."

"Maybe with the lab you could design more?"

"Perhaps, if they have the correct materials to build a few more."

Aaric said, "Well, I still have mine. You're welcome to it." He removed the Matter Arranging Device from his wrist and handed it to Maubrey.

"Wonderful," Kamsten stated.

"Yes," Maubrey interrupted, "but testing them at such a distance could be dangerous. Plus, they've never been used outside of Zanchier, so we have no idea how, or if, they will work."

Bain added, "Well, there's one way to find out. We can test mine later when we go back to the castle."

Sebena added, "Not without me you don't. I don't need you disappearing, never to return."

"You can use Grandfather's and we'll vision walk together."

"Vision walk?" Sebena asked confused.

"Yes, the MADs allow you to envision where you want to go and transport to that place."

"Really?" Sebena asked surprised. "That sounds wonderful; no need for air-rovers, or a temperamental Baiskreet. But why have you not used it since returning if it began to work again?"

"Well, I wasn't sure what the technology was in this world. Someone seeing me disappear and reappear in another place could have caused some problems for me."

"Yes, you are right about that." Sebena stated.

They all chatted a little longer before excusing themselves from Aaric's and Neitha's company to head to the castle to see about using the lab, Sebena's promotion, and to discuss with the new general all the things which had taken place over the last week.

# Chapter 20



Bain thought about the discussion he and Sebena were about to have with the general, and his mind began to think on all the repercussions that discussion could have.

"Sebena, how about we hold off telling the general about time-traveling. I don't have a good feeling about letting him know about that just yet. It could have major ramifications should it go wrong."

"Sure, but I don't see how."

"The militaristic advantages to such a discovery could be a serious temptation for a man in his position. I'd rather just keep that quiet."

"Well, all right then, I will speak to him alone. But how will I explain my decision to not take the Command position?"

"I don't see why you shouldn't take it. Who knows when or if another portal will open. We could be here for an indefinite period of time."

"True; you make a good point. All right, I shall take the position. Perhaps it will allow me even more time to be able to keep a closer eye on you." She smiled at him, knowing he understood her meaning. She turned to Kamsten and Maubrey.

"Would you two like to come along and speak to the General about using the labs?"

"Absolutely," Maubrey added emphatically. He and Kamsten followed Sebena across the courtyard.

Bain grinned as he watched them go in search of General Bridger. He then turned and walked out to the training yard and found Mercer and Guidriun sparring with one another.

"Good morning, boys." Bain smiled as he approached.

Guidriun and Mercer stopped what they were doing to greet their friend.

Mercer replied, "Morning. Where have you been all night?"

Bain grinned. "Oh, just spending time with family and friends."

Guidriun grinned crookedly. "Is that what you're calling Sebena now?"

Bain smiled at the man, avoiding any further discussion. "Careful, we don't want people to know about us. So, what's the plan for today?"

They nodded then Mercer shrugged. "Same as always I suppose, sparring, then over to the breeding grounds."

"How about we all go grab a pint of barley-wine after dinner tonight?" Bain suggested.

They both smiled and nodded in agreement.

Mercer added, "Sounds good to me. It's been a while since I had a pint.

Guidriun laughed out loud. "Merk, you just had more than several pints yesterday at the festivities."

Mercer smiled even bigger. "I said a while. I didn't say how long ago that was."

The men laughed at their friend's attitude and continued with sparring until time was called by Captain Nigel, excusing them to the breeding grounds for Baiskreet care. There they saw Sebena up on the observation platform with her new cloak with the addition of the gold-outlined, blue stripe to her shoulder patch, which signified her promotion and new status as squadron commander.

Guidriun and Mercer stopped at their Baiskreet paddocks and Bain continued on to the Kriesletrope den. As he got closer he could sense Karalises presence.

*'Enlightened One,'* Karalis greeted mentally, *'You've returned yet again. Come see my offspring, for today two hatched!'*

Bain quickened his step, hurrying through the gate running toward the nest at the forest's edge. Neeanne, the Kriesletrope trainer and breeder was also there, smiling from ear to ear at the new births. She turned to look at him as he approached. He smiled as he slowed, Neeanne jumping up and down in excitement, and clapping her hands.

"Bain, look at them. Aren't they beautiful?" Neeanne turned back to the hatchlings. "Twins," she said breathlessly.

Bain asked, "Do they normally hatch two?"

"No, not really. They can lay several eggs at once, but often only one is viable. This is very unusual." Neeanne said, almost screeching with her excitement.

"Really?" Bain asked, surprised. "I've seen several new batches of hatchlings in all the other Baiskreet pens. Some even had up to six new babies."

"Yes, well, that is normal for the other breeds. But the Kriesletrope being the largest and most majestic breed, lends to almost always only hatching one young. Too many of this breed can lead to a catastrophic war for dominance and all of us lower food chain creatures would suffer greatly from it." She smiled at him, knowing the images she must have planted in his head.

"Wow, I can see what you mean." Bain watched the colorful hatchlings mill about the nest, their scaly, iridescent-looking skin reflecting a multitude of colors as the sunlight bounced off their glistening hides. Bain looked at Karalis who stood regally, looking down at his offspring, obviously proud that he had lent to the birth of two new Kriesletrope.

Bain's eyebrows shot up as he watched Karalis prance around, strutting and preening himself like a pompous king, preparing for a parade where his devoted worshipers would bask in his presence. Bain smiled at the show. He looked over at Karaliene, who seemed tired, and laid her head down upon the edge of the nest, her eyes fluttering closed.

Bain asked Neeanne, "Is Karaliene all right?"

"Yes, I believe so. Hatching one egg is tough enough, and she has two very proud, very rambunctious, very competitive hatchlings for which to tend."

He and Neeanne watched the twins roll around on the ground, playing and nipping at one another as the field behind them filled with other people who came to witness the oddity of the Kriesletrope birth. This of course only added to Karalises' pomp and circumstance as he sat proud and tall beside his sleeping mate, looking out over the masses that had come to gawk at his creation.

Bain wasn't sure what was more fun to watch, the hatchlings or Karalises display of pride.

*'Why shouldn't I be proud, Enlightened One?'* Karalises voice bounced around in Bain's skull.

Bain communicated back. *'Oh, from what I understand, you should be. I wasn't judging, just enjoying the display.'*

*'Yes, well, again, you must control who you let into your head, or you may likely regret your new abilities to speak with us creatures.'*

Bain looked confused as he walked closer to Karalis and looked up at him. *'Why do I need to be careful? Can other creatures alter my thoughts?'*

*'No, but you can give away much of your plans to enemies.'*

*'How?'* Bain certainly had no idea how the thoughts in his head could lead to somehow harm himself or others.

Karalis indignantly released a puff of smoke and roared, Bain hearing it as laughter. *'My, you are a rather ignorant human aren't you? Do you truly believe you are the only one of your kind who can speak to us?'*

*'Well, of course not.'* Bain said, rather put out. *'I know several people with the same ability.'*

*'And are all those humans good beings?'*

*'I don't know, but I believe the ones who I know are.'*

*'Surely you understand that not all who have the gift of enlightenment are trustworthy.'*

Bain understood his meaning now. *'I suppose there are people out there with less than honorable intentions who may also have the gift.'*

Karalis harrumphed. *'Yes, and if those humans can speak to us creatures, then they can also see into your own mind. You must learn to block others out if you wish to keep your secrets.'*

Bain nodded. *'Thank you, Karalis, for your wise instructions. But how do I do that? I'm new to this whole telepathic communication.'*

Karalises large head slowly dropped to within a few feet of Bain as one large eye peered at him. *'Concentrate, Enlightened One;*

*you must always guard your thoughts and your mind. You must practice blocking out others.'*

Bain shook his head, not fully understanding how he was supposed to do that. Especially when there was no other person he could get help from. Then he thought about Jilly.

Karalis nodded and blinked. *'Yes, the young telepath who just arrived. She can help you train to block out mind scanning of others who will seek to harm you.'*

Bain looked at Karalis and audibly said, "I forget you can read my thoughts, even when I'm not speaking to you."

*'Not all are as powerful as I, but most Baiskreet can do this. And if their loyalty is to an Enlightened One who is not so trustworthy, you could be in great danger of revealing so much of what you do not wish for others to know.'*

Bain nodded his thanks. *'Thank you for your instruction Karalis, and once again, congratulations on siring such a beautiful and majestic set of twins.'*

Karalis beamed with pride once again as he straightened to his full stature, stretched, and sat watching over his young and the crowd of humans gathered about them.

The workday had completely changed with the birth of the twins, and so Bain knew he could vanish without detection or much questioning from his superiors. Bain turned and began to walk across the paddock, his actions catching Sebena's attention, a questioning look on her face.

Bain grinned at her and waved nonchalantly, careful not to draw too much attention to their interaction. He decided to go in search of Jilly, hoping she could help to train him on how to block out or to know if others were reading his thoughts. He hopped onto an air-rover which was sitting at the edge of the paddock, hoping it wasn't one belonging to one of the captains, and set out to the seaside hotel.

Sebena watched Bain go, curious as to his destination. She turned back to the twin Kriesletrope which pranced and played, a worried look on her features as the largest, obviously the male, was already displaying dominant qualities. They may soon have to take the buck to the wilds of Eathreon.

Sebena's attention was drawn to Karalis, who let out a loud roar and stared at her, puffs of steam and smoke rising from his nostrils, his breathing suddenly harder than just a few moments earlier, like he suddenly was under duress.

Sebena wondered if Karalis understood her thoughts, much like the girl Jilly could speak to the creatures who obeyed her; appearing to understand her words. She had watched Bain and Karalis interacting earlier and it looked as though the two were having a conversation.

*Surely not?* Sebena thought.

Karalis nodded to her, glaring at her like he would make a pile of ash of her at any moment. Sebena watched him closely as he watched her, making certain her mind stayed clear of thought. Her attention was soon drawn back to the young male Kriesletrope who snapped at his smaller, more vulnerable sibling, already proudly prancing, and preening about as the other hatchling slunk off to curl up under the protective wings of its now watchful mother.

Sebena noticed the exchanged look of concern between Karaliene and Karalis as they both watched the new little male, who was thoroughly enjoying all the attention of the onlookers.

Sebena commanded loudly. "All right, show time's over; everyone back to work. Karaliene is certainly tired and will have enough to keep her busy without worrying about any of you getting stepped on or used as a plaything for her young."

The group of people began to disperse and head back to their own fields and Baiskreet. Sebena glanced back at Karaliene who appeared to nod thankfully at her. Sebena's brow knit in curiosity. Then she looked at Karalis, who watched her, but not with the same grateful look that Karaliene gave her, his was one of uncertainty. He turned away from her and, taking his large nose, nuzzled at the young buck, pushing him into the nest with his sibling, beneath the protective wings of its mother as Karalis himself curled up in front of the nest, once again cautiously watching Sebena as she walked away.

Bain soon arrived at the seaside hotel, finding Jilly and Dot playing down by the water with the other telepaths.

Bain greeted them. "Jilly, how are things here?"

Jilly smiled brightly. "Great, now that my friends are back."

"Good to hear, I'm glad everyone seems to be recovering well." Bain watched the children, or young people now, playing at the water's edge with Dot, who jumped around like a pup, happily chasing and being chased by everyone else.

"He seems to be enjoying all the attention."

Jilly laughed. "Yes, who knew he was so playful; it makes me wonder at his age. It was just the two of us for so long, and he was always so watchful and protective. I think he sensed my fear and loneliness."

Bain nodded. "Yes, it's those senses that I'd like to speak to you about."

Jilly looked at him confused. "Did Dot or I do something wrong?"

Bain smiled reassuringly. "No, nothing like that. But ever since you gifted me with telepathy I'm having trouble controlling my thoughts."

"Oh, how so?" Jilly asked, confused.

"I understand that there is a way to control others from reading your thoughts. I need to learn this to protect my mind."

"Oh, yes, so sorry, Bain. It was something that we just naturally learned as we aged. You need to learn how to access certain compartments of your mind. Find a place where you can openly discuss things with others mentally, then lock that door when you don't wish to communicate. You have to always be in control of your thoughts. You can't let your emotions, or feelings, take over. Calm and control will be your best friend."

Bain exhaled loudly. "I've never been very good at either of those traits. I tend to fly off the handle and sometimes wear my feelings on my sleeves. How am I supposed to change my own behavior so drastically?"

Jilly patted his arm. "It takes time, meditation, and concentration. Eventually it will become second nature to you."

"Do you think you can teach me how to do this?"

"Sure." Jilly looked around, spotting what appeared to be an unused stretch of sand just a ways down the beach. "How about we meet over there in the more private area each morning at dawn. It should be quiet and tranquil, and the lull of the ocean waves should help you to stay calm and give you a rhythmic balance to follow."

Bain smiled brightly. "Thank you, Jilly. That will be most helpful."

Bain left and headed back to Castle Dihendra and his guard position. He would have to skip breakfast to be able to meet Jilly each morning, but it would be worth it. He could swing by the dining hall and grab something easy and quick to eat on his way to the hotel. They usually kept fruits, vegetables, protein bars, and water-skins filled for the recruits. It seemed as though Bain's life was growing fuller and busier by the day. How would he explain what he was doing and where he was going to Sebena? Would she understand how he could now speak with the creatures?

# Chapter 21

**Castle Dihendra, Evening, Day 9**

Sebena watched Bain returning from wherever he had disappeared to earlier. He pulled the air-rover into the parking area and stepped down.

"Recruit Brinley."

Bain heard Sebena's voice behind him and turned to address her.

Standing at attention and saluting, Bain said, "Commander Zentrialle." His hands fell to his side, and he stood unmoving.

A slight smirk curled Sebena's lips as she leaned forward and whispered, circling around him as she spoke. "I think I'm really going to like my new position."

Bain tried not to grin at her playful words full of dominance and control.

"Ma'am," Bain said, "you were already my captain, and commanded the same respect."

"Yeah, but this jumping to attention just at the sight of me is definitely a little different, Recruit." She stopped moving and stood directly in front of him. "Where have you been, Recruit Brinley?"

Bain still stood at attention; quite aware he couldn't move until given the at 'ease command'.

"To the hotel to see my friends and family, Commander."

"Oh." Sebena nodded. "At ease, Recruit Brinley."

Bain exhaled heavily and relaxed, looking down at her. She grinned slightly at him, trying not to draw too much attention to them.

"Follow me, Recruit Brinley."

Sebena turned from the room and briskly walked away, Bain scurrying to catch up to her. She moved fast for a shorter, smaller woman.

Sebena walked to a door on the Commander's floor, unlocked it with her new set of keys, and stepped into a room, ushering Bain inside after her and closing the door.

Bain stepped further inside the room, realizing it was her new Commander's quarters. He turned to speak to her and found himself locked in her arms as she planted an intense kiss on him. Bain leaned into her, fully participating in the embrace. They soon pulled apart and looked at one another.

Sebena smiled broadly from ear to ear. "I've been waiting to do that all day. This command position may be harder than I predicted. I thought I would have a bit more down time, but everyone watches me and wants advice, commands, and plans for everything!" Sebena let out an exhausted breath and collapsed onto the sofa in the small seating area of her large room.

Bain smiled at her and went to sit beside her. "Sorry, Commander, that you find yourself pulled in so many directions."

She looked at him. "No Commander here. Here I'm just Sebena. Your Sebena."

She leaned into his arms, resting her head on his chest as they snuggled together, a sigh of contentment escaping both of their lips. Bain's head lay upon hers, as the fruity scent of her shampoo wafted through his nostrils. They sat there quietly for a few minutes just enjoying the feel of one another's arms and the companionship of it.

She soon leaned back and stared up into his face. "So, we just saw your family this morning. Why the need to go back this afternoon?"

"I needed to see Jilly about something."

Sebena watched him for a minute, a question coming to her mind. "Did it have anything to do with the strange conversation, or whatever it was, I saw taking place between you and Karalis earlier?"

"You noticed we were communicating?"

She sat up straight, turning to him. "I figured that was what was happening, though there was no movement from either of your lips."

Bain sighed heavily. "When I went to look for my family and found some of them on the southern islands, Jilly was able to give me the ability to speak to the creatures."

Sebena sat up on her knees, confusion on her face as she looked down at him. "How is that possible?"

"I'm not sure. I just know that when I came back, Karalis could sense that I had changed and began to speak to me."

"Really? Saying what?"

"Well, he asked me to fly with him to catch the general and the corrupt commanders."

"So that's why you were on him." Sebena said, deep in thought. "Can he read all minds?"

"I don't know, but I wouldn't doubt it. He even knew about Jilly and she has never seen him, or he her."

"Well, today I felt like he could sense my thoughts. I was concerned about the young buck's already aggressive nature toward his twin sister and thought about taking him to Eathreon. This thought seemed to agitate Karalis, and he watched me continually afterward, looking as though he wanted to roast me where I stood."

"It is possible."

"Can Jilly give me this gift too?"

Bain shook his head in uncertainty. "Sebena, it isn't so much a gift. I have to meet with Jilly every morning to learn to control my thoughts from other readers. You may wish you didn't have it."

"I doubt that very seriously. Besides, it would be vastly helpful if I could speak to the creatures, and other telepaths as well."

"Perhaps, but I don't know if I like the idea of you being able to read my mind."

She bristled at this. "But you can read mine? Besides, what do you have to hide from me?"

Bain threw his hands up. "Nothing, I promise. Besides, I haven't figured out how to read other people's minds. Just communicate with the animals."

"Well then, I want to try it as well. What time are we meeting Jilly?"

"Before dawn. Oh," Bain quickly stood up, pulling her to her feet. "speaking of meeting, I told Guidriun and Mercer that I'd meet up with them for drinks after dinner."

"Mind if I come?"

"I don't, but I'm not sure how the boys will feel about hanging out with the new Squadron Commander." He smiled at her.

"They'll just have to get used to it. Remember, where you go, I go."

Bain grinned down at her, and before stealing another kiss said, "Yes, and I'm glad of it."

They broke apart, with Sebena hurriedly changing into something more comfortable while Bain went to the Barracks to do the same. They agreed to meet in the dining hall, hoping to find their friends there. After locating the boys, they went into Dihendra Rhial, walked into *Brecker's Breach*, up the stairs, and took a seat on the upper veranda once more where Sebena had taken him when they had first met.

Guidriun and Mercer oohed and aahed.

Mercer stated, "Wow, we feel important."

Sebena looked at them with angst. "Boys, when you become acting guard patrolling around the rhial, you too will have access to this veranda without the aid of a superior."

Mercer leaned back in his chair, rubbing his chest and stomach in a macho way. "I guess we can chalk this up to an intensive training session then."

Everyone laughed at him.

Brecker soon appeared with four iced mugs and several bottles of barley-wine for their table. They sat for the next several hours enjoying each other's company, the icy drinks, and the rich flavor of Brecker's special blended barley-wine until the hour grew late and they stumbled all the way back to the castle. Sebena was more skilled at holding her barley-wine, but Mercer was pretty skilled as well. Between the two of them, they managed to drag Guidriun and Bain to the barracks and throw them into their beds.

"Goodnight, Commander Zentrialle," Mercer said, his attentive stance swaying a tad, and his saluted elbow tilted a little toward the ground.

Sebena grinned then soberly said, "At ease, Recruit Rand." She nearly laughed out loud when he smiled brightly and collapsed backward onto his own bed, his legs hanging off the side, his arms stretched out beside him, and a silly grin still plastered on his face.

As she walked upstairs to the third floor toward her new room, and inserted her key into her door, she heard her name.

"Commander Zentrialle."

She turned abruptly, taking a stance of attention. She saluted and said, "Lieutenant Commander Vertrite."

Vertrite walked closer to her, a look of stern disappointment on the woman's features. "Commander," she began, "it has come to my attention that you are consorting with your recruits."

"Just trying to keep up open communications and morale, Ma'am."

"As a past captain over the squadron, that sort of thing may have been acceptable then, but now that you are a commander your behavior is frowned upon. If you wish for your troops to take you seriously, you have to be above them all. And that includes whatever relationship you have going on with Recruit Brinley. Do I make myself clear?"

"Yes, Lieutenant Commander Vertrite."

Vertrite turned and walked away, and Sebena let out a held breath and fell against the wall of the curved, two-foot, recess that stuck out from each door in the castle's interior rooms. She gathered herself, opened her door and walked into her room. How was she supposed to sneak off with Bain every morning now with Vertrite breathing down her neck? Maybe she could figure out a way to keep the woman busy while she and Bain took care of business? Perhaps Guidriun and Mercer could help with that. Sebena got ready for bed as a plan formed in her head. She lay down on her bed and tried to close her eyes for the few hours of sleep that would likely evade her for the remainder of the night.

Sebena woke Guidriun and Mercer when she woke Bain for their early morning meeting with Jilly. She explained what she and Bain had to do, leaving out the whole mind-reading part, instructing them to com-call her if Commander Vertrite came looking for her. They would all have to be on constant alert if she and Bain were going to be together and have a chance of time-jumping together as well. If their plan at keeping Vertrite busy failed, then she and Bain would just have to leave the castle and live a normal life until he was called to time-jump again. She was not about to let him go without her, no matter what happened.

With Bain's grandfather's Matter Arranging Device that Bain had given her yesterday morning, they just had to find a secluded place, turn on the device, and walk through to the other side of Dihendra Rhial. Jilly waited for them on the beach, the beast known as Dot, lay curled up on the sand asleep.

Sebena looked at Bain after they walked through the MAD's open portal.

"That was so amazing! If we had such technology for the guard it would make things much easier to navigate the territories."

Bain smile, "Maybe, but it could cause a lot of chaos too."

They walked over to Jillian and Bain made proper introductions.

"Jilly," Bain said. "You remember Sebena."

Jilly smiled, "Of course, who could forget you."

Sebena smiled at her comment, then, never being one to beat around the bush, said. "I wish you to give me the ability to speak to the creatures as well."

"Oh," Jilly said, a bit taken aback. "I can try, but I can't promise that it will work. Not all minds are prepared for such things."

"I believe mine will be. I'm certainly open to trying it."

"Yes, many people would like to have the ability, but it can be overwhelming at times."

"I understand that, but it can also be extremely useful as well."

"Well, all right, but you have to promise not to tell anyone I did this for you. It could really lead to quite a mess for me."

"I understand."

Jilly looked at Bain and gave him a stern look of disappointment which Sebena caught.

"Bain didn't willingly tell me. I noticed him communicating with Karalis, and then later, it felt like Karalis could read my thoughts as well."

"Karalis?" Jilly asked, looking at them both questioningly.

Bain explained. "A creature here in Dihendra known as the Baiskreet."

"So that is who I've been reading. I have been sensing a lot of other creatures since being here on Dihendra, but one presence is very prominent."

"Really?" Sebena asked, surprised.

"Yes. Well, concerning your mind, perhaps it will work since you have such a keen sense of observation, but there are no promises."

Jilly stood in front of Sebena, and as she had done for Bain, put one hand against Sebena's temple, and the other to her own. She concentrated for a few seconds, speaking into Sebena's thoughts. After nearly a minute of concentration and calling to her telepathically, her voice broke through. *'Can you hear me, Sebena?'*

Sebena smiled. *'Jilly?'*

*'Yes.'*

Sebena's eyes popped open and she pulled the girl in a big hug.

Jilly was startled at first, then began giggling. "Sebena, we'll need to make sure it took without my having to touch you."

"Oh, sorry." Sebena let her go and stood still. "Now what?"

Jilly looked at her without audibly speaking. *'Sebena, can you hear me still?'*

Sebena smiled brightly and answered telepathically. *'Can you hear me?'*

"It worked!" Jilly said.

Sebena looked at Bain, a giddy look on her face.

Jilly stood before them both. "Now comes the hard part. Controlling what and who you hear from, and stopping others from entering your thoughts, mind, and memories."

"How do we do that?" Bain asked.

"First, look to the sea to calm and quiet your thoughts. Watch the waves come and go. Listen to the sounds of the ocean around you. Now, close your eyes and focus on the rhythmic sound of the waves crashing on the shore, then ebbing back to the sea. Find a place in your mind where you are calm, relaxed, and in control of your thoughts and feelings. Your emotions can betray you, so don't let them show. Picture an empty room in your mind, one where you can open and close the door."

Bain and Sebena stayed for thirty minutes listening to Jilly's instructions before using the MADs to return to the castle.

As soon as they appeared, Sebena slunk away to her command post while Bain went to the training fields. Hands on training with the Baiskreet was going so well, that flight training had started, taking the place of morning sparring. The recruits of Squadrons twelve through fifteen were racing to the Baiskreet fields, excited for flying exercises. Several different recruits from each squadron worked in the different paddocks and everyone had their favorite beast; everyone in a hurry to claim their favorite Baiskreet with which to climb on its back and take to the air, all hoping that they would be accepted by whichever beast they chose.

Mercer decided that since he had spent the last week nursing the Brundwedim, Brutus, he now had a special bond with the creature. Guidriun chose the Copasedrom known as Corpse. He was familiar with riding the beast when he returned it for Bain several days back when he had left the island in search of his family.

Bain however felt Karalis calling to him once more as he ran through the training grounds, dodging excited recruits, all mounting Baiskreet and taking to the sky.

Karalis waited for him at the overhead bridge as Bain ran, jumped down upon his back and the powerful beast was soon in the air, looping, and soaring with the rest of the other Baiskreet.

The people of Dihendra Rhial all looked up, pointing toward the castle, and exclaiming in excitement over the flight training. This was a quarterly appearance for the rhial. The harried, unorganized first day of actual flight training created an interesting spectacle in the sky above them and the castle. Baiskreet screeched and flew in all directions, some people even fell off the backs of their Baiskreet, fortunately caught mid-air by one of the many watchful captains and commanders who oversaw the chaos of first day flight with humor.

# Chapter 22

**Castle Dihendra, Day 10**

Several recruits ended up in medical with small injuries due to their inability to stay on their Baiskreet, or how to navigate around the creature's abilities. One poor guy's Brundwedim was digging through the mountainside and his rider forgot to turn on his protective shield to keep the rocks from hitting him. It wasn't until he was beat black and blue that he realized his mistake.

Several other riders of the Triastrium breed forgot their filtering masks, and the creature's ability to emit a euphoric causing gas made them fall from their backs, acting higher than the moons of Harilhia for the next thirty minutes. They all had to be kept under lock and key for a while until they came to their senses. There was a lot of teasing for a solid week; a lesson well learned to never again neglect the use of their filtering masks.

Many Verassuan riders were shaken from the creatures back during ground thrashing episodes, making them sore and some even sick to their stomachs from the violent vibrations the creature created. Others were a bit air-sick, not used to the speed with which many of the Baiskreet could fly, especially the riders of the Copasedrom, Lurepture, and Nassureptic breeds.

The Durnestrum with its pungent odor made several riders sick to their stomachs and hoping to be paired with a different breed in the future. The medics decided to test potential riders with sinus issues to pair with the creatures in the future. Likely they would have to issue air filtering masks to this breed's rider's as well.

And then there were the Viigisur riders, some who neglected to clip their safety harnesses to their creatures saddle and tumbled off their backs when it went to scale a cliff side or building.

There were many stories related to the neglect of using necessary equipment or the lack of learning the abilities of their chosen Baiskreet before jumping on their backs and taking to the air.

The Captains of the squadrons often took bets on who they thought would fail Baiskreet rider training day; many being publicly reprimanded by their commanders who really didn't care about the betting, but they had to keep up appearances for the sake of the injured recruits.

Weeks passed with rider training growing more successful and the Baiskreet and their riders beginning to move in uniformed patterns.

General Bridger, Lieutenant Commander Vertrite, Sebena and all the other commanders watched the captains lead the recruits who were soon to become acting guards of Dihendran territories.

General Bridger stated, "I have to say, this group of riders, particularly the Twelfth Squadron have learned much quicker than any squadron before them."

Commander Vertrite added, "I believe sir that it is because of Recruit Brinley, and the quick recognition of his abilities by Commander Zentrialle."

Sebena was surprised by her praise of both of them, especially after the ripping she had given her weeks before, and how closely she seemed to watch Sebena since.

Bridger replied, "I do believe you are correct Lieutenant. Commander Zentrialle and her Squadron seem to have an advantage over the other three sky patrol squadrons. I believe a short weekend pass is deserved by the sky-rider troops. They've trained long and hard, and with great vigilance in learning their creatures since the day one debacle."

Vertrite replied, "Yes, sir, I agree. Commander Zentrialle, see to it that all sky-rider squadrons, their captains, and commanders receive a three-day reprieve, beginning at the end of this week. Each squadron will take a separate weekend allowing the best performing group to have first leave and so forth. We can't leave our defenses completely barren all at once."

"Yes Ma'am, Lieutenant Commander Vertrite." Sebena saluted, excited that she and Bain would be able to escape for three days of unmonitored activities.

Bridger interjected, "Commander Zentrialle, it seems that some of the hatchlings from several weeks back are showing aggressive and untrainable traits and will need to be flown to Eathreon. Take several of the commanders, a few captains and some of the more promising recruits along for the delivery. We have a  rather large rejection group this year and you will need more help than normal."

"Yes General." Sebena thought for a moment. "But concerning the Kriesletrope buck. The young male's attitude has not gotten better, and I am afraid that Karalis may not take kindly to us removing his male hatchling from their paddock."

"What makes you think this; has Karalis gotten out of hand?"

"Well, no sir, but I've noticed a particular protectiveness over the young Kriesletrope. Karalis would be quite unmanageable should he choose not to cooperate."

General Bridger watched her closely, unsure what her concern was. "We've never had any issue with either of the Kriesletrope Baiskreet. Why should we now?"

"I think it has to do with the twin hatchlings. Karalis is showing very dominant, protective traits over them, particularly the young buck."

"Well, see to it that he is controlled, Commander."

Sebena did not want to hear that. The General and Lieutenant departed leaving Sebena and the other commander's on the platform, all of whom were giving her apologetic looks and words of encouragement as they passed her by to go about their daily assignments.

She sighed heavily. Good news followed by horrid news. Karalis already did not like her, and this was going to be hard. They may have to tranquilize him in order to remove the buck which was something she knew would not go over well once the tranquilizer wore off. Karalis could cause all of Dihendra serious trouble should he so choose, and making the king of the Baiskreet angry would be a very dangerous possibility indeed. And of course the nasty little job would land in her lap as her responsibility. When would she learn to keep her big mouth shut? Perhaps Bain could communicate to Karalis the need to remove the buck to Eathreon. Of course it would have been very irresponsible to ignore the buck's aggressive nature. He was movable as a hatchling but as an adult Kriesletrope it would be impossible. At two weeks old he was already bigger than a few of the other adult breeds, and much more aggressive and dangerous.

Sebena squared her shoulders, took another deep breath, and went in search of Bain, Captain Nigel, and several other captains, commanders, and recruits. She would gather those for the Eathreon trip, then deliver the news of the leave orders for the sky-riders. Hopefully they could make the trip to Eathreon quickly and be back in time for weekend leave since her squadron would get first leave privileges.

Sebena walked to the training fields to communicate the orders to the troops; her mood definitely dampened by the trip orders to Eathreon.

She stood on the platform above the three-hundred plus recruits, captains, and commanders, all of whom waited to hear what she had to say. She called out the captains, commanders and recruits required for the trip, and as they made their way to the platform for special orders, she announced the General's decision and reward for the sky-rider troops, giving them their leave weekends in order. When she had finished her announcement, the troops below erupted in cheers and whoops for the next few minutes as excitement moved throughout the grounds.

Sebena stood before the twelve recruits, four captains and three commanders and explained the orders General Bridger set upon them. Bain asked for permission to speak. Sebena granted it.

"Commander Zentrialle, moving the Kriesletrope buck may well be disastrous."

"I know this, Recruit Brinley, but orders are orders."

"Did you…" he stopped realizing the breach in protocol. "Commander, did you explain to the General the attitude of the adult male Kriesletrope?"

"Of course I explained, Recruit Brinley, and I was given the instruction to subdue and control Karalis."

Bain looked at her briefly with a shocked look on his face; quickly changing it to a blank expression.

Sebena said, "Any more questions?" No one spoke. "All right, we'll head over to the paddocks where we will gather the Baiskreet to be moved, prep our Baiskreet to ride, then head out for the trip to Eathreon. Recruit Mercer, Recruit Guidriun, go along with Captain Nigel to request provisions to be prepared for the trip and ready to go in two hours. The rest of you, come with me to prepare the wild ones, then you can be excused to gather your personal items for four days of traveling."

Everyone nodded and went about their orders. Bain watched Sebena out of the corner of his eye. Once they were closer to the breeding grounds and everyone split up to take care of different Baiskreet, he asked her, "Sebena, how do you plan to get Karalis to release his only male hatchling to the wild lands of Eathreon?"

"I was hoping you'd have a plan for that, Bain."

"Me? Why me?"

"You are his bond-rider. You said so yourself that he called to you."

"Yeah, but that doesn't mean he'll listen to me."

"Well, let's hope he does, because I have no other clue or plan how to do this. If we sedate him, he will be livid when he comes out of it. He'll likely destroy everything and everyone just out of spite."

Bain thought about the first time he rode Karalis and the joy he witnessed in the massive beast, and how Karalis had admitted to wanting to destroy every one of the traitors just for fun.

"You're right. There has to be a better way to go about this."

As they approached the paddock Karalis stood waiting, sensing their approach. His defiant stance and glaring stare made Sebena and Bain uneasy.

"Karalis," Bain called, "General Bridger has ordered the removal of your male hatchling."

Karalis laughed. *'I care not for the orders of humans.'*

Sebena added, "Still, you know the buck is dangerous. He won't live well here near the city. He has to have his best chance and that isn't here."

Karalis glared at her even more. *'I knew you had become enlightened.'*

Sebena nodded to him in answer.

Karalis added. *'You're telling me his best chance is at Eathreon. He is too young. He will be overtaken quickly by the wild Baiskreet and killed. My hatchling will stay with me.'*

Sebena shook her head and said, "You know he can't stay here. He's uncontrollable and untrainable, Karalis. It's too dangerous this close to the rhial."

*'Perhaps it is, but only to you humans. There is no danger for my buck. Nothing can or will harm him as long as I am alive.'*

Sebena sighed heavily, knowing this would not go well. She looked at Bain and motioned to him to jump in any time to help.

Bain looked at the Kriesletrope family. Then he turned to Sebena. "Do you have to have a Kriesletrope breed here at the grounds?"

"I don't know. I don't suppose we have to have one. Why?"

"Would the General approve of the release of them all?"

Sebena shook her head. "I'm unsure, Bain. Let me com-call and see." Sebena turned away to make the call to the general, returning soon.

"General Bridger said that if their going was the only way to secure the safety of Dihendra Rhial, then fine, but we would have to replace the breed with another one."

"How do we do that?"

"We would have to capture a wild one from the lands of Eathreon."

Bain doubted that would be an easy task. "I have a feeling our *weekend* of leave just got canceled, at least for those of us making this trip."

"That about sums it up," Sebena stated.

Bain turned to Karalis. "Karalis, king of the Baiskreet, you have been given your freedom to go to Eathreon with your hatchling."

Karalis laughed again. *'Given my freedom? My freedom has always been my own. We only stayed because life here was simple. Once Karaliene was with child, she needed a safe place to hatch our eggs. Being raised by the humans here has made that easy, feeding us, and tending to our every need. But I suppose it is time to move on. We will travel with you to Eathreon and take our place among the wild ones. It is time I ruled over the other Baiskreet in the wild lands and raised my hatchlings as true, free, Baiskreet of Harilhia.'*

Bain and Sebena looked at each other, pleased that Bain's idea went over well.

Sebena called to the recruits. "Bring the straps to secure the hatchling."

Karalis roared louder than anyone had heard yet. *'You will not strap my hatchling! I will control what is mine!'*

*Sebena raised her hands in the air in defeat.* "Fine, but he is solely your responsibility."

*'Yes, he is!'*

Karalis glared at her, his dislike of her evident in every fiber of his being. His snarl vibrated as a growl escaped his curled lips, wisps of smoke rising from his nostrils as if he instantly wanted to set her ablaze.

Bain said telepathically, *'Karalis, Sebena is my mate. She is only doing as she is told. Please, do not harm her.'*

Karalis turned toward him. *'Your mate is weak in soul and spirit if she is only doing what is based on another's orders.'*

Bain's words became audible. "Do you not expect the other Baiskreet to listen, obey, and respect you as their king?"

Karalis thought for a second. *'Of course I do.'*

"Well, here, humans have the same type of rulers and kings, and they must obey as well. She is being loyal to her rulers, just as the other Baiskreet are loyal to you."

Karalis looked at Sebena then back to Bain. *'I understand what you are saying. Just know that I do not trust her and I will be keeping my eye on her.'*

"Fair enough," Bain stated.

Sebena gave Karalis instructions for their leaving and when to have his family ready for the two-day trip. As she and Bain turned to go back to the barracks to pack, she said, "Now, all I have to do is look up a replacement Baiskreet to take their place and then catch a pair."

"Sounds easy enough," Bain said sarcastically.

"Exactly." Sebena exhaled loudly, grinned sideways, and took the stairs quickly to her quarters on the third floor as Bain turned toward the barracks quarters on the second level.

# Chapter 23

**Traveling to Eathreon, Day 22 on Harilhia**

As Bain and the others headed out of the castle to meet once again at the breeding grounds, Maubrey and Kamsten were coming across the grounds from the castle.

"Bain!" Maubrey yelled.

Bain stopped and looked at his friends. "Hey, what are you two doing here?"

Maubrey replied, "We were working in the tech room up in the castle when I had a thought."

"You could have com-called," Bain said, stopping to speak with them.

"Yes, well, this is a bit more intensive, not to mention, we decided we need to stay closer to you."

"You can't exactly follow me around the castle all day."

"No, but, with what I've discovered, I figure we need to stick as close as possible. I've figured out a way to tell when a storm is coming, and what the intensity will be."

Kamsten interrupted, "Well, almost."

Maubrey looked at her, "True. It's only in theory but it will require more study. And to do that, we need to stick close by you. If you jump without us, then, we may never see you again."

"Well, thing is guys, we are just about to leave on a four-to-five-day trip to deliver some Baiskreet to Eathreon."

"Deliver what to where?" Maubrey asked, confusion written on his face.

"The creatures we ride here just hatched eggs weeks back and the ones that are untrainable are delivered to the wilds of Harilhia."

"Oh, do you think the powers that be will let us go along? I'd like to see this Eathreon." Maubrey asked excitedly.

"I don't know, Maubrey, it could be dangerous. Plus you've never flown before."

Maubrey seemed excited by the idea, while Kamsten's face fell in angst.

"I'd love to give it a try. Since we've left Zanchier, my adventurous spirit has perked up considerably."

Kamsten jabbed Maubrey in the ribs with her elbow. "His has, but mine is quieting down," she replied.

"I'll check with Sebena, but this is not going to be a fun trip I'm afraid. Plus we are transporting some dangerous animals."

Maubrey happily stated, "Well, at least we'll be surrounded by castle guard who will be able to protect us."

Bain sighed. "Okay, but don't say I didn't warn you. Do you have enough supplies in your packs for at least five days?"

Maubrey smiled brightly. "Oh yes, since we decided to tail you, we carry most of our belongings on our backs. Of course, since we were kidnapped and held prisoner for almost a year, we don't have much anyway."

Sebena suddenly appeared beside them, a question on her face. "Ready to go, Bain?"

"Yeah, but Maubrey and Kamsten want to tag along."

The look on Sebena's face was one of apprehension.

Maubrey quickly added, "We won't be any trouble."

She looked at him strangely. "I highly doubt that. Besides, this will be a long, hard, trip."

"Like I reminded Bain only moments earlier, it can't be any more difficult than a year in prison and being tortured."

Sebena winced. "Fine. But we are leaving now. Are you both ready to go?"

"Absolutely," Maubrey stated happily. Kamsten rolled her eyes, unsure this was a good idea.

"I'll pair you both with other riders who have larger Baiskreet that can carry two people over such a long distance." She turned to Bain. "Take them in the barracks and grab two more travel packs for them to use, then stop at the kitchen before that and ask them to quickly add food for two more for the trip. Pick up the food on the way out and meet us at the breeding grounds."

Bain nodded. "Certainly, Commander."

Maubrey teased Bain, "Commander ehh?"

"She is my superior, and the superior of everyone on this trip; including you two." Bain turned and walked briskly toward the castle.

Maubrey grinned. "Oh, absolutely. Kamsten and I will be on our best behavior."

Kamsten grabbed his arm to hold him back and looked at him.

"I have no behavioral issues," Kamsten said offensively.

"I know dear; it was just a figure of speech."

"Well speak for yourself. I'm not crazy about this impromptu trip."

"It'll be fine," Maubrey assured her.

"It better be, because if I die on this trip my spirit will haunt you the rest of your days. And if we die together, I'll still haunt you; forever." She glared at him in warning, her eyes squinting and fists clenched at her side.

Maubrey stretched his neck, trying to clear his throat from the constriction that suddenly choked him, realizing Kamsten was not happy with him volunteering them to make a trip across Harilhia on the backs of winged creatures for the next four or more days. But he couldn't let Bain disappear for days knowing there was a chance he could disappear through a portal, forever. This was the opportunity of a lifetime to study time-travel and the space-time continuum.

Maubrey laughed nervously as he said, "Yes dear, a…and I'll happily let you." They turned and walked quickly, trying to catch up to Bain.

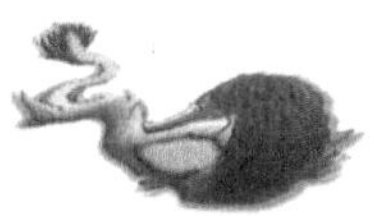

The group of twenty-two travelers mounted their Baiskreet with the four commanders and their Baiskreet leading the group. The eight cages which contained the untrainable hatchlings were lifted into the air with attached chains and carried by the larger Baiskreet. Several of the larger cages and hatchlings had to be carried by two Baiskreet. Karalis of course was above the grunt work of such tasks, and he and his family flew alongside the others. He and Karaliene seemed to be having trouble corralling their own young, particularly their overly-excitable buck; the very reason they had chosen to leave Dihendra.

Hours had passed as the band of travelers flew over the mountainous terrain below. Bain watched in amusement as Maubrey twitched, twisted, and wiggled in his seat behind Captain Nigel, seemingly very uncomfortable with sitting for so long on the back of the Baiskreet. Bain had also chuckled when they had just taken to the sky and poor Maubrey got air-sick, nearly up-chucking his breakfast. His current state of discomfort seemed to give Kamsten some gratification, although earlier during his sick bout, Bain could tell she did feel some compassion for her fiancé'.

Sebena, who led the group, gave the signal to land for lunch and bathroom breaks. When the large troop managed to find a valley in which to land, Bain along with everyone else, chuckled as poor Maubrey slid to the ground, his knees almost buckling under his weight.

Kamsten walked over to him to offer her assistance. "Here, Sweetheart, let me help you over to that rock to give you something to support yourself."

"Oh, thank you, darling. I…I don't think my legs will work on their own. I think everything is asleep from the waist down," Maubrey said, gladly accepting her support. After he leaned on the rock, he noticed that she didn't seem affected by the flight or the hours of sitting in one position.

"You seem to have handled this trip quite well so far."

"Yes," Kamsten sighed, smiling. "It's quite invigorating flying."

"Well, why don't you have any of the same issues I'm experiencing?"

"I'm not sure. Perhaps my countenance is just stronger than yours. Plus, the person who I'm riding with said she has a great little trick she's learned during riding for long periods of time."

Maubrey leaned in, ready to hear anything that might help him over the next two days. "Really, what is it?"

"Her Baiskreet, on command of course, can vibrate its body, giving a feeling of relaxing massage as you ride. Keeps the blood flowing to the lower extremities of the body."

"I don't suppose all the other Baiskreet can do this?"

"I don't think so. She did say it was specific to her breed."

Maubrey grinned begrudgingly. "Oh, how awesome for you. I don't suppose you'd want to trade with me for a while?"

"Nope." She patted him on the shoulder as she walked away to grab her and Maubrey's packs for lunch.

Less than an hour later, Sebena instructed everyone to tie a bandanna around their necks or slip on their guard issued head cloths. Then, they were back in the air once again. Not long after, the scenery below began to change. Everyone new to the trip watched the turbulent scene below with worry. Large, thick, swampy-looking pools of water bubbled and churned as steam rose above them, creating a thick cloud in the sky which lent a putrid scent to the air. What sparse vegetation that existed below them was thin, scraggly, and barely alive. The landscape was a barren one, with sharp rocks, and dark caverns. Death and despair seemed to mark the desolate territory.

Bain rode up next to Sebena with a questioning look. She grinned at him and offered up an explanation.

"This area is known as the Gaslands. Not much can survive in this territory. It can be quite deadly with all of the steaming, churning, swampy waters, which can be quite hot at times."

"Where does the smell come from?" Bain asked, his lips curling in disgust.

"Likely the ground beneath the waters. Its swamp gasses for the most part."

"There isn't another way around this place?" Bain asked; hopeful.

"Not without adding another two full days to and from Eathreon to the trip. This land is about twenty miles wide going east to west, and only about five north to south, which is the direction we are traveling. "

"Got it." Bain nodded. "Hold your breath when you can, and grin and bear it."

Sebena laughed at his words. "Pretty much the attitude you need to make it through here." She slipped the fabric around her neck up and over her face, the rest of the group following her actions. It offered little, but some relief from the smell.

They both turned in their saddles to look back at the others. Maubrey's pale skin seemed to take on a green tint, as did Kamsten's. Some of the new recruits were even growing pale. The only person who got through the Gaslands without issues was Reannan, the woman whose filter-mask helped her with the rank odor of her Durnestrum. She just smiled and waved at everyone else who groaned miserably and looked her way. They turned and spurred their Baiskreet on faster to try to escape the putrid gases quicker.

Bain watched as Karalis and his family flew higher up than the rest of them, likely trying to avoid the smell. Bain realized they couldn't fly too much higher with the weight of the cages adding strain to some of the Baiskreet.

An hour later they were out of the gasses and desolation and flying over a completely different scene. The ground below them turned to rolling, green, grassy knolls, sparkling blue streams that looked to stretch for miles, and large trees that appeared to house a race of smaller people. The fields were striped with rows of lush, thick, gardens full of fruits and vegetables. Children in colorful brightly colored clothing ran below them, waving their arms madly about their heads, leaping and jumping with excitement; perhaps at seeing the Baiskreet or just other strange people in their somewhat isolated world. The valley seemed to be tucked between the Gaslands and another mountainous, ominous-looking, terrain ahead.

The hour grew late as the sun began to dip behind the ever-approaching mountain ahead of them just as Sebena gave the signal to land. After everyone slid off the backs of their Baiskreet Sebena gave them their next orders.

"We'll make camp here tonight so pitch the tents and make a fire for dinner and warmth. We'll hit Traitors Pass in the morning after a good night's sleep."

Maubrey asked, "Excuse me, but isn't it a little hot to need a fire?"

"It is now, but as soon as the sunlight disappears completely, the winds sweeping down into this valley off Crestfal Mountain gets quite cold. Trust me when I say, you need to bundle up tonight."

"Yes Ma'am," Maubrey said, saluting as though he were a castle guard conscript.

Kamsten rolled her eyes and began helping some of the others to assemble one of the tents. Maubrey soon joined her as others began making fires for warmth and setting up kettles for hot coffee to ward off the cold winds.

Bain asked Sebena another question as they worked. "Why do they call the area we are going through Traitor's Pass?"

Sebena shrugged. "I'm not sure; I've never asked."

After chores were done, and people and animals fed, they all sat around the fires wrapped in their blankets, with steaming mugs of hot coffee in their hands. Large tarps had been draped around the cages to keep the caged animals warm, and the rest of the Baiskreet huddled around the outer-rims of camp and the glow of the fire. Their thick, scaly backs facing the mountain and helping to block the winds from their riders and campsite. Karalis and Karaliene huddled together in a circle, head to tail, their two hatchlings tucked tightly between them. One of Karalises large paws lay over his buck, keeping him firmly in place.

Commander Asletrum, one of the older, more experienced men in the group, having overheard Bain and Sebena's earlier conversation, decided to give an explanation.

"I heard your question earlier, Recruit Brinley, and I have an answer if you'd like to hear it."

"About the name of the pass?"

"Yes, precisely that."

"Sure."

Everyone else nodded they would like to hear it as well.

"Well, from what I remember hearing when I was a young boy, it all started with a pilgrimage hundred's of years ago. Two separate families who had been life-long friends decided to make the trip from the lowlands just north of Eathreon, before it became overrun with Baiskreet and their kind were all killed. Both men and their wives feared for the safety of their children and future generations and wanted to make the journey to find the fabled, beautiful fields and rolling hills of Serenity Valley, the name given back then to the small village we passed earlier. These two families, along with hundreds of others, struck out on foot for the long journey. Many had wagons and were fortunate to have Hobblings to help pull their belongings across the sometimes rugged and dangerous terrain. But others had to lug and pull their own wagons, their whole family pitching in to help. They traveled this way for days, as the Hobbling-pulled wagons made much faster time than those on foot and they arrived at the high, steep, wall of rock in the early daylight hours. No one was prepared to find the daunting mountain of Crestfal looming dark and cold before them. As everyone made camp at the base of the mountain, preparing for the night ahead, those on foot arrived just before nightfall, falling onto the ground, tired, and spent from their long, hard walk. The sun disappeared below the horizon, and the cold winds began to howl off the mountain, blowing through their camp. Many of the men, women, and children who were without wagons or any sort of cover froze to death in the night winds. The next morning the survivors spent no time gathering bodies or honoring those who had lost their lives in the cold of night."

"Why didn't they bury the dead?" Mercer asked.

"To avoid wasting time crossing Crestfal Mountain. You see, they knew that if they wasted any time at all, and they were stuck on top of that mountain when the sun went down, they would all surely freeze to death. For if the winds blew that cold at night in the valleys, then it would have to be much worse at the mountain's peak."

Mercer and a few others nodded their heads in understanding as Commander Asletrum continued.

"It was every family for themselves as they all moved as quickly as possible to get across the mountain while the sun blazed warmly overhead. People stepped over each other, knocked others who moved slower out of the way, and pushed their own ever faster. It was said that as night began to draw closer, some people even selfishly ran off, leaving their slower wives, husbands, elderly, and children behind as fear of freezing to death gripped their already selfish, cold hearts."

Someone interrupted. "This can't be true."

"Oh, I assure you, it's very true. Man's true, selfish, nature, especially when faced with certain death can spur even the kindest-hearted soul to true treachery," Commander Asletrum stated. "Now, where was I. Oh yes, we were crossing the peak. The two families who were steadfast friends pushed and pulled one another over, fortunate that their Hobbling's had survived the night before due to their thick and woolly pelts. But as the wagons crossed over the ridgeline of Crestfal one of them suffered damage. A wheel got lodged into a deep crevasse, and they were stuck. Their friends tried helping for a while, but one father, realizing the hour was growing later and the wheel was not moving, decided to abandon his friends and scramble off the mountain before his own family suffered a frozen, icy death. The pleading and mournful cries of the family left behind could be heard echoing off the walls of the mountain as the traitorous others moved on, and that family, along with so many others, was never heard from again. Those few people who made it off the mountain labeled the path that they had used to cross it as Traitors Pass, since so many traitorous decisions had to be made to survive that trip. No one else has dared to cross Crestfal Mountain on foot again, and the small valley, once known as Serenity, came to be called Perfidious Valley, in remembrance of that fateful journey."

Sebena spoke up. "But the area is called Resolute Valley, not Perfidious or Serenity."

"It is now. Many years passed and the old ones died off, along with the teachings of caution and treachery. New people were put in charge and they didn't like the name Perfidious because to them it stood for negativity and deceit, so they renamed it Resolute Valley."

Maubrey chuckled a little nervously. "You're a great story-teller, Commander, but I wonder how much of that is true."

"All of it. In my village it was ingrained into our very beings as children on how NOT to treat others," Commander Asletrum stated.

"Surely some of the story was…embellished for dramatic effect," Maubrey added.

"Not a single word," the commander assured him.

Bain tossed a small stick into the fire, watching the sparks float upward. "History forgotten and rewritten," he stated bluntly, wondering how long it would take for Zanchier's history to be overlooked as well. The once beautiful, wild, somewhat just world, now surely nothing more than a pirate's playground. Worse yet was the Scaithers, under the twisted, perverse rule of Riglan Mortruff. He shook off the dark thoughts as everyone quietly finished their hot coffee and slipped away to their own tents to wait out the cold, windy, dark night with thoughts of Crestfal Mountain and Traitor's Pass flitting through their dreams.

# Chapter 24

**Day 2 to Eathreon, Day 23 on Harilhia**

The night before had been cold and long, as the wind off the mountain howled and shook their tents. But with the morning's arrival and the sun's rays breaking over the mountain, the air warmed so quickly that it seemed as though the freezing night had simply been a dream. Bain couldn't fathom how the temperature could change so drastically in just minutes. It was something that puzzled Maubrey's and Kamsten's brilliant minds as well. Bain could see them passionately discussing how such a phenomenon could take place as they waited to mount the Baiskreet for the second day of their journey.

Bain wondered what else he was yet to discover about Harilhia, the planet he had no clue he had lived on for his entire life until less than a month ago. They had all assumed that Zanchier was the only life anywhere, having never seen another person outside of Zanchier before. Their society, as advanced in some technologies as they had been, was completely ignorant to other things, having been landlocked for so long, and letting fear trap them inside their own world. He decided then that he would never let fear of the unknown stop him from doing anything. He wasn't prone to fear anyway. His years at the LSS had taught him to be strong, brave, and honest. They had fought to protect and did well for so many years until the Scaithers grew too powerful and many people were forced to seek sanctuary elsewhere, many able to find a way out of Zanchier. He of course had inadvertently walked into a time-portal and was now on the adventure of a lifetime.

He looked at Sebena, a small grin coming to his lips as he watched her. She was unlike any other woman he had ever met. Direct, honest, strong, and fearless, yet kind and caring; beautiful barely described her, in both body and soul. She noticed him watching her and she winked at him. Bain smiled at her and finished putting away his tent and supplies.

Sebena had instructed them to prepare for the day's long journey without stopping, so everyone made certain their dried food, snacks, and water-skins were easily accessible.

Soon they were all in the air and heading across the dark, desolate mountain. Everyone looked over the sparsely vegetated landscape. Not much could survive such drastic temperature changes every day, and so what trees and vegetation that did exist were twisted and battered from their struggles on Crestfal.

Bain saw no signs of life, which didn't really surprise him. He couldn't imagine any living creature being able to survive in a place as barren of food and life; everything must eat after all.

The journey across the mountain was only about an hour's flight, then they traveled over grassy plains, marshlands, and then the coast of a great sea. They flew for hours, unrelenting with nowhere to land. It was well past noon before any land was visible, but Bain could see a small island coming into view. Perhaps that was Eathreon.

Sebena gave the signal to land and they all soon dropped down to the island. It was lush and green, and palm trees lined the shore and thick jungles covered the land with cliffs and hills blending into the greenery. Mountains could be seen in the distance, and the lonely call of a single bird could be heard somewhere amongst the trees.

Sebena said, "This is a temporary break. Eat, stretch, and relieve yourselves. The next leg will be just as long, but the end result will be Eathreon."

Guidriun asked, "How will we know when we reach it?"

The commanders all chuckled. Commander Asletrum answered. "You'll know, Recruit Brunzfeld. There's no mistaking the wild lands of Eathreon."

Guidriun shrugged and nodded in a nonchalant manner, accepting that they knew what they were talking about. It did give him some apprehension and excitement all at the same time as his imagination kicked in and possible images of this strange new land filled his head.

Sebena gave them an extra thirty minutes to tend to all the caged creatures and to recover from the long flight before making them prepare for the last, long journey.

"Load up everyone and get comfortable if you can. There isn't much to look at as far as scenery goes until we get there; all open water from here out, except for a few smaller islands along the way."

Sebena watched everyone nod and prepare for the last leg of the trip. But this wasn't your standard drop and go mission as in the past. They would actually have to find a safe place to spend the night if they didn't manage to capture a new breed to replace the Kriesletrope. She noticed Karalis suddenly looked at her, and she could feel him in her head. Then, he began telepathically speaking to her.

*'Don't worry, Commander. I, king of the Baiskreet, will find you your replacement.'*

Sebena replied, *'What if the wild Baiskreet don't recognize you as their king?'*

Karalises' laughter sounded as a roar to the others, catching everyone's attention. Bain watched the interaction between them with interest, knowing something was going on.

*'I will show them my might, power, and majesty, and they ALL WILL bow to me, make no mistake.'*

Sebena shrugged and nodded at him. *'Well let's hope that your might and power will show up and show off when we have to secure your replacement, or else all these people here may die.'*

Karalis looked at Bain. *'I care not for human lives, except the Enlightened One. I will help if only to spare his life. If the rest of you benefit from his good fortune, then so be it.'*

Sebena looked at Bain with a slight grin. *'I agree, his life IS worth it.'*

Her Baiskreet took to the sky, followed by all the others.

Karalis watched her with interest before leading his own family into the air. *'Perhaps she isn't as selfish as I thought.'*

Karaliene looked at him. *'Bain is her life mate, Karalis. Of course she would do all to protect him. Just as I would you and our hatchlings and as you would do also for us.'*

Karalis looked surprised by her statement.

Karaliene continued. *'Can you not feel the connection between them? It is as strong as our own. I don't know how you missed it.'* Karaliene flew ahead a bit to guide their wayward hatchlings in the right direction.

Karalis watched Bain, and then Sebena. They didn't seem like they were mated, even though Bain had once defended her to him. But human emotion was a fickle thing. Baiskreet mated for life; and he had seen the way most humans changed life mates more frequently than Baiskreet laid eggs.

The trip was made in thoughtful and mostly exhausted quiet, except for the occasional exclamation by Maubrey. Who, although he had gotten used to flying by now, his seat was still a tad uncomfortable and he would twist and turn as best as he could to bring feeling back to his sleeping legs.

"I'll never be able to stand again," he said dramatically. "There's likely permanent damage to my spinal column with the way I'm sitting."

Bain smiled and turned to him. "You insisted on coming, remember?"

"Yes, well, had I known how tortuous this ride would be, I might have changed my mind."

Sebena said, "I warned you it was long and hard."

"Yes, but that isn't the same as torturous. No one says what they actually mean anymore." Maubrey huffed.

Kamsten giggled at his display of self-pity. He could be so over-the-top with his personality when he was uncomfortable.

"Maybe, but what you consider to be torturous is only uncomfortable for others, and yet others might still fully enjoy a trip like this," Sebena argued.

Bain smiled and added, "I'm enjoying it."

He could feel Maubrey's steely gaze of unpleasantness boring into his back.

"Traitor; and here I was thinking you were my friend, Bain Brinley," Maubrey mumbled, causing those who could hear their words to chuckle.

Kamsten laughed as well. "Good grief, Maubrey, it isn't that bad."

"Say's the woman who's Baiskreet essentially massages your buttocks whenever commanded." Maubrey moved again, trying to get more comfortable as everyone else laughed.

Sebena yelled, "All right, quit your whining, we're basically here, but keep high in the air, away from the water below, or you might inadvertently become dinner for something quite large and ugly."

Everyone looked around, realizing they had all flown into a thick fog bank. They could begin to make out a large cliff jutting out over the water as the fog began to clear.

Suddenly, as they rounded the cliff-side, they faced land and one of the most spectacular scenes any of them had ever seen. There was a collective gasp as exclamatory remarks shot out from the mouths of all the new recruits.

"Yes," Commander Asletrum said, "it still takes my breath away every time I see it."

Sebena smiled brightly at the majestic, wild beauty of Eathreon. It never failed to impress her either.

The falls that erupted from the sporadic placement of trees at the top, spilled over into the ocean water's below, and they ran high, and vast. From their seats, a half-mile offshore, they still couldn't see if or where the falls ended along the coastline as the land twisted and turned in many places.

The falls were a varying, staggering blend of smaller and larger ones, all mixing together. Large slabs of rock jutted out in certain places as the water ran shallow over them, spilling and splashing onto another platform below that one. The water was so clear that the sun sparkled off the movement like glistening jewels all along the area. The wild ocean waters churned and crashed against the lower levels of the falls, and in some places larger rocks; some which looked to be sharp; jutted out of the ocean floor upward toward the sky. Thousands of wild sea-birds in many different breed, sizes, shapes, and colors flew from level to level, bathing, drinking, and then flying down to the ocean to nab a fish or two for dinner.

As they flew closer, they followed Sebena who led them to land in a large grassy area which sat near the top of the falls where everyone could dismount.

Sliding from the backs of their Baiskreet, they all stood at the top of the falls, taking in the sights below and all around them.

"I could live here!" Mercer stated, smiling.

"It looks beautiful, but it's just as deadly, so keep your wits about you," Commander Asletrum stated.

They all watched as Karalises' hatchlings romped and played along the rocky shelves of the falls, chasing birds and an occasional fish or two.

"Now what do we do?" Guidriun asked.

Commander Asletrum answered. "Normally, we just release the untrainable into the forest, but since we need to acquire a replacement breed, we need to quickly find one we might be able to handle."

"How do we wrangle a fully grown Baiskreet to transport?"

Sebena said, "We don't, we grab hatchlings: one of each sex so they can be bred."

"Won't the parents of said hatchlings be a LITTLE upset that we are stealing their offspring?" Mercer asked.

Sebena nodded. "More than likely, yes. Plus, we need to get the hatchlings quickly before nightfall or none of us will likely be alive by morning."

Maubrey nervously asked, "Wh…what do you me…mean we won't be alive by morning."

"We call this the wilds of Eathreon for a reason. No one inhabits these lands. It's full of Baiskreet; wild, untrained, meat-eating Baiskreet. Normally we drop and fly to one of the smaller islands  further south for the night."

The color drained from Maubrey's face, realizing what she was saying. He gulped loudly, choking on his own saliva as it got stuck in his tightening throat.

Commander Asletrum said, "I suggest we release the hatchlings, and fly inward in search of a suitable breed."

They opened the cage doors, allowing the caged creatures their freedom, watching as they quickly took flight into the cover of the forest, likely sensing the danger in the new place.

Bain looked at Karalis, making sure to communicate by telepathy so the others wouldn't know they could speak to the creatures. *'Any suggestions on acceptable breeds?'*

Karalis roared loudly and shook from his head to the end of his tail. Then he turned to his own young buck, dipping his head low and growling. The buck bowed his head and shied away from his massive, commanding father, his eyes cutting up to look at Karalis, as though pleading for mercy.

Bain turned to the others. "I think he wants us to follow him."

Karalis lifted off the ground and everyone else followed, Karaliene and the hatchlings sticking very close to him.

They flew over the heavily forested area below, an occasional body of water appearing here and there. They could see wild Baiskreet sailing through the air far off in the distance in several directions. Karalis let out a loud roar, and they noticed the Baiskreet in the distance quickly dropped below the tree canopy.

Sebena yelled to Bain, "You think that was a warning or something?"

He shrugged. "I don't know. Maybe he's just announcing his arrival."

"I wonder if that's good or bad?" Sebena stated.

Karalis soon began to drop toward the ground and they could see a large, open, rocky, area below. They also noticed another very large Baiskreet emerge from a dark cavern on the edge of the area. It looked in their direction and roared loudly at the intruders. Karalis landed in the center of the area, as other Baiskreet appeared from the edges of the surrounding forest. The large creature emerging from the cavern was another Kriesletrope, but he looked battered and beaten. Scars stretched across his face, back, and he even had a few tears in one wing. His coloring, once bright and beautiful as Karalis was dingy looking and dimmed, likely from years of fighting to keep his position as king of the Baiskreet.

Karalis stood tall and erect as the other Kriesletrope fully emerged into the light. He had some scales on his chest and other sparse areas across his hide that still reflected the light, giving evidence of his once brilliant, coppery, color. He was large, like Karalis, matching him in size, yet didn't quite have Karalises' majestic appearance.

The Baiskreet which began to circle the area began to tweet, chirp, and gurgle. The sounds began to grow as if they were anticipating something was about to happen.

The riders began to feel the agitation and nervous behavior of the Baiskreet they rode upon.  Their creatures began to dance about, and Sebena and the others cooed to them to calm down, patting their necks and backs.

Bain said, "I think we might want to back out of the way here. I believe there is about to be a throw-down between these two, and I for one do not want to get in the way."

Sebena looked around, realizing they were surrounded by wild Baiskreet, some that were paying more attention to them than they were the Kriesletrope Kings. "I'm not sure there is a safe place to go."

Everyone noticed what she was talking about.

Commander Asletrum said, "All right everyone, assume an outward facing formation keeping your backs to one another for as long as possible. Show a united front and perhaps we can avoid any surprise attacks."

Just as they did as instructed, the two Kriesletrope roared loudly at one another, their once glowing scales turning to darker shades of color as they charged. The crashing of bodies echoed off the rock walls and surrounding trees as Karalis and the wild beast battled for position of king. Screeching and roaring was heard from the onlookers as though they were all rooting for their favorite opponent. Bain knew this was a fight to the death, and that Karalis would not give up easily, especially with his family's future on the line. But Bain knew nothing of the wild, menacing-looking Kriesletrope. The creature looked as though it had battled many times, and apparently had overcome its opponents to hold the position of king.

They rolled on the ground, biting and scratching at one another. Karalis grabbed the other by the neck with his large mouth and slung the beast against the rock wall of the cavern it had exited earlier. It stood and charged Karalis knocking him over as it bit and scratched at him, tearing a few scales loose. Karalises' tail spike opened in defense as he shot several at the beast on top of him, planting some of them in its back. The beast roared in pain, scratching desperately to remove them. As it busied itself reaching around with its mouth to extract the spikes, Karalis got to his feet and roared, releasing a streak of fire from his belly, singeing the other king. It took to the air to avoid the blaze and Karalis grinned and took off after him. The two met in the air and collided once more, their wings flapping to keep them up as they twisted and turned in battle. Spikes flew from tails and many Baiskreet on the ground ran for cover to avoid being struck by a stray spike. Some made it, some did not, and they yelped in pain, running into the forest to lick their wounds.

Mercer shouted, "I don't think we are in a very safe place guys!"

"I agree with Merk!" Guidriun stated.

"All right, everyone scatter for some kind of cover," Commander Asletrum yelled.

They all took off in different directions, many trying to stay together in groups of two or three. Now their own Baiskreet were in ground battles against the other wild ones that had gathered to watch the battle of the kings.

The rider's Baiskreet hadn't really ever battled wild creatures before and so Sebena wondered how or if they were going to survive this. On top of all of these little skirmishes, they were supposed to locate a new breed to take back. She tried to keep an eye open for something small enough and unusual to take back as they all fought for their very lives. One good thing about the fight was that each of the wild Baiskreet knew no loyalty, and therefore even fought amongst themselves.

As she dodged yet another attack she saw Karalises' young buck slip away from Karaliene as she fought to protect herself and her young.

Sebena cursed under her breath and took off into the air after the buck which seemed to be flying toward Karalis and the battle he was fighting. She watched as another Baiskreet saw the young Kriesletrope take to the air and decided he'd make a decent meal. Sebena urged her Baiskreet faster as she had to dodge others flying at her in the air. Karalis noticed Sebena flying toward his now airborne buck, not sure of her intent now that he had no protection. He then noticed another Baiskreet with the same intentions, and fought hard against the old, tattered king for the throne. The wild Baiskreet was about to lay his talons into the buck when Sebena and her creature laid a line of fire onto his hide, sending him off in another direction. She chased after the beast that turned, screeching at her, but still intent on the easy mark. Karalis roared loudly, struck the old king through the chest and into the heart with his tail spikes, allowing him to fall to the earth in a loud, earthshaking thud. He then flew toward the Baiskreet which dared attack his young and quickly slayed the beast. He nodded thankfully to Sebena who returned his gesture with one of her own.

As the old king lay there, his breath stilling in his chest, Karalis landed, placed a large paw over the dying king, and let out a mighty roar. All the Baiskreet stopped their attacks and fled in fear, many appearing to bow as they backed away into the thick forest.

# Chapter 25

Karalis was good to his word and located several different young hatchlings whose mothers were apparently killed in today's battle. They would need taking care of anyway, and there was no grieving parent to miss them.

Sebena asked him, *'What breeds are these hatchlings?'*

Karalis replied, *'The yellow are Ipimsoltanis, the sea-green are Lapaguamar and the white breed are Nevaltrium. You now have three new breeds to replace mine for your Castle Guard. Surely your king will be happy with that.'*

Sebena nodded and bowed slightly. *'I'm certain he will, thank you, Karalis.'*

Bain stepped up to speak to him. *'Good luck to you and your family here in Eathreon, Karalis. I'm certain we'll see you again in the future.'*

*'That is doubtful. I sense a storm coming. Your future awaits you elsewhere Enlightened Ones.'*

Karalis looked at Sebena as well when he made the statement.

Bain and Sebena looked at one another with eyebrows raised.

The group of riders lifted into the air with the newly caged breeds to begin the return journey to Dihendra. Tonight they would fly to one of the remote islands about an hour away, get a good night's sleep and head out in the morning toward Crestfal Mountain.

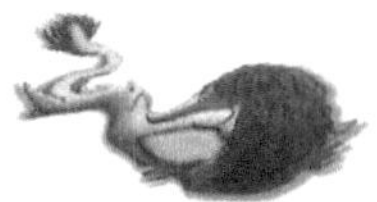

Morning came early on the small sparse island and the team loaded up once more and journeyed toward Crestfal Mountain, making it over and to the outskirts of Resolute Valley before sunset.

Many from the village ran to greet the travelers, excited to see people in charge of the deadly beasts their ancestors had fled from in fear hundreds of years before.

As the valley people got closer they realized they were a small race by nature, basically dwarfs. The children were particularly small, so much so that Bain feared for their lives.

"Maybe we should limit their proximity to the Baiskreet. I'd hate for an international war to start over a hungry beast thinking the children to be big-footed Lopers."

Sebena and the others smiled. She replied, "Too true. These children are very small indeed."

They held up their hands to halt their progression as the excited children ran ever closer, and the adults of Resolute ran to catch up to them, snatching them up off the ground to prevent them from getting any closer to the beasts.

One taller and more rotund man stepped forth. His tall hat sat a bit sideways on his head, and it was covered with baubles from nature and some smaller cogs and wheels from some machine from the past. He had a wide nose, scruffy beard and mustache, and long scraggly hair. He wore a vest over top a very loud colorful shirt that looked as though it had seen better days, and the hem of his shin length pants were tattered.

As a matter of fact, nearly the entire village appeared to dress the same way, although most everyone else's clothing was in better shape and they appeared to be more groomed.

"Greetings, travelers. Are you friends, or foes?" the little man asked, peering around them at the massive Baiskreet behind them.

"Commander Asletrum of the Castle Guard of Dihendra," the commander stated, a smile on his face as he stepped forth, bowing slightly, and extending his hand in a friendly gesture.

The small man beamed proudly as though he were a foreign dignitary. He took the commander's hand and shook it vigorously.

"Pripfore Berryworth at your service, village head and leader of Resolute Valley. Are you and your friends in need of lodging or supplies for your journey?"

"Not at all, Sir," Commander Asletrum elegantly stated; managing to impress Pripfore Berryworth with his manners. "We only need to stay here in this part of the valley to rest our Baiskreet and our weary bones. May we refresh the Baiskreet with water from your stream?"

Pripfore smiled brightly. "Of course. The stream is not ours to own, we share it with all nature and manner of creatures. Help yourselves. Will you and your friends be needing food? We have plenty as we are celebrating the abundant harvest the four moons has rendered this year. Our festival was just about to begin. You are all welcome to join, though, since your beasts are so large, they will have to stay here you understand."

"Thank you for your kind invitation, Sir. We would be delighted to join you in your celebrations." Commander Asletrum bowed and turned to some of the recruits. "Four of you will need to take first watch and stay with the Baiskreet, then others will relieve you within the hour to allow you to attend the celebrations as well. I'm sure I don't have to tell you all to be on your best behavior. We don't want to inadvertently offend our hosts." Four recruits agreed to stay behind first, with the village people taking them food and a beverage akin to barley-wine. Then every hour they would change out, allowing everyone about an hour or two of celebrations of which to partake. The Captains and Commanders of course were allowed to stay the entire time. The festival lasted all night with food, drink, music, and the occasional ruckus and rough-housing, then as midnight approached, everyone excused themselves, thanking their kind hosts for the hospitality and returned to their camp.

In the early hours of morning, before the sun came up, a storm strong enough to wake everyone blew through the area. As Bain, Sebena, Maubrey, and Kamsten gathered together outside discussing the storm's strength, several portals began to open.

Bain looked at his friends and they all looked to him, knowing he needed to decide which portal to take.

Bain wasn't sure what to do; he supposed he just needed to decide based on feeling. They all split up temporarily to grab their supply packs.

Sebena ran to speak briefly with Commander Asletrum to explain.

"Sir," she saluted as she slung her pack across her back. "It's time for me and my friends to leave."

"What do you mean Commander Zentrialle? Leave where?"

"Can you see the glowing lights appearing and leaving throughout the field? Those are time-portals Sir, and Bain has traveled through them before. It's time he and the others left, and I'm going with them."

Commander Asletrum watched the glowing lights appear and slowly fade away with each strike of lightning.

"If that is what you feel you should do Commander."

"It is Sir. Will you and the others return our Baiskreet?"

"You'll not be taking them with you?"

"No sir, we aren't sure what we will find on the other side, so it's best to travel lightly. Please, Sir, if you can, keep this to yourself about our time-traveling. Bain fears the world isn't ready for everyone to know. Specifically those who hold powerful positions."

"I'll do my best, and safe Journey, Commander Zentrialle. Give the others our farewells."

Mercer and Guidriun watched, wishing they too could go but unsure whether it would be wise. They waved goodbye to their friends as Bain, Sebena, Maubrey, and Kamsten all disappeared in a flash of light after they walked through a portal and were gone, likely forever.

Those left behind looked around at one another, unsure what to make of what had just happened. As dawn broke, and the storm subsided, Commander Asletrum gave strict instructions to keep what they had seen quiet. Only a handful of them knew what truly had taken place, and they all agreed to keep it to themselves. Besides, who would believe them anyway? The story they would share with anyone who asked, was that the four missing people had perished in Eathreon during the Baiskreet battle to find the new breeds.

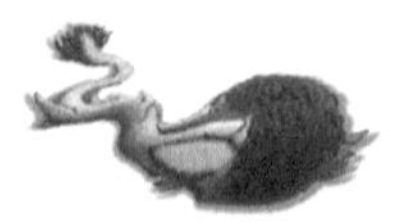

"Adwyn, hurry up!"

"We're coming, Grandmother!" Adwyn yelled over the sound of the thunder and lightning. She, her oldest son, and her husband Marshal who carried their youngest son on his hip, rushed to make the jump before the portal closed on them.

Adwyn had been raised by her grandparents since she was little. Her parents had been killed in an accident, and she had been thrust on them. Little did she know then that her grandparents were world-jumping, time-traveling adventurers of the highest caliber. When she had been forced to go with them the first time, she wasn't happy, but she soon discovered so many things that boggled the mind. Things, places, and creatures no one would have ever believed were real. When she met Marshal Burke on one of their trips in her twenties, he had followed her home and got stuck in their world. Her grandparents had taken pity on him and took him in. After years of training to be a time-jumper, he and Adwyn eventually ended up falling in love. They had two children. Hiram was their oldest child of sixteen, and Carter, their second and last child, was three. Since Adwyn had struggled with other failed pregnancies before him, young Carter was the apple of his great-grandparent's eyes.

Sebena motioned them forward quickly. "Hurry up or we might get stuck here, or worse, somewhere else. Your grandfather will not be happy about having to track you all down again!"

They jumped through the portal, rain pelting them, just before it closed.

Marshal said, "Where is Bain anyway?"

"He's already gone on ahead to meet with Maubrey and Kamsten. Time is short, I'm afraid Maubrey doesn't have much time left. Their family is gathering at their home as we speak."

The four of them rushed through the forest and the ebbing rain, hoping to make it before their grandfather's lifelong friend passed away. After many years of time-traveling with Bain and Sebena, Maubrey and Kamsten had settled down in the Irish countryside in a later time period where so many more scientific advancements had been available. They had raised three children and five grandchildren together. Their youngest grandson Ryan Halloran was special. As a highly functioning autistic young man, he had shown much promise as a scientific genius even at a very early age, and Maubrey and Kamsten had spent much of their older, aging years with their daughter and her husband nurturing young Ryan's gifts.

They walked through the door of the house, the quietness sending chills up Sebena's spine. Maubrey and Kamsten's life had been filled with laughter, adventure, and mishaps with some of their crazier inventions, but it had never been so quiet before. She could hear speaking coming from Maubrey's bedroom. She stood in the door frame watching Bain sit by his old friend's bedside as Kamsten lay beside her dying husband. Tears began to streak Sebena's cheeks.

"Well, old friend," Maubrey coughed, "it's been an adventure. One that I never dreamed of all those years ago when you first started working at the LSS in Loradin."

Bain nodded and patted Maubrey's hand. "Yes, we've had many adventures together, and I wouldn't have missed any of them for anything."

"Sebena might have something to say about that," Maubrey laughed weakly, causing him to cough.

Sebena walked into the room and sat on the foot of the bed behind Bain. The rest of their family gathered around the bed to say their goodbyes.

Maubrey looked over at Kamsten. "It looks like it's up to the young ones now to take over our time-traveling adventures."

"Perhaps, if they choose that life." Kamsten smiled sadly.

"Is it ever really a choice?" he asked. "Adventure calls to our kind. It's in our very blood."

"Not all of our children and grandchildren see it that way. Poor Ryan is scared to leave his room most days, much less time-travel," she chuckled softly.

"He'll do great things for mankind. You just wait and see Kammy-girl." Maubrey patted her hand that lay on top of his.

They smiled at one another happily, knowing the life they had built together had been a good one.

Little Carter struggled from his father's grip and wobbled over to Bain, climbing onto his grandfather's lap.

Bain smiled at the lad, Maubrey did as well. They all sat together until the hour grew late. The children grew tired and curled up in the other rooms of the house while the adults all waited and said their goodbyes to their beloved father, grandfather, and friend.

Bain and Sebena went to sit beside little Carter on the sofa. Carter woke and crawled onto his grandfather's lap, sleepily looking up at him.

"Read the story about Wren, Grandfather."

Hiram whined in protest. "Not again, Carter." He rolled his eyes and flopped into a side chair; his sixteen years of age protesting hearing the same old story for the hundredth time.

Bain gave Hiram a stern look, then looked down at the little one on his lap and stroked the boy's hair. He reached into his satchel which he carried with him everywhere and pulled out the old journal he had started all those years ago, on the planet of Harilhia, on a distant southern island while searching for his family. He looked around at all the blessings in the room. The creator had been very good to him. He smiled, got comfortable in the chair, and began to read.

"My unexpected adventures." The title read. "It all started one cold winter day in the mountains of Xantifal when I was nineteen years of age. One fateful afternoon, I saw a mysterious, glowing light in Storm Valley..."

The End

Find out if Bain ever finds his family in the world of Time-travel. You can read more about Bain and Sebena's journey's in the second book starring Harper and Wilkins, Bain's parents, and his siblings.

Thanks for reading my books, and I hope you enjoy the adventures. If you don't mind, please leave my book a review. You can do so on my website located on the about the author page.

# About the Author

SG Boudreaux homeschooled her three children for over twenty years. She still teaches her youngest special-needs, forever student, with her two oldest now graduated. She enjoys music, especially playing the drums with her ladies group for special events, writing, creating new creatures for her books, learning new things, gardening, animals, and all things beach related. She and her husband of twenty-eight years live in the country in Louisiana; unfortunately not near a beach. She is the next to youngest of eight children; five older sisters, one older brother, and one younger adopted sister.

All her works are published through Zanchier Publications, an imprint of S.G. Boudreaux.

You can find out more about her Blog, her books, and current events at www.sgboudreaux.com. You can also see all current titles and their information at www.zanchierpublications.com

You can follow her on the listed social media accounts: Facebook/S.G.Boudreaux, Instagram@sg_boudreaux, Youtube,@ SG Boudreaux X@SGBoudreaux, Tiktok@Sgwrites, or sign up to receive email notifications at - www.sgboudreaux.com

Her previous series of books are clean-reading, fiction, fantasy, and time-travel. You can contact her at the email address in the front of the books or through her website.

# Other Books by SG Boudreaux

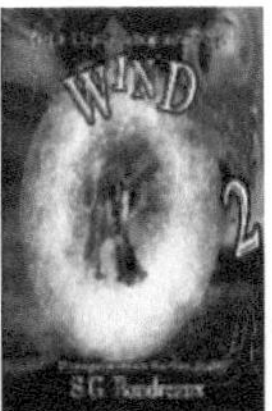
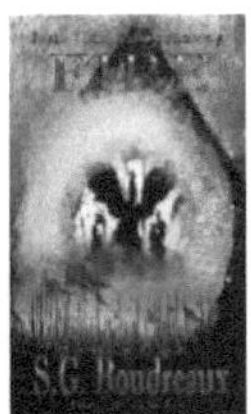

## Non-fiction titles by Shawna Boudreaux

Thank you for your continued support, and I truly hope that you enjoy my line of clean reading, fiction, fantasy, novels.